"Sure am glad you're here, Jack. That damn dog won't let us anywhere near the body."

"Dog? What dog?"

"Didn't you know?" Quent said. "I thought that's why you was here. There's a vicious dog in the car with the judge. Mattera fact, looks to me like maybe he's the one that kilt the old man. His throat's all shredded."

Roark's face was now visible through the side window of the Cadillac. He was panting. He saw us and began to bark.

"See?" Sheriff Flynn had followed us. "He's a vicious maniac."

The bark of the "vicious maniac" turned into a high-pitched whine. Deep wrinkles started to form on his troubled forehead. A look of fear clouded his big brown eyes.

"Funny, what I see is a cold, frightened animal who doesn't know what's going on."

Another loud bark came from the Cadillac. Officer Fisher, or Fletcher, raised his shotgun. But before he could take aim, I stepped in and knocked the barrel up, accidentally smacking him hard on the cheek. He slipped and fell backward. As he went down, I snatched the gun away.

"Understand this," I said, "nobody shoots that dog while I'm around."

Also by Lee Charles Kelley

A Nose for Murder

LEE CHARLES KELLEY

MURDER UNLEASHED

AVON BOOKS
An Imprint of HarperCollins*Publishers*

This book is a work of fiction. References to real people, events, establishments, organizations, or locales are intended only to provide a sense of authenticity, and are used fictitiously. All other characters, and all incidents and dialogue, are drawn from the author's imagination and are not to be construed as real.

AVON BOOKS
An Imprint of Harper Collins*Publishers*
10 East 53rd Street
New York, New York 10022-5299

ISBN: 0-06-052494-4
www.avonmystery.com

First Avon Books paperback printing: January 2004

Printed in the U.S.A.

10 9 8 7 6 5 4 3 2 1

This book is dedicated to the memory of my father, Jack Kelley.

Acknowledgments

Thanks to Gail Neiderhoffer for a whole damn lot of things, mostly being a great friend, a great dog owner, and for letting me play her piano from time to time.

Thanks also to Jerry and Delia Kass for their generous, positive feedback, writing-wise, and their gracious and warm-hearted manner, human being-wise. Thanks, too, to their dog Magee for being such a good boy and for licking my face.

Thanks again to Tom and Kirstin, and to Roark, their boxer dog. And to Joel and Marcia, and their beagle Maggie. And to Thomas and Mareane and their great Dane Achille, who, in a way, is the inspiration for the character "Hooch" in this book. Thanks also to my good friend Ann and her Maltese, Suzie Q, for sharing their home, however briefly, with me and Fred.

Special thanks to ex-NYPD detective Melanie Weiss for her technical advice, as well as her helpful and oftentimes creative ideas. This book wouldn't be as good as it is without her.

I also need to thank Jocelyn at Veterinary Clinic of Chelsea, Gina at Yorkville, Kolie, Althea, Dawn, and Cherese at Ansonia, Marcia at Heart of Chelsea, Ann at Calling All Pets, Helen at DUMBO Pets in Brooklyn, Randy at Whiskers, Deborah at Animal Attractions, Carolann at University Animal Hospital, the staff at Creature Features, Chaya at Desktop Depot, Rick and Lockwood at Crocodile, and Tom at Murder Ink!.

Thanks again to my agent Frances Kuffel, without whose vision and persistence this series would never have materialized. Thanks, too, to my editor at Avon, Erin Richnow, the cheeriest person I know, no matter how much I pester her with my sometimes gruff and ornery questions.

Extra special thanks, as always, to the other half of my heart and the better part of my soul. Her name is Dana.

And a big bone to Fred, the best dog in New York.

CORRECTIONS

There were a couple of mistakes in the first edition of *A Nose for Murder,* the first book in this series, that need to be corrected. The biggest mistake (for me) comes when Jack says that he and Jamie were listening to Townes Van Zandt sing, "If I Could Only Fly", which is actually a Merle Haggard song, written by D.M. Fuller. However, I'm almost certain that Fuller wouldn't mind having the song mistaken for a Van Zandt number.

When I wrote that chapter I was thinking of "To Live Is to Fly", a great Van Zandt song.

"When we were kids, our mother told us
that dogs can sense a person's vibration—
whether they have a good vibration or a bad one.
That's where the song "Good Vibrations" comes from,
from what my mom told us about
dogs when we were kids."

—Brian Wilson

MURDER UNLEASHED

1

The colored balls clicked and scattered across the green felt. Jamie had made a good break. Annie Deloit poured a glass of ale and handed her husband Darryl the empty pitcher. Annie—with red hair and pale skin—was a little plump, though not unattractively so. In fact, she was quite pretty, with luminous green eyes. Darryl—slender, African-American—had coffee-colored dreadlocks, short and well-trimmed. He also wore wire-rims, a neat goatee, and had a smooth, high forehead and an easygoing smile. The couple—in their early thirties—were holding hands.

It was a Friday night at Gilbert's Publick House. We were sharing a pitcher of Newcastle Brown Ale to ward off the winter chill, and doing our best to ignore the loud blues band: the singer was trying too hard to sound like Joan Osborne, and didn't have the voice for it. Jamie and I were playing eight-ball. The bet was whoever lost had to be the other's "love slave" for the rest of the night. Jamie was up, two games to one.

"What is it now, best three out of five?" I asked.

"That's right, hotshot. Unless you're chicken?"

"Nah," I said, admiring the tight curve in Jamie's jeans as she leaned over the table and stroked her cue. "Besides, it makes no difference to me whether I win or lose."

She tossed her long, chestnut hair over one shoulder of her tan cashmere turtleneck, and gave me an up-from-under look. "Are you trying to be Zen about this, Jack? Because it's not—"

"I'm not being Zen. It's just that I've *always* been your love slave. You know that. Not just for Valentine's Day."

"Ahhh," Annie sighed. Jamie unleaned herself from the pool table, came over to where I stood, took a fistful of my Irish fisherman's sweater, and gave me a long, deep kiss.

"That was nice, brown eyes," I said. "Now, let's get back to shooting pool." She laughed and got back to shooting pool.

"So, Jamie," Annie had to shout to be heard over the music, "when are you two love birds getting married?"

Darryl shook his head, shushed her. Annie gave me a look. "You mean you guys haven't even *talked* about it?"

"Nope," I said, "*thankfully* the subject has never come up."

Jamie glared at me from over her shoulder.

"Besides, honey," Darryl waved at a cloud of smoke coming from a nearby table, "Jamie's still married, remember?"

"Oh, that's right. So, what's holding things up, James? When will your divorce from Oren be final?"

Jamie took a shot on the fifteen ball. It rolled into the far corner pocket. She walked to the back of the table, tilted her head in my direction and said, "Ask Sherlock, here. He's the one that had my divorce attorney put in jail."

"After all," I laughed, "he did *kill* a couple of people."

"The bastard," said Darryl. "Who wants more beer?" Annie raised her hand, and Darryl went to the bar for a refill.

While he was gone, Jamie made three in a row, then missed an easy shot on the twelve ball. A tall, sandy-haired man in a tan leather jacket came over and asked Annie to dance. She told him she was married. "What, to that black guy you're with?" Annie said yes. She also told him that "that black guy" was a cardiologist. The sandy-haired guy seemed to think it meant someone who sells greeting cards for a living.

I sank the six, then, while I was eyeing the table the band

took a break, and Carl Staub—mid-twenties, tall, with black, curly hair and blue eyes (like me)—came through the front door. He saw us, took off his scarf and gloves and came over to say hi; how was our trip to the Bahamas, wasn't it a drag to come back to all this ice and snow, how are things at the kennel, etc.

I made the appropriate noises, then he and Jamie started talking about a missing judge and I stopped listening. One of the reasons I moved to Maine was to get away from cop talk.

A barmaid walked by. Carl stopped her and ordered coffee to go, then said, "Can I buy you guys a drink?"

"Sure. I'll have a Macallan's—neat. Jamie's driving."

Jamie and Carl went back to their conversation. The table gave me nothing, so I finessed the cue ball into a spot between the four and the one, leaving Jamie without a shot.

"You're up," I said, interrupting their conversation.

She came over, looked at the setup, snicked the cue ball softly against the ten, leaned against the table, took a sip of Diet Coke. "So, why do *you* think Judge Merton disappeared?"

"Beats me. Who's Judge Merton?"

Annie chirped in, "It's been all over the news."

"Yeah, well, I don't pay much attention to the news." Another reason I left New York. I dropped the two then made a scratch while sinking the seven and it was Jamie's table again.

"Oh, Jack, come on," Jamie said, sinking the ten, "how could a sixty-year-old, State Superior Court judge just vanish into thin air somewhere between here and Augusta? You have to admit, it's an intriguing mystery."

"No mystery at all. His car probably skidded on the ice and he ended up in a ditch somewhere. Or, I don't know, maybe he ran off to Venezuela with his legal secretary."

Carl looked at Jamie, puzzled. "Venezuela?"

Jamie shrugged, chalked her cue. "It's better not to ask."

The barmaid came back with my scotch and Carl's coffee.

"Well, I don't know," Carl said, tamping down the plastic lid on his cup. "The State Police have checked and rechecked every road between Camden and the capital for the last two days. There's no trace of him or his car." He pronounced the last word "cah," as most good Downeasters do.

"Yeah, well, they'll find him sooner or later," I said. "Him and his 'cah.' " I took a sip of the Macallan's. "This is nice, Carl. Thanks." He told me I was welcome. I thought of something and said, "Wait a minute, what kind of car are we talking about here?"

"A new Cadillac Deville, why?"

"Well, Cadillacs come equipped with GPS. Has anyone tried to track down his car through the OnStar system?"

Carl nodded. "Yeah, but it's been disconnected."

"Disconnected or just not working?"

"Uh-oh, Jack," Jamie said, "what does that look on your face mean?"

"Well," I sighed, "if his car's GPS isn't working, there are only four possibilities: the first one is that the judge called the company and had it turned off . . ."

Carl shook his head. "We checked on that. He didn't."

"Okay, then the other possibilities are that the system malfunctioned somehow, which isn't very likely, those things are built to last. Another possibility is that the car was in a terrible accident, I mean the kind where it rolls over and over, again and again, and the chassis is ripped apart, which means whoever was driving the car—presumably the judge—is, in all likelihood, critically injured or dead. The last possibility is that someone who knows cars deliberately unhooked the wires leading to the GPS system, which also suggests that the judge is dead, or else he would've reported the car stolen or car-jacked. The only thing is, in *that* scenario his death wouldn't be accidental. It would be a case of cold-blooded murder."

There was a moment of silence, or the closest one can come to silence in a crowded bar on a Friday night.

Jamie said, "Well, I hope you're wrong about that, Jack."

"So do I, honey. So do I."

2

Jamie asked Carl if he'd like to stay and join us, but he said he had to get home to the wife. After he left, we went back to our game. Jamie sank the eight ball, Annie drained her glass, Darryl came back from the bar with a fresh pitcher, but we decided to call it a night. Jamie wanted to go back to my place to collect on our bet. So we put on our parkas and said our good-byes to the Deloits, who waved gaily and started scuba-diving their way through the next round.

As we went out the side door, we heard two people arguing just outside the bar. The band's lead singer—a short, pretty, Eurasian girl, early thirties, with heavy makeup and pink hair—was yelling at a tall, scrawny older guy dressed in black Levi's and a fatigue jacket. I knew him. It was Farrell Woods. He was making placating gestures at her but she was furious and wouldn't stop yelling: "You burned me, man! You burned me!"

"Take it easy, Tulips," he said, his breath making clouds in the cold night air. "There's a lotta shit goin' down—"

"I don't care about your problems, man. All I want is . . ." She leaned in close, jabbed a finger in his chest. I couldn't hear the rest.

I held the door open for Jamie. A blast of cold air stung our faces. "Another drug deal gone bad."

"God, it's brutal out there."

Woods said, "If you're in such bad shape, why don't you talk to your friend Eddie?"

We left the fracas behind us, heading for Jamie's car, which was parked in the lot on Sharp's Wharf. I wondered if the "Eddie" that Woods had just referred to was Eddie Cole, a drug dealer who'd been making threats to kill Jamie, (due to the fact that he used to be her soon-to-be ex-husband's coke dealer, and in an effort to get him into treatment she'd threatened to have Cole put in jail. She'd never gone through with it, but Cole still, apparently, held a grudge.

"How do you know that's a drug deal?" Jamie asked.

"That's Farrell Woods," I said, "remember? He deals marijuana."

The salty night air nipped at our ears and noses. Jamie brrred and hugged me tightly to keep warm. It didn't help any, although it did feel nice. "But how do *you* know him?" she said. "You told me you never—"

"I tried it once in college, but I prefer using my brain to think with." Then, looking over my shoulder at the two of them, still arguing, I reminded Jamie of how I knew Farrell Woods:

He'd been a dog handler for the K-9 corps during the war in Vietnam. Now he lives in Belfast, along with a pack of about a dozen beagles. He drives down to my kennel every month or so to try and hit me up for a job. He also sells pot to the local high school kids, which is why I've never given him one. A job, that is. Plus the back of his camper shell is covered with bumper stickers and decals promoting the legalization of hemp.

"Just the kind of thing I want parked in my driveway when clients show up in their Grand Wagoneers and QX-4s to drop off their dogs for the weekend."

Jamie shrugged. "I remember him now. And who knows? Some of your clients might like the convenience of being able to drop off the pooch and pick up a little weed at the same time."

I had to laugh. "You're probably right. But see, that's another headache I don't need—to have him dealing the stuff on my property, you know? Especially with Leon around."

She nodded. "How are things going with that?"

"I've got another hearing in family court next month."

Leon is my fifteen-year-old foster son, at least temporarily. He's also another reason, at least partially, why I moved to Maine. I first met him while investigating a multiple homicide in Harlem. His older brother, his mother and father and a younger brother, just two years old, were all killed by drug dealers. Leon and his younger sister Althea were spared. The sister was spending the night with her grandmother, Grace, and Leon was hiding in the closet. He saw the whole thing through a crack in the door.

It was a revenge thing. The older brother was marginally connected to members of a rival gang. The killers thought he knew more than he did and decided to ice him. They threw the rest of the family in for free. We had the bastards nailed, but a dirty judge threw out our case and the only way to get a conviction was for Leon to testify. The trouble is, or was, that if he *did*, he'd be another casualty within forty-eight hours. The DA insisted on using his testimony, and I insisted on not. Shortly thereafter I took early retirement, bought the kennel I now call home, and took Leon with me, along with his grandmother's blessing.

In January the case was reopened, the dirty judge retired (thanks to the help of my old friend Lou Kelso, who's a private investigator in Manhattan), and Leon was off the hook. The State of Maine had other ideas about our current situation, so I had to fight my case in family court.

"The sad thing is," I said, "he's really good with dogs. Woods, I mean, though so is Leon, come to think of it. But as for hiring him, you know, I just can't afford to run the risk of him being stoned during an emergency."

Jamie gave me playful look. "Maybe you should go back there and get *us* a joint. After all, it *is* a holiday."

"Very funny. Besides, he doesn't have any right now."

We got to her car—a green Jaguar sedan her father had given for graduation from medical school. "How do *you* know?"

"Why else would Tulips be so upset?"

"Tulips? Who's Tulips?"

"The singer—at least that's what he called her. Besides, we don't need drugs. I get stoned just looking at you."

She sighed, leaned into me, and put her arms all the way around my chest, hugging me as tightly as she could.

"Jack Field, sometimes you say the nicest things."

"Meaning sometimes I don't?"

She looked up and nodded—kind of sadly, it seemed to me.

I was about to kiss her when a shot rang out. I heard the ping of a bullet ricocheting off metal. It came from the back of the bar. We looked over and saw Farrell Woods throw Tulips to the ground. Then he scurried behind a Dumpster. Another shot hit the Dumpster, another ping.

I shouted, "Hey!" at no one in particular. I had no idea where the shots were coming from, but wanted to provide a distraction. Then I realized that Jamie and I might become the next targets, so I grabbed her and we crouched next to her car, hoping it would serve as cover.

We heard a car door slam, a screech of tires. I jumped up, hoping to get the license, but all I saw was some sort of black sedan peeling off onto Bayview Street and out of sight.

"Stay here," I told Jamie. "I'm going to check on Woods."

"Jack," she said, running after me, "I'm a doctor, remember? If he's been shot, I need to take a look at him."

"He hasn't been shot," I said.

"How do you know that?"

"Because both shots hit the Dumpster."

We got to the back of the building in time to see Tulips run back inside the bar. Woods got up, dusted himself off, saw us and said, "I'm okay, Jackie boy. Don't call the cops."

"Are you serious? Someone just tried to kill you!"

"Yeah, well, you let me worry about that, man. Okay? Anyway, whoever it was missed me. And even if he hadn't . . ." He unbuttoned his coat and pulled up his wool turtleneck to show us the flack jacket he wore under his clothes.

"Oh, man. What the hell is going on?"

"No time for that now. I'll catch ya later." With that, he ran to his truck, got in and took off, leaving me and Jamie standing there, looking at each other.

We called 911 on Jamie's cell phone, then waited around, like the good citizens we were, to give our statements to the two Camden police officers who showed up five minutes later. A crowd had gathered outside, but no one except Jamie and I knew anything. The cops took our statements and got ready to leave. They didn't even look for the two bullets.

As they headed back to their radio car I said, "Where the hell are you going? This was an attempted murder!"

One of them shrugged. "Hey, if Farrell Woods wants to file a complaint, fine. Till then, there's nothing we can do."

They were about as interested in what had happened as the Dumpster was. Maybe less. After all, the Dumpster had been shot twice.

3

Later, while we were asleep in my bed—with Frankie, my black and white English setter, lying on top of our feet to keep warm—the phone rang. Frankie snuffled. Jamie groaned and put a pillow over her head. I fumbled for the receiver.

"Hello?" I said.

"Is she there, Field?" a gruff voice asked.

"Yes, Sheriff. Just let me unlock the handcuffs so you can speak to her." I took the pillow from Jamie's head and handed her the phone. Frankie wagged his tail, once.

"Handcuffs," she said, "very funny. What *time* is it?"

I turned on the lamp, nearly knocking over the dozen roses I'd given Jamie earlier. Frankie grunted, opened one eye, then closed it. "A little after two," I said, steadying the vase.

Jamie pulled her hair back, took the phone, said hello to her soon-to-be ex-uncle-in-law, paused, then said: "What? No, that's just his idea of a joke." She listened a moment and her face fell. She sighed, uh-huhed, took the Lord's name in vain twice—once for the Father and once for the Son—then said, "No, I've got my car. I'll meet you there."

She handed me the receiver, swung her long naked legs over the side of the bed, and reached for one of my T-shirts. "They found Judge Merton's car." She shimmied into my shirt. "God, it's cold in here. In a ditch outside of Union."

She flipped her hair back with the backs of her hands then got up—hugging herself to keep warm—and went toward the bathroom.

Frankie got up too, circled once, then quickly moved into Jamie's spot while the sheets were still warm and fragrant with her scent. "So, was I right?" I asked, stroking Frankie's ear. "Was he murdered?"

"Well, yeah," she stopped in the bathroom door, "you were right, Jack. Uncle Horace said the judge's throat had been cut to shreds. So for now it looks like a homicide. Though it won't officially be *anything* either way until I say so, remember?" She went into the bathroom and closed the door.

"Well, I'm sorry you have to go out there." I had to raise my voice to be heard over the sound of running water.

She poked her head back out. "Darling, I have to *pee*. If we're going to have a conver*sation*—"

"Just leave the door open."

She looked at me like I was nuts. "No *way*." She went back inside. "Anyway, I'm still mad at you."

This was the first I'd heard of it. "Mad at me for what?"

I got no answer. I got up, went to the door, and waited for the sound of the water to stop running. Instead, I heard a loud crack, coming from somewhere outside the house. It was followed by a long, shimmering crackle. The toilet flushed, Jamie stuck her head out the door. "What was *that*?"

"I don't know. Probably a branch on the willow tree, breaking under all that ice. Why are you mad at me?"

She propped the door open, washed her hands, then dried them on my terry-cloth robe, which hung on the back of the door. "You're the hotshot psychologist—slash—detective; you tell *me*. Why does this always feel like the warmest room in the house?"

"I don't know, the hot water pipes? Could you use that

towel instead of my robe? And I'm an *ex*-detective, remember?" She finished drying her hands on my robe, then took a toothbrush from the holder over the sink. I said, "*And* an ex-psychologist. I gave them *both* up to do something a little more honest."

"Hah! Dog training? That's more honest?"

"The way *I* do it, it is. And I still can't believe those cops wouldn't stick around long enough to look for the bullets."

"I know." She squeezed the tube at the wrong end, then put it back, leaving the cap off, as usual. "You know, I'm a little worried about Darryl and Annie. Mostly Darryl, since I think he's just drinking to keep her company. But if you must know, I'm really worried about *us*." She started brushing her teeth.

"Us? Well, don't worry. We're just going through our dominance phase." She shot me a look, her mouth foamy with toothpaste. "Sure," I said, "that's what all these jokes about the handcuffs and love slaves and stuff are all about. The cathexis phase—which lasts about three months with most couples—is coming to an end. Now we're engaged in an unconscious sexual dialectic over who's going to control our relationship."

She laughed so hard she almost choked on her Crest. She rinsed and said: "That is about the *stupid*est thing . . ." She dried her mouth on the back of my robe and was still laughing as she began brushing her hair. She took an elastic thingie off the doorknob and pulled the hair back into a ponytail. "Anyway, I thought you didn't believe in dominance."

"Not in dog training. It's a purely sexual behavior. And what sex has to do with teaching a dog to sit on com—"

"Okay," she said, pushing me out of the door, "then who wears the pants in this relationship, you or me?" I told her I didn't care. She shook her head. "Wrong answer, Jack."

"Okay, then *I* do. So, get back in bed right now!" I went

back to the bed myself, got under the covers—it *was* cold—and slapped them for emphasis. Frankie wagged his tail, nervously.

Jamie picked her jeans up off the floor, came over to the bed, and kissed the top of my head. "Nice try, but that's not what I'm mad about." She stroked Frankie's neck and ears. He rolled over on his back, hoping for a tummy rub. She obliged. I was about to ask her again what I'd done to upset her, and she said, " 'Thankfully,' " then put on her jeans and began buttoning them. "Remember? When Annie asked if we'd talked about getting married? You said the topic had 'thankfully' never come up."

"Oh, *that*." I felt my face flush. "That was just a joke. And by the way, next Valentine's can we go someplace quiet instead of to a pool hall with a bunch of your friends?"

"A bunch of my friends," she snorted. "Jack, we were there with *one* other couple. You are such a misanthrope. And the thing is, I want us to have a social life. So far, Darryl and Annie are the only people I know who actually *like* you. You've alienated almost everyone else in my life."

"That's true. Except Jonas and Laura." (Jamie's divorced parents.) "They're both crazy about me."

She took my hand. "Yeah, they are. Probably only because *I* am. Anyway, I've been thinking it over and I think the only reason you're attracted to me is because I'm unavailable." She began looking around the room. "The minute my divorce goes through, you'll lose all interest in me. Have you seen my bra?"

"Oh, come on," I said, pointing to the bra, which was hanging on the brass bedpost. "I *adore* you, you know that."

She took off my T-shirt and began doing that wonderful thing women do when putting on their bras; breasts bobbing, shoulders and elbows flying. "What are *you* looking at?"

"Nothing." I continued with Frankie's tummy rub.

She flipped her ponytail up, then put on a thermal T-shirt

and turtleneck sweater. "I mean, think about it—why else would you be single at your age?" She flipped her ponytail back down.

"My age?" (I'm forty-one, Jamie is thirty-two.) "You know, I love the way you flip your hair around like that."

"Really? Because I was thinking about getting it cut. I guess I won't now. And the answer is simple. You're attracted to unavailable women." She'd worn one pair of socks to bed. Now she picked a second pair off the rug and began putting them on. "You know, I'd really like to meet one of your old girlfriends; if you have any—you never talk about them—but if you *do* have some, I'm sure they'd all agree with me."

"Well, you may get your wish soon. And if you're so mad at me, then what just happened a couple of hours ago?"

She let out a disgusted sigh, like I was a total idiot, then looked around for her boots. I pointed her toward the door. "It's *Valentine's*," she said as she went to get them. "You think I'm going to let a little thing like being mad at you get in the way of my having some great sex?"

"So it was great, huh?"

"Un-huh." She sat on the edge of the bed and began putting on her Timberlands. "Besides, I had to collect on our bet. I won at pool, remember? So, what wish am I going to get?" She looked around the room. "My own underwear drawer? Some closet space? Maybe a space heater?"

I felt my face flush again. "I hadn't thought about it."

"Well, I'm getting tired of living half at my mother's house and half here. Maybe I'm just tired of the cold. So? What wish am I going to get?" I told her that Kristin Downey, an ex-girlfriend from my grad-school days at Columbia, was coming to town. "Ah-hah!" She wiggled her eyebrows. "The plot thickens. Well, I hope you're planning to let me meet her."

"I don't think I could avoid it. She'll be staying in the

downstairs bedroom." She gave me a look. "Well, she *will*. So, is that all I'm good for? Great sex?" I said.

She ran her fingers through my hair. "Don't be silly, sweetheart." She grabbed my beard and tugged on it, then got up and went to the door. Over her shoulder she said: "Don't wait up. I won't be through till morning."

I heard her footsteps on the stairs, then the front door closed. I cuddled up next to Frankie and told him: "You know, she wouldn't be half so cocky if she knew I'd played those last three games of pool left-handed." He said nothing, he just sighed.

A few minutes later Jamie reappeared, tiny snowflakes on top of her blue knit cap and on the shoulders of her yellow nylon parka. She had her car keys in one mittened hand and her gray medical examiner's kit in the other. She looked like a little girl who'd missed the last school bus. "It was the oak," she said, "not the willow. Your branches are blocking my car."

4

I started up the Suburban and Jamie got in, but I thought it a good idea to take a moment and let Leon know where I would be. (Leon stays in the guest cottage, a recently renovated carriage house, which sits recessed between my two-story Victorian home and the kennel building. The renovations were done by one of my dog training clients, Dorianne Elliot.)

I knocked on the door and went right in. I knew he would be asleep, which he was. I turned the light on. He woke up and blinked at me. "Yo, Jack. What's up?"

The two Pomeranians, Scully and Mulder, crawled out from under the covers and looked at me. Scully, the red female, barked once, then both dogs shook themselves in unison. Scully and Mulder, both ten, are owned by the Toland family, but they spend most of their weekends at the kennel. Leon likes them.

I told Leon what was up, then let him and the two dogs go back to sleep. When that was done, I got into the car and Jamie and I headed out to the open road.

Once the heater warmed up, she folded her arms across her ME's kit, leaned back and closed her eyes while I concentrated on not sliding off the mountain. We'd had an ice storm two days earlier; the third one that winter. It was followed now by a light snow, which made the trees and utility lines look like something out of a fairy tale, but made the back roads and even the main highways precarious, to say the least.

"I'm glad we took the Suburban," I said as I tried to slow down for a right turn at the intersection in Hope. "This way we can kill ourselves in four-wheel drive, instead of two."

I pumped the brakes half a dozen times, but all that happened was the car suddenly spun around in circles for about forty yards before coming to a stop on the far side of the crossroads, facing the opposite way. I sat perfectly still, both hands on the wheel, my arms tingling with tension, my cheeks and the tops of my ears burning with adrenaline. I took a moment to let my body vibrate with the quiet throb of the engine and let my mind soak up the silence of the country road.

Jamie opened her eyes. "Stop showing off, Jack," she yawned, "we all know you studied stunt driving at the Police Academy."

"The funny thing is," I laughed to relieve the tension, "I never actually went through the academy." I took a long, deep breath and gunned the engine to five miles an hour, hoping to make the (now) left turn at a more reasonable speed.

Jamie yawned again and said, "Oh, that's right. You were hired by the NYPD as a hotshot psychologist right out of Yale Medical School."

I somehow made the turn onto Route 105, and said, "So, are you still mad at me or is it your father this time? Or both?"

"What are you talking about?"

"I'm a hotshot psychologist, remember. You know very well that Jonas and I both went to Harvard—thirty years apart, of course. And he didn't drop out his second year like I did. Anyway, I figure you said 'Yale' just now as a dig at him or—"

"All right! I'm bugged at the old man, okay?"

"Okay. What's he been doing?"

"It's more a question of what he's *not* doing. He's supposed to be at home, recuperating, you know." I reminded her that I did know, then asked again what Jonas had been doing to upset her. She sighed. "I don't know, I think he's been trying to live up to his image as one of the top thirteen richest doctors in the U.S. What are you laughing at?"

"Your father. He didn't quite make it onto the top *ten* list, so he pretends there's a top *thirteen*. Which one is he?"

She glared at me. "Thirteen," she said, then she started to laugh too. She then explained that Jonas had not only donated a million dollars to Rockland Memorial—and as a result felt he had the right to ask his daughter, who was on staff, to run errands—he'd also invested heavily in a research facility just outside of Portland; studying neurotransmitters. "He's even asked me to run down *there* for him a couple of times. Plus he's making deals with Ian Maxwell, this crazy billionaire inventor—"

"I know who he is. He's the guy who invented that thing, what's it called?"

"I don't know. He's invented a lot of things. Meanwhile, they're working on a top secret, radical new way to perform brain surgery, and Dad wants me to be involved in that too. Like I'm supposed to fly over to Ian Maxwell's private island for a meeting at the drop of a hat because Dad can't go?"

"Honey—why don't you just say no to him?"

"Have you ever tried to say no to my father?"

"I *have* said no to your father. Of course, he didn't listen to me, but I did *say* it."

"Exactly." She stared at the ice. "I'm also worried about Darryl. I think he may be becoming an alcoholic, like Annie."

I shook my head. "I think he just realized that nagging her is the wrong approach. It's like dog training—"

"Be serious. To you, *everything* is like dog training."

"I *am* serious. If you're trying to break a dog of a bad habit, the worst thing to do is tell him no. The best approach is to show him that you value his instincts, then teach him how to channel his energy into a substitute activity; like chasing a tennis ball, say, instead of the cat. Is this where we turn?"

"No, about a half a mile further. What do a cat and a tennis ball have to do with Annie's drinking?"

"Nothing, I guess. I was just thinking that maybe Darryl's been *acting* self-destructive to mirror Annie's behavior. It probably won't work, of course, unless helping *him* get well becomes a substitute addiction for her. She's a nurse, right? Anyway, that's all that these twelve-step programs are. They're just replacement addictions for—"

"Gee, if only everybody in the world would listen to the great Jack Field, all of their problems would be solved."

I noted her sarcasm, remembering a little too late that her soon-to-be ex-husband's cocaine habit had ruined their marriage.

We skated to a stop at another three-way, with a flashing red light reflecting off the ice-laden trees. "Right or left?"

"Right. Don't you know your way around yet? You've only been living here for two years."

"It's all this ice," I said, making the turn. "I can't tell if I'm in Maine or if we're living on Mars."

"And why did you drop out of Harvard? You never told me."

"I didn't?" She shook her head. "Well, when my mom died and I went home for the funeral, I never made it back to Cambridge."

"How did she die?" I must have had some kind of look on my face because she said, "I'm sorry. Maybe I shouldn't ask."

Now was not the time to tell her about my mother's battle with mental illness, or her suicide. "No," I said, "of course you can ask. It's just a topic that's better suited for another place and time, that's all."

We drove in silence for a while, then Jamie made a hmphhing sound and said: "Kristin Downey. What an awful name. It's so fucking pretty. I hate her already. What's she like?"

"Who knows? She used to be the jeans and T-shirt type."

"Is that the type you like?"

"No, you're my type. You and only you. Would you get off it please?" She agreed to stop talking about it, but I knew it was only a matter of time before the subject came up again.

It did feel nice, however, to know that Jamie was jealous. But the fact that it felt good to me also made me feel a little guilty and ashamed. Jealousy is a painful feeling, and I never want Jamie to be in pain over anything if I can help it.

5

A few miles past Union, on State Road 17, we came to a dairy farm. Jamie told me to go easy and I slowed to a crawl.

We came around a long, gracious curve and saw the orange lights from a tow truck, the red lights from an ambulance and two sheriff's Jeeps, and the blue lights from three State Police cars, all making multicolored nimbi in the falling snowflakes.

They were parked on the right side of the road, on a broad, level stretch of ice between the highway and a high plank fence surrounding the dairy farm. On the left side of the road was a narrow ditch where a dark green Cadillac sat, its front bumper kissing a brake of ice-laden quaking aspens. It was tilted at a slight angle, blocking the driver's side door; a door the driver wouldn't be needing any longer. A group of figures stood in a semicircle of flashlights to our left, forming a tableau about twenty feet from the passenger door of the Cadillac. Their breath made bright clouds in the cold night air.

A deputy suddenly appeared in the edge of my headlights and tried to wave us by. I recognized the compact figure of Quentin Peck, stopped and rolled down the window.

"Nothing to see, sir," Quentin said. "Just drive on by."

"Hi, Quent. How's it goin'?"

"Oh, hiya, Jack." His tobacco eyes glittered. He flashed me a quick, nicotine grin, then tilted his head sideways and beamed in at Jamie. "Hey, how are ya, Dr. Cutter?" Jamie said she was fine. Quentin nodded with his chin then pointed down the right side of the road with his flashlight.

"Just pull 'er up there on the other side of Flynn's Jeep." I started to tell him I wasn't going to pull 'er up on the other side of Flynn's Jeep, or anywhere else for that matter—I was just there to drop Jamie off—when he looked over his shoulder at the Cadillac and said, "Sure am glad you're here, Jack. That damn dog won't let us anywhere near the body."

"Dog? What dog?" I looked at Jamie.

She was as puzzled as I was.

Quent said, "Didn't you know? I thought that's why you was here. There's a vicious dog in the car with the judge. Mattera fact, it looks to me like maybe he's the one that did it. You know, kilt the ol' man. His throat's all shredded."

A tall, imposing figure detached itself from the tableau and moved toward my Chevy Suburban. As it did, a narrow beam of light snicked across my front license plate, caressed the top of my hood, and, a second later, a female voice as dry and matter-of-fact as John Wayne's said, "What's the trouble here, Deputy?"

"No trouble, Sergeant. I'm just letting these two know where to park."

"Oh, sorry." The John Wayne voice warmed and the beam of light traveled across our faces. "Is this the daughter?"

Quent said, "Uh, no, ma'am. That's Dr. Cutter—"

"Hi." Jamie leaned across me. "I'm with the state ME's Office. This is Jack Field. He's a hotshot dog trainer."

"Hotshot," I said, "that's your favorite word tonight." I turned to the female trooper. "As a matter of fact, I'm one of the top thirteen dog trainers in the United States." The trooper seemed puzzled. Jamie dug an elbow into my ribs.

"Well, it's lucky you came by," the trooper said. "Animal Control slid off the road outside Cooper's Mills. It'll be a while before they can get a tow. Maybe you could give us a hand with the dog? I'm Sergeant Loudermilk, by the way."

The flashlight moved away from our faces, my eyes adjusted, and I could see that Sergeant Loudermilk had short, dishwater hair tucked under a State Police hat, a big horse face, bright red cheeks, and watery blue eyes. She held out a gloved hand. I shook it. She said, "Ow!" and pulled it away.

"Sorry," I said. I didn't think I'd shook it that hard.

"It's okay. It's just cramping up from the cold." She shook it. "Think you can do anything with the dog?"

I was about to respond in the negative when Quent grunted, "Good luck. He already attacked me and Trudy Compton."

Jamie said, "I thought Trudy was a switchboard operator."

"She is," Quent said. "She's studying to become a deputy, though. Tonight was her first patrol."

"Poor thing. Is she okay?" Jamie asked.

"Ah, she's all right," Quent said. "Just spraint her ankle's all. She's over there." He pointed toward the ambulance where Trudy, a tall, black deputy, sat on the back bumper, her ankle wrapped in a bandage. Two paramedics—one male, one female—were sitting inside, drinking hot coffee, which steamed around their tired, empty faces.

"Well, I'd better go have a look." Jamie got out and headed that way.

I told Sergeant Loudermilk I wasn't equipped to handle a strange dog. "What kind is it, anyway?"

Quent said, "A boxer. Belongs to Ron and Beth Stevens."

"You mean Roark?" I said.

"Oh, that's right," Quent recalled, "I seen him out at your kennel that time I brung Emma over to get her trained."

"You know the dog?" Loudermilk asked. I said I did; he'd boarded with me a few times. I asked her what he was doing in the car. It turned out that Beth Stevens, the owner of the dog, was Judge Merton's daughter, then she repeated

Quentin's theory of the case. "Near as we can figure, the dog attacked the judge while he was driving. The man's throat is all ripped up."

I thought it over. "Well, I can tell you for a fact that the dog didn't do it," I said. "He wouldn't hurt a flea."

"You ain't seen the body, Jack," Quent said. "Me, I had a quick look through the door. It wasn't a pretty sight."

Loudermilk snorted. "Lookit, maybe you oughta park your vehicle and then we can talk." She turned and walked away.

I let out a long sigh and shook my head. The last thing I wanted was to get mixed up in another police investigation. Of course, all I was *supposed* to do was secure the dog and go home. The trouble is, certain habits die hard with me. I knew that if I hung around this particular crime scene long enough, I'd be unable to keep myself from getting involved somehow. Screw it, I thought. Just take care of the dog and go home. I put the car in gear but was interrupted by a beeping sound. The tow truck was backing its way toward the Cadillac. I hung my head and sighed. See what I mean? I thought. Then I called out to Loudermilk and waved her back. She came over and folded her arms across her ample chest, giving me a look.

I shrugged a smile. "Look, maybe I'm wrong about the dog, okay? But if I'm *right*, you might want to hold off with that tow truck. You know, until you can search the area for tire tracks, footprints, trace evidence? I don't know if you're familiar with a little thing in law enforcement we call clues?" I may have had a slightly sarcastic tone in my voice.

Loudermilk thought it over, then yelled at the tow truck. "Hey, Lenny! Let's hold off for a bit, okay? We got a hotshot animal expert here to take care of the dog."

6

After I parked the Chevy and came around the front of Flynn's Jeep, I overheard him on the two-way, "What do you mean you're not sending anyone till after sunup?" There was a pause. "No, I'm not gonna sit around in the cold waiting for one of your newspaper's lazy-ass photographers to come take my picture. They never heard of flashbulbs?" He thought it over. "Well, I *may* be here, I may not. Depends."

"Hello, Sheriff. Election year, huh?"

He glowered at me, then signed off. "What are *you* doing here, Field?"

I shrugged. "Jamie's car was blocked by some fallen branches. Why didn't you say anything to her about the dog?"

He shot me a look, then twitched his big salt-and-pepper mustache. "Why do you think?" He wrestled his potbelly out of the car. "Damn mutt's lucky we didn't shoot him already."

"Oh, that'll win you a lot of votes—killing an innocent dog."

Before he could hit me, Jamie and Sergeant Loudermilk came over. Then—after we'd all gotten how cold it was out of the way—Sergeant Loudermilk walked us across the road to where the others were standing. She introduced us to an Officer Fisher or Fletcher, a nervous young buck holding a shotgun, and an Officer Smith who held a thermos and cupful of coffee.

Roark's face was now visible through the side window of the Cadillac. He was panting. He saw us and began to bark.

"See?" Flynn had followed us. "He's a vicious maniac."

The bark of the "vicious maniac" turned into a high-pitched whine. Deep wrinkles started to form on his troubled forehead. A look of fear clouded his big brown eyes.

"Funny—what I see is a cold, frightened animal who doesn't know what's going on, or what he's supposed to do about it."

Jamie said, "For what it's worth, Uncle Horace, Trudy says the dog didn't actually attack her. She was just startled by him and slipped on the ice."

"Would you two like some coffee?" Loudermilk asked. We said yes. Loudermilk turned to go back across the road, slipped, caught her balance, and as she did, a loud bark came from the Cadillac. Officer Fisher, or Fletcher, raised his shotgun—just as a reflex: I doubt if he actually intended to shoot through the window. But before he could take aim, I stepped in—somewhat reflexively myself—and knocked the barrel up, accidentally smacking him hard on the cheek. He slipped and fell backward, knocking his head on a rock. As he went down, I snatched his gun away. Officer Smith looked over, shook his head at the rookie, then took another sip from his thermos.

The kid glared up at me and said, "Hey!" then took a gloved hand away from the back of his head. In the moonlight his blood looked like black shoe polish.

Loudermilk sighed and said, "Your turn in the ambulance, Fletcher," then took the shotgun away from me.

Jamie said, "Thanks a lot, Jack. With you around we never run out of patients."

"Depends how you spell it," Flynn said.

Jamie helped Fletcher to his feet, then followed him as he ambled to the ambulance.

Loudermilk explained to me—quite patiently, I thought,

under the circumstances—that my only reason for being allowed at the scene was that Animal Control couldn't make it for another couple of hours or so and that I was familiar with the dog. "But listen here, if you don't behave yourself—"

"I appreciate that. I just want it understood that nobody shoots that dog while I'm around."

"Well then, maybe you'd better leave," Flynn said.

"Let me handle this, Sheriff." She sucked a tooth and said, "Listen here, Mr. Field, you know as well as I do that Officer Fletcher wasn't going to shoot that dog."

Smith said, "Hah!" We looked over at him. He kind of blushed, said, "Uh," then pretended to clear his throat. "I think I got something stuck in my windpipe."

I turned back to Loudermilk. "And, no, I don't know that for sure. Look, just let me handle the dog and get him out of your way, okay? Then you can get on with your investigation."

She rolled her tongue around in her cheek for a bit, nodded, then said, "Okay, then. You need anything?"

I asked her to have everybody turn off their flashlights and headlights and go back across the road and get inside their vehicles. I also asked if she could find me a blanket.

"What's the matter, Field, you cold?"

I ignored Flynn's sarcasm.

Loudermilk said, "I've got one in the trunk." She went around the back of her vehicle but stopped short when she put the key in. She seemed troubled about something. She gave me a suspicious look. "What do you need the blanket for?"

"It's less lethal than buckshot." She didn't understand, so I explained. "Look, if the dog decides to charge me, I'll throw the blanket over his head. That should stop him, or at least slow him down long enough for me to take control. And it won't hurt him or kill him like getting shot would."

She did that thing with her tongue again, rolling it around

in her cheek. Maybe she had a loose filling. "Are you sure you don't want to wait? Animal Control has all the equipment—"

"I know; the catch pole, the padded suit, the stun gun."

Jamie came back from the ambulance. She dug an elbow in my ribs. "All *he* needs is his charm. Isn't that right, hotshot?"

"Yeah, and if that doesn't work, at least I know there's a doctor in the house. And didn't somebody mention something about coffee? I take mine black."

Loudermilk opened the trunk and gave me the blanket, then went to get our coffee. While she was doing this, Jamie and Flynn started up a conversation about Jamie's soon-to-be ex-husband (and Flynn's nephew), Oren Pritchett, who'd just come back from a treatment center in Arizona and was going to NA meetings every day in Portland. I got bored with the topic so I took my coffee a ways down the road to "visit" a tall maple tree. When I came back, Jamie was mad at me again.

"What did I do now?"

"Don't play dumb with me, Jack."

Everyone else was inside their vehicles. Jamie and I were walking back to the Chevy; she to get inside, start up the heater, and stay there while I secured the dog, me to find some treats and a tennis ball. The headlights, flashlights, and roof lights had all been turned off. The moon was high, though, almost full; shedding plenty of icy, winter light to see by.

"I'm told you've been acting like you're in charge of this whole investigation."

"Honey," I said, "you're the one who's always pestering me to put my detective skills to good use, saying how you *want* me to get involved in your little murders."

"*My* little murders? And I don't care if you get involved in them or not." She stopped. "Well, that's not true. Actually,

I'd love it if you would. But just—*please*—try not to piss people off. Is that too much to ask?"

I opened the passenger door to let her in. She picked up her ME's kit, got in the car, and put it in her lap. I stood there, holding the door open.

I said, "If anyone's pissed off it's only because they're wrong and I'm right."

She shook her head and sighed. "See? That's exactly the kind of attitude I'm talking about."

"Can you grab me some liver treats and a tennis ball from the glove box?"

She did as I asked.

"Anyway, why yell at me? All *I* want to do is get Roark out of that car and go home. Okay?"

"Okay." I was about to close the door when she said, "Honey?" Her face looked small again, like that little girl who missed the school bus. "Are you sure you're going to be okay? I mean, how certain are you that this dog isn't dangerous?"

I smiled. "Well, unlike certain local law enforcement personnel, I don't jump to conclusions. But I'm about as certain that Roark isn't dangerous as I am that *you're* not."

"That's not very comforting, the way I feel right now."

"You'll get over it. You're just a cupcake at heart."

She tilted her head, then gave me a superior smirk. "You're forgetting who won at pool tonight."

I put the liver treats and tennis ball in my pocket and said, "Yeah, but only because I started playing you left-handed after I won that first game." I was about to close the door, then noticed that her eyes were burning.

"I don't believe it." Her voice was hoarse with emotion.

I was stricken with fear. "Are you really upset?"

She was breathing hard, staring at me with pure hatred. "Oh—yeah. I am *never* . . . never, *ever* speaking to you ever again. Ever." She let out a long breath.

I didn't know what to say, but I didn't get a chance to say anything. Sergeant Loudermilk came over and tapped me on the shoulder. "Can we get on with this?" she said.

"Sure," I said.

"Screw you, Jack," Jamie said, and slammed the door.

Loudermilk said, "Whoa, what's the matter?"

"I'm not sure. It's either part of an ongoing unconscious sexual dialectic or someone has a bad case of PMS."

"I heard that," Jamie said through the window.

7

Unlike Jamie—or *any* woman who's angry at her mate—most dogs will bite only as a last resort. It's kind of a paradox too, since the urge to bite is at the core of a dog's most positive social instincts. This idea flies in the face of conventional wisdom, of course, which says that a dog's social instincts revolve around issues of dominance and submission; who's alpha and who's not. But in my opinion—and in the opinion of more and more experts these days—there is no such thing as an alpha dog. No canine has any desire to be alpha, and no ability to form a social hierarchy based on concepts like rank and status. (Dogs don't think conceptually.) My belief is that the pack is actually a self-emergent heterarchy, in which the behaviors of the individual dogs create the social structure; the social structure doesn't control the individual behaviors.

Besides, all dogs *really* want to do is to chase things and bite them, which is the foundation of their prey instinct. And canine social behavior is inextricably linked to prey drive, particularly the need to hunt large prey.

Think of it like this: when a lone wolf bites into a fleeing rabbit, the crunch of bone and flesh between his teeth and jaws is a highly pleasurable thing. But when that same wolf—working in glorious synchronicity with his pack-mates—bites into a galloping deer or a cornered elk and feels the moist, hot, massive flesh tear away from the animal's heaving body, while his packmates are all emotionally aligned to the same purpose, and are all filled with the same wild emotions, that, my friends, is pure ecstasy.

I should know. I was a wolf in a former life.

This didn't make my journey across the road to Judge Merton's Cadillac any less nerve-wracking. I'd dealt with aggressive dogs before. I'd even been bitten four or five times, though most of the incidents were accidental. A high-strung standard poodle named Ozymandius once tried to grab a tennis ball from my hand and bit me on the thumb instead. A poor, neurotic boxer named Spike did the same thing to my arm. (Either I moved at the last second or he had bad aim.) My saving grace with Roark was I knew that he liked to play fetch, which is why I had a tennis ball in my pocket just in case I couldn't lure him out of the car with the liver treats.

I had another thing on my side—a sensible caution based on a studied understanding of a dog's den instincts. You see, there's this thing about dogs and doorways. The dominance crowd believes that a dog who goes through a door ahead of you is trying to be alpha. Supposedly one of the perks of being the top dog is being the first to go through any opening. The truth is much simpler (it always is): whenever a dog senses movement at the threshold of the den, his bite reflex is automatically stimulated. Why? My theory is that crossing thresholds is a risky business; there might be danger just outside the den door when you leave, there might also be danger lurking inside when you come home. A canine's bite reflex has to be right up on the surface, available to use, whenever he leaves the den or whenever someone else comes in. This is the only reason some dogs and wolves snap at others who go through a door ahead of them. It has nothing to do with being alpha.

I remembered all this as I approached Roark, ending up about four feet from the passenger side of the car. By this time he was a barking, snarling maniac—just as Flynn and

Quentin Peck had described him. The car door was the same for him as the door to a wolf's den. He was ready to guard it with his life. Any attempt by me, or anyone else, to get inside that car, or to even put a hand through the door, would result in bloodshed. Offering him a liver treat would lose me a finger. Teasing him with a tennis ball, then throwing it across the ice, would have no effect. The question was: How could I entice him to get out of the car voluntarily?

I couldn't. I realized I'd have to *force* him out somehow. I wished for a moment that I'd waited for Animal Control. Having a padded suit on, even wearing just the arm pad, would certainly help. I had a quick mental image of Roark grabbing hold of my padded arm with his teeth, the way attack dogs are trained to, and that's when it hit me: tug-of-war. Screw the liver treats, screw the tennis ball, screw the army blanket. All I needed was something Roark could sink his teeth into. Then—once he was fully committed to playing tug-of-war with me—I could yank him out of the car and onto the ice. Presto!

I searched my pockets for a tug toy or a bandanna. Then I noticed the tassels of the ragg wool scarf Jamie's mother, Laura, had given me for Christmas and thought, "Shit, there goes a perfectly good muffler." I untwirled it from around my neck and had a perfect tug toy.

I opened the door, and as soon as I did, Roark faked a lunge at me, but stayed inside, as I knew (or hoped) he would. I began teasing him with my makeshift tug toy, waving it around the door, trying to entice him to grab hold of it. He was more intent on growling and snarling at me, though, so I began praising him as I danced the scarf in front of his nose. The praise was not to reward him for trying to kill me, but to make him feel that we were on the same side; that we both wanted the scarf "dead." I even threw in a few fake growls of my own, to let him know that the two of us were killing the scarf together.

It worked. He stopped focusing on me and grabbed the scarf and pulled on it, hard. In fact, he pulled *so* hard he almost yanked me into the car. I don't know how, but I managed to stay upright. We played tug for a few seconds, me praising him and doing my fake "play-growl" the whole time, and then I used the scarf, and leverage from the open car door, to pull Roark's ass outside and onto the icy ground. He lost hold of the scarf, then grabbed it again. What a silly goose. He wanted to kill me a moment earlier, now he was helping me "kill" my muffler.

I let go of the scarf and praised him for beating me—which is how all tug-of-war games should end; you always praise the dog for winning—then, while he shook his head around as if breaking the neck of the fallen scarf, I took hold of his leash, which he'd been wearing while he was in the car, and began to lead him gently up the side of the ditch, stopping for just a moment to take a look inside the vehicle. Just as I'd thought, there was almost no blood visible on the judge's spent air bag.

I was startled by an unfamiliar sound. I looked across the road and saw that everyone was standing outside their vehicles, applauding. Everyone except Jamie and Sheriff Flynn.

I gave an embarrassed wave, then walked Roark across the road to the Suburban. Loudermilk met me there.

"Nice work, Mr. Field." She reached down to pet Roark's head. He wagged his tush, happily. He seemed to like her.

"Call me Jack. And yeah, I was lucky, I guess."

She nodded and asked if I wouldn't mind keeping the dog at my kennel for a few days. I said I'd be glad to, and she said she'd drop by later to take care of the official paperwork.

I put him in the back of the vehicle and gave him a tennis ball to chew on for when he'd finished destroying my muffler.

I came around the front and got into the cab of the truck. Jamie's face was cold, empty of emotion. "I'll need to get some swatches from the dog, in case there's any blood on his jaws."

"Want me to do it?"

"No. Legally, you *can't* do it, you're not an ME or a CSI." She looked back at Roark. "Unless you think he's going to bite me."

"He won't bite." I smiled. "Any more than *you* would."

She ignored me, then put on a pair of latex gloves, got a squeeze-bottle of distilled water and some cotton swabs from her kit, and went to the back of the car. When she'd finished her swatches, she came around to the front of the car to put them in a brown paper bag. She unrolled some white tape and sealed the bag, then wrote on it with a Magic Marker. She did all this standing next to the car, with the door open. "All set."

"Listen, honey—"

"Don't talk to me."

"Oh, just get over it, all right? You know you're going to have to get over it eventually." She said nothing. "You want a rematch? Okay, I'll play you right-handed this time. Or we can *both* play left-handed. Will that satisfy you?" She almost chuckled. "Or we can both play with one hand tied behind our backs." She started to laugh. "Or we can play with both hands tied behind each other's backs. Wouldn't *that* be fun?"

She couldn't keep it in any longer. It wasn't that funny, but it released a lot of tension. After a while she got in next to me and said, "Okay, so you made me laugh. But you're not getting off that easy. Incidentally, nice work with the dog."

I said thank-you.

"Uncle Horace is pressuring me to reconcile with Oren. That's why I'm acting this way. I don't mean to be such a bitch about everything. I am being a bitch tonight, aren't I?"

"Are you kidding? I'm not going to answer that."

"Smart boy." She smiled, then sighed. "He's been clean

for a couple months now, and Flynn thinks if I give him another chance it'll improve his recovery."

"Un-huh. And what do *you* think?"

"I don't know. I told Uncle Horace I'd think about it."

I was stunned. "What do you mean, you'll think about it? What's there to think about?"

"Don't look at me like that, Jack. I don't know what's going to happen with us. I'm scared we're not going to make it. Your ex-girlfriend is coming to live with you, and—"

"She's not coming to *live* with me, she's just going to be visiting for a few days. That's all."

"Really?" She wanted to be convinced, wanted me to say something tender and permanent. That's when I realized this was just a game on her part, a game that she herself didn't realize she was playing. She said, "What are you *laughing* at?"

"You, you knucklehead. You realize that if you get back together with Oren, that means *we* have to break up."

"I know." She seemed serious. "Would that bother you?"

"No, not much. Only in endless, infinite amounts. What is *wrong* with you? Of *course* it would bother me."

"It would?"

"Are you kidding? I would be emotionally eviscerated."

"Then why did you say 'thankfully' when Annie asked if we'd ever talked about getting married?"

I sighed. "It's called banter, you should try it sometime. Look, don't you have a body to examine?"

She nodded, unlatched the door, but let it sit there, half open. She smiled. "So, how's your racquetball game, hotshot?"

"What? I don't know, I haven't played in years."

"Good, I'll schedule a court. If you can beat me at racquetball, I'll forgive you for playing left-handed at pool."

"And what if I lose?"

She gave me a look. "Don't worry. I'll think of some way to make you pay me back. Maybe I'll borrow a pair of handcuffs from Uncle Horace and really make you suffer." She got a playful look on her face, unzipped my parka and tried to twist my nipples with both hands, but my sweater was too thick.

Suddenly, a bright arc of headlights came swooping through the windshield. We shielded our eyes, and then, after the headlights went off, we looked outside and saw Ron and Beth Stevens climbing out of a Camden police cruiser.

Sergeant Loudermilk came over to meet the couple. Ron put his arm around Beth's shoulder but she flinched and moved away.

Loudermilk, who was a good six inches taller than Ron, pointed to the judge's car but didn't allow Beth to go in that direction. She just ushered them back toward the police car. Before they could get inside, more vehicles showed up; and there appeared a sudden crush of reporters and TV crews. Loudermilk, Flynn, Quentin Peck, and the others motioned the vultures away from the scene, showing them where to park. A few of them got through, poking microphones into Beth Stevens's face. Finally, Loudermilk got the couple into the back of the Camden cruiser, where they sat staring morosely at the scene.

Jamie sighed and turned to me. "Life sucks. You know?"

"Not life, honey. Homicide detail. That's why I run a kennel now, remember?"

Then I heard a familiar sound; one that always sends shivers of pleasure up my spine, for some reason. I looked in the back of the truck and saw Roark, lying there, grunting with pleasure, happily chewing away on his favorite new toy; a dirty old tennis ball. He looked up once and stared off into space, as if he were trying to remember something he *should've* been doing; guarding his den, perhaps? He couldn't seem to think of what it was, though, so he just went back to chewing his ball.

8

The next morning was bright and cold. I spent the early part of the day clearing dead branches and dealing with glitches at the kennel. Mrs. Murtaugh, who's in charge of the salon, had back pains again, so I sent her home to lie down, which meant I had to ask Sloan to come in and help D'Linda with the grooming—Saturday is our big day for it—and they don't like each other. D'Linda (short, stocky, with a big florid face and overworked straw hair) is—as Sloan would put it—"trailer trash," while Sloan (twenty-one, tall, slender, with hair and eyes the color of wet sand) is—in D'Linda's words—a snob. They're both right.

I spent the morning refereeing, then at eleven I took Frankie and Roark out to the play yard. Frankie was more interested in finding the best place to pee than he was in playing. Meanwhile, Roark was in a very playful mood, which is always fun to see in a boxer. He'd start off by doing a play bow, enticing Frankie to move toward him. If Frankie did, Roark would spin his body around in a full circle then take off like a rabbit—his back end in third gear and his front end in first. If Frankie wouldn't chase him, he'd come back at full speed and do a flying nip at Frankie's butt as he passed by. That usually got Frankie out of his urinary coma (and got me laughing), and then Frankie would start barking and running after Roark, who—I swear—had the biggest and happiest smile you've ever seen on anyone's face. (They say dogs don't smile but I know better.)

When they were tired enough, I took Roark back to the kennel and took Frankie inside the house, then left D'Linda in charge, while Leon and I went into town to play a little one-on-one at the high school gym. When we pulled into the parking lot, I saw Beth Stevens's husband Ron sitting in a parked car, talking with a female student. They looked like they'd been playing a little one-on-one themselves. After we finished our game, Leon said he wanted to meet some friends at the library. I didn't stop him.

At one I had a training session with Dorianne Elliot and her German shepherd, Satchmo, so I drove to West Rockport, where her construction company is located.

Dorianne Elliot's husband died ten years ago, leaving her a load of debt and a contracting business, which she knew next to nothing about. After the funeral was over, she rolled up her sleeves, dug in her heels, and, in typical Maine fashion, learned everything she could about her husband's business and began to run it herself. In two years she was out of debt. In three she was making a profit. And in five she was making twice the money her husband ever had. Her only problem was Satchmo; if he wasn't interested in coming to her, he would ignore Dorianne when she called him.

I pulled into the gravel parking area in front of the big galvanized steel Quonset hut that housed her offices. She and Satchmo came out to meet me as I got out of the car. We made the usual pleasantries, then she took me around back.

"I have something I want to show you. Remember, you said I should stop taking Satchmo jogging with me? That what he really needs to do is to run full speed for twenty minutes a day?"

I said I did.

"Well, I cleared an area behind the office where we can play Frisbee every day. He loves it!"

She showed me a fenced-in, rectangular area behind the offices and the equipment sheds. It was covered in ice, just like the rest of Rockland County, but she had sprinkled some sand on top of the ice to give Satchmo better traction. She opened the gate and we went inside.

There was a plywood rack, waist high, with two wedge-shaped bins attached. Each bin had a plywood top to keep the rain out. Satchmo went straight for the rack, barking and wagging his tail. There were Frisbees and Aerobies in one bin, and some balls, a tennis racket, and some tug toys in the other.

Dorianne told me she'd built the rack in such a way that Satchmo couldn't get at any of his toys on his own. He had to wait for her to open one of the bins and reach down into it to get the toys out.

"Why did you do that?"

"Because," she tapped me backhanded on the stomach, "you told me that all access to his hunting drive has to come through me, remember? Besides, it keeps everything dry when it rains."

"So what's the problem with his recall?" I asked.

She got an Aerobie out and began teasing Satchmo with it, as I'd taught her to do. "It's these damn Aerobies. They fly great, but sometimes they catch the wind and go over the fence. And when they do, he just stands there, barking at the fence, and won't come back, no matter how much I call him."

"Ah-hah. We need to plug his drive back into you."

She shook her head. "I'm sure you know what that means, Jack, but I haven't the foggiest idea what you just said."

"What it means is: he's more interested in the toy than he is in you. We need to make him feel that his only access to the toy comes through obeying you."

"Okay, but how?"

"How would you like to have Satchmo, while he's in the

process of running full speed after the Aerobie or a tennis ball, stop, turn on a dime, and come running back to you, even faster and harder than he does when chasing the toy?"

She laughed a sour laugh. "Well, as long as you're granting wishes, how about getting me in on some of the contracting business for Ian Maxwell's dream house?"

"I'm sorry?"

"Yeah, me too. I've been a little bummed, since my neighbor—" she pointed to a building next door "—Moon MacKenzie, is doing all the finish work on the place."

I looked up at a hand-carved wooden sign, with old-fashioned lettering overlapping a big quarter moon, painted blue. I'd always thought, when seeing the sign before, that it was a two-man operation: So-and-So Moon & So-and-So MacKenzie. Turns out they were just one guy.

"Okay," I said, "but I still don't—"

She got a sad, faraway look in her eye. "Although I should probably wish him well, considering all the trouble he's been through in the past couple of years."

I got my fifty-foot lead out of the inside pocket of my down vest, hooked Satchmo up to it, and asked her to explain.

We walked toward the center of the play area and she told me that Moon MacKenzie was an accomplished finish carpenter, and that Ian Maxwell (the billionaire inventor who was in business with Jamie's father) was in the process of building a house on a private island somewhere in Penobscot Bay. MacKenzie had been hired to make the custom stairways, banisters, and mantelpieces.

We got to the center of the play area, and she went on to tell me that MacKenzie's troubles of the past few years included the death of his daughter in a drunk driving accident, back in October, and the fact that she got pregnant when she was seventeen by a married cop who later refused to pay child support until she sued his ass in family court and won.

"Ah, gee, that's terrible. Is he a decent guy?"

"Who, MacKenzie? Well, he's temperamental and a bit volatile, but yeah, underneath it all, he's a pretty decent guy. That cop is another story. And she was such a good girl too—Marti. Straight A student, college scholarship, the works."

"Well, my heart goes out to him. A drunk driver, huh?"

"Yeah, he's on trial right now, in fact."

"Well, I hope they fry the bastard. Figuratively speaking, of course. Now, let's get started."

I told Dorianne that the first exercise wasn't going to make any sense.

She laughed. "Yeah, I remember you said that last time."

"But what we did got him to stop scavenging, right?"

She nodded her head in wonder. "The minute he sees a piece of food on the ground, the first thing he does is look up at me. He totally forgets the food. It's amazing."

"Even though what I showed you didn't make any sense."

"That's right."

I began to teach Satch and Dorianne three simple exercises that took less than two minutes each, not including the time it took to explain them. And when we were done, about ten or twelve minutes later, Dorianne was able to get Satch, while he was in the middle of chasing a ball, to turn on a dime and come running straight back to her, even faster and harder than he'd been running while chasing the ball.

After we'd finished, Dorianne said, "Am is supposed to do this every day?"

I laughed. "No. If we did it right, I'll only need to proof it once, which I am going to do right now." I teased Satch with the Aerobie, then threw it. Before he could get fifty feet, I shouted, "Ho! Satchey, come!"

He turned in mid-chase and came running back to me at

full speed. “Okay, that’s it,” I said. “You can mail me a check.”

“You’ve got to be kidding.”

“Nope. Try it right now.” I tossed her a tennis ball.

“Okay,” she said, unconvinced, “here goes nothing.”

“Make sure to tease him with it first.”

She did, then threw the ball, and Satchmo went after it.

“Okay,” I said, “call him.”

She did, and Satchmo tried to turn on a dime in mid-chase, but slipped and skittered on the sandy ice. Still, he stopped chasing the ball and, finally, when he got his balance, came running back, fast and furious. I tossed Dorianne the tug toy.

“This is unbelievable!” she said, laughing and playing tug with the wild and happy dog.

“It’s all in the drive, my dear, it’s all in the drive. If he forgets tomorrow, I’ll come out again and he’ll remember it pretty quick. He’s a good boy! Aren’t you, Satchmo? Who’s the good boy!” He came running over, jumped up and kissed my face. “What a good boy!”

9

When I got back to the kennel, there were two strange vehicles in the drive. One was a red Volvo station wagon, apparently belonging to the Asian girl Farrell Woods had called Tulips the other night, because she was pacing next to it and smoking a cigarette. She was wearing a cheap knock-off of a bomber jacket with the usual fleece collar, but the leather was artificially aged and it was cut in a more feminine fashion than the real thing. She also wore large hoop earrings, a black newsboy's cap, stretch jeans, and too much makeup. There were ten beagles barking and baying in the back of her car.

"Shut up, goddamnit," she yelled at them, but it had no perceptible effect.

While this was going on, Frankie came running up to me, doing his happy dance. I got out of the car and stroked his head.

The other strange vehicle was a light green state Animal Control panel van with the back door open. A tall, burly, mostly bald man with an absurdly large blond handlebar mustache was trying to get Roark inside. The guy was wearing chinos, a tattersall shirt, a red knit tie, and a green down vest. The boxer boy was not cooperating. In fact, he seemed terrified of the man.

"Thank god, you're here, Jack," D'Linda said. She was smoking a cigarette on the front step of the kennel building.

She was in tears, her mascara running. "This man says he has permission to take Roark away and have him put to sleep."

"Like hell he does." I went over and took Roark's leash. Or tried to—the guy wouldn't let go. He had huge hands, the right one of which sported a class ring on the ring finger. His grip was strong, but I looked up and saw his eyes were the color of caramel. "This is a vicious dog, sir," he said.

The "vicious dog" flinched and squinted his eyes every time the man spoke or shifted his weight. "Yeah, he's awful vicious." I reached one hand down to pet Roark's head for a second. When I stopped, he nudged me with his nose.

The guy stroked his mustache with his left hand, then dropped it at his side. "I'm not going to argue with you about this, sir. This dog is a danger to public safety, and is scheduled to be put down immediately."

Frankie came over and licked the guy's free hand. He must have liked the flavor of his mustache wax.

He pulled his hand away. "Get your dog away from me."

"Frankie, leave it," I said, and he did.

"That dog should be on a leash."

I laughed. "Are you kidding? This is private property. You're the one who should be on a leash."

He huffed. "I am a public official, and if you continue to interfere, I'll have you taken away in handcuffs."

I laughed. "Yeah, provided you live long enough."

He was startled. "Are you threatening me?" He sounded genuinely surprised. He was a good five inches taller than I am (I'm six-one) and he was built like a beer truck. Being threatened was probably a rare thing in his experience.

"Let's call it a polite warning, shall we?"

The beagles yipped and howled. D'Linda and the singer from Gilbert's stared at us. Me and Mr. Mustache stared at one another. Then, without breaking eye contact, I said over my shoulder, "D'Linda, go inside and get my gun. We have a thief on the premises."

"Gun?" she said. "What gun?"

"It's in my top desk drawer. Now, go get it."

She went inside. The guy's caramel eyes started to melt. He let go of Roark's leash, looked down at his L.L.Beans, then strode toward the front of his vehicle. As he got in he said over his shoulder, "I'll be back. With the police."

As he drove off, the quaint sound of barbershop quartet music came floating out of the van; "Down by the Old Mill Stream," I think it was. (I found out later that the guy was a member of the Maine Barbershop Quartet Society—which not only explained the music, but the absurd mustache as well.)

I waited until the state van turned onto the county road, then gave my attention to Tulips. "Can I help you?" I said.

"What was *that* all about?" she said.

"Murder and politics. What are you doing with Farrell Woods's dogs in your car?"

"What? No, no. These are *my* dogs, man."

"Oh really? What are their names?"

She tried quickly to think up (or remember) the names of the ten beagles, and as she did, D'Linda came back outside.

"Jesus, Jack, that was scary." She laughed. "I thought for a minute you actually had a gun in there."

"Nah, I was just bluffing. What's Farrell Woods's phone number?"

D'Linda blushed. "How should *I* know."

"Because you buy pot from him."

"Me? Who told you that? Did Sloan say something?"

"No, I just know." I turned to look at Tulips but continued speaking to D'Linda. "Can you go call him for me? And take Roark with you and give him something to eat."

"But, Jack, he won't eat unless I stand inside the kennel with him the whole time." (It was true. Like a lot of people, Roark doesn't like eating alone.)

"Then stand inside the kennel with him."

She shook her head disgustedly and took Roark into the kennel building.

I gave Tulips a look. She chewed her lower lip.

"Okay look," she said, touching my arm, "they're Farrell's dogs—I admit it. But he had to go out of town suddenly and he asked me if I'd drop them off here." Unlike her singing voice, her speaking voice had a sweet, melodic quality.

"So when D'Linda calls him right now, he won't answer?"

She took a long drag on her cigarette, tilted her head, then pulled a bit of tobacco off the end of her tongue—the usual stall. "Well, he still has to pack and shit, so—"

I laughed. "You're a lousy singer but you're an even worse liar. This wouldn't have anything to do with the fact that he burned you on a drug deal last night, would it?"

"What? How did you know about—" She made a nice save. "—about me being a singer?"

"I was at Gilbert's the other night. I heard you sing, or try to. I also overheard you and Farrell arguing. And saw the two of you almost get shot. Now it looks to me like you're trying to get back at him by kidnapping his dogs."

"No way." She threw down her cigarette. It lay there on the gravel, smoldering. I stepped on it. (Why do women never put their cigarettes out properly?) "Okay, look," she stepped closer to me, put her hand on my arm again, then softened her voice by a decibel or two, "first of all, I just want you to know that I'm not a bad singer when I have the right material. Okay? It's just that my voice is better suited for Billie Holiday type stuff than what we have to do down at Gilbert's." She sang a snippet of a Billie Holiday song—"Fine and Mellow"—and she was right, her voice fit it perfectly.

"Second of all, okay—me and Farrell had a little disagreement about what was paid for and what got delivered. But we worked that all out. Now I'm just here trying to do him a favor. He's in trouble and he told *me* you were the only guy he trusted with his dogs. But, if you don't want 'em . . ."

I sighed. Maybe she was wearing me down with the ripple effect of one lie after another. Maybe I was just worried about what might happen to the beagles if I didn't take them. Maybe I felt like I was the only person along the Maine coast who wasn't going around trying to steal or kidnap or shoot other people's dogs that day. Whatever the reason—I caved in. "Okay," I said, looking inside the car, "have they got their leashes on?"

"Leashes?" She made it sound as if I were from Mars.

"Yeah, leashes. You've got ten crazed beagles inside your car. As soon as you open the door, they're going to run off in ten different directions. We'll be lucky to track them down to Canada, Florida, and California."

"What are you, nuts?" she said. "These are Farrell's dogs, man. They *listen*."

With that she opened the back door. All ten beagles jumped onto the gravel drive and started to run off in ten different directions, just as I'd predicted. Then Tulips shouted, "Ten-hut! Beagles in formation!" and they all came running back—forming a makeshift canine military unit right in front of her.

I could swear a couple of them actually saluted.

"Okay," she said, "now I can remember their names, now that I'm looking at them face-to-face. Farrell named them all after singers or musicians that he likes. Except for those who had previous homes—they each came with a name attached. Okay," she looked down at the little squadron, "starting from the left we have Gracie and Janis, named, obviously, after Grace Slick and Janis Joplin." Both dogs were smallish, tricolor beagles, and each had a white tip on the end of their tail. They seemed almost indistinguishable from one another except that Gracie had a slightly larger head. "They love to hang out together. In fact, they're almost inseparable. The next one is Lucy . . ." Lucy had a speckled tan coat and green eyes and seemed uncertain as to what was expected of her. She wagged her tail nervously. "She's their tagalong. Then comes Petey and Wampus. Petey is named after Peter Green, who you've probably never heard of."

"I have, actually. He was one of the founding members of Fleetwood Mac. He wrote the song 'Black Magic Woman.' "

Tulips smiled and touched my arm. "It is so *cool* that you know that. God, you and Farrell would get along so great together."

She looked back down at the beagles. "Next comes Wampus, I have no idea where his name comes from." Petey and Wampus looked just like Grace and Janis, only stockier. "Petey and Wampus are Grace and Janis's brothers," Tulips said. "They never go anywhere without the other one.

"Let's see now, this is Maggie . . ."

Maggie was another tricolor with a white-tipped tail, but unlike the others, she had a white comma-shaped spot on her back, almost over her left hip. She was sniffing furiously at the ground in front of her.

"She's got quite a nose, doesn't she?"

Tulips nodded. "Boy, does she ever. And I don't know where her name comes from, but I always remember her from that Rod Stewart song." She sang, " 'Wake up, Maggie, I think I've got something to say to you . . .' "

"Hey. You *do* have a nice voice."

"Thanks. She's a little bitch, this Maggie. The only person in the group she ever got along with was Brian Wilson, but he's dead. A hawk got him one day, poor little guy."

"A hawk?"

"Yeah, he got eaten by a hawk, can you believe it? Then there's B.B. King and Smokey Robinson, which you can figure out for yourself, and Jimmie, which I always thought was for Jimi Hendrix, but then Farrell told me it was for this old-time country music singer, from like the twenties, that no one has ever heard of except for Farrell and someone named Merle Haggard."

I laughed and didn't even bother trying to explain to her that Jimmie Rodgers was known as the "Grandfather of Country Music," and that Merle Haggard was—well, never mind.

"And finally, this little guy," she pointed to a puppy, probably ten months old or so, "his name is Townes Van Zandt."

Shocked, I said, "He named one of his dogs after Townes Van Zandt?" Unlike the others, the dog's tail was totally white.

"Yeah, you heard of him?"

"Yeah, I've heard of him. I used to collect his records." I looked at the puppy. "So, when he calls this dog," the "he" being Farrell Woods, "he says, 'Townes Van Zandt, come!' and the dog comes?"

"Of course."

Townes Van Zandt wagged his little white tail when he heard me call his name.

"And they know all their commands?"

"Are you kidding? Hah! Farrell should be on Letterman with these dogs. They do absolutely everything he says."

I couldn't resist the impulse. I crouched down and said, "You all stay, *stay*! Townes Van Zandt, come!" The little puppy came wiggling over to me. I picked him up and let him lick my face, which he loved doing.

My god, I thought, I'm going to be living inside a master's thesis on American musicology with these dogs. I said, "How come he hasn't named any of them after Greg Brown?"

"Oh, he would," Tulips said, "but he says he'd need a bigger dog. So, can I go now?"

"Yeah, in a second. I just want to know that Farrell is all right. I mean, after the shooting the other night and all."

"Yeah, man. Wasn't that a drag? I mean, Jesus, I thought it was all over for sure."

"So is he okay?"

She shrugged. "He's kind of incognito, if you know what I mean. But he's handling things, so it should work out. So, can I go now? I've gotta meet somebody."

I said she could.

10

I got the ten musical beagles situated in the laundry room—the one in the house, not in the kennel—then tried to put a call in to Sergeant Loudermilk. The dispatch operator said she was out somewhere, cruising in her radio car, but that she could pass along a message if it was important. I said it was.

"Some idiot from the Governor's Office was just here," I told the operator, "attempting to remove and destroy a key piece of evidence in the investigation into Judge Merton's murder."

"He was murdered? But I thought his dog was the one who—"

"No, he wasn't. And Roark isn't the judge's dog. He belongs to the judge's daughter."

"Okay, whatever. I'll contact the sergeant right away and have her call you."

"Yeah," I said, "please do."

I was busy cleaning the dog hair out of my snow boots a few minutes later when the telephone rang.

Sergeant Loudermilk said, "Did you tell the dispatch operator that Judge Merton was murdered?"

"Well, *wasn't* he?"

She sighed, though it sounded more like a low growl. "At this point, our official position is that the death came about as a result of mauling by an aggressive and dangerous dog."

I laughed. "Well, that explains why this idiot from the Governor's Office was just here threatening to kill Roark."

"Grant Goodrich was at your kennel already?"

I felt my neck go up. "Now, hold it. That sounds like you knew about this beforehand. Why didn't you warn me about him?"

There was a pause. "I didn't know he'd be on this so soon, I just knew, when you mentioned someone from the Governor's Office, that it had to be Goodrich. He runs the Dangerous Dog Task Force. They track down and destroy vicious dogs throughout the state. Pit bulls, mostly. And Rottweilers, I guess."

"There's no such thing as a vicious dog."

She snorted. "Tell that to the Governor's wife. Her niece was mauled five years ago, which was when—"

"—they started this task force. Fine. And I'm not saying there aren't aggressive dogs out there, I'm just saying they're not vicious. That's the wrong word. It implies an intent to do evil. And, unlike guys like Goodrich, dogs *can't* be evil."

"Fine, whatever."

"And another thing . . ." I was about to explain that Rottis and pit bulls can be two of the sweetest breeds on the planet—though I'm always careful around chows and Akitas—but I interrupted myself. "How did Goodrich know Roark was here?"

Another pause. "I don't, um, I don't know. Maybe the press got hold of that information somehow."

"How *would* they, unless you told them?"

She huffed. "I certainly did not."

"Un-huh."

"Now, listen here, Mr. Field, I think I've had just about enough of you and your attitude. Right now, I am a key investigator on this case, and if you're going to continue—"

"Fine, I apologize. Just get that dog-killer out of my hair," or you'll have another murder to investigate, I wanted to add, but stifled myself. It would be imprudent to let a State Trooper hear me threaten to kill a government official.

"I'll do what I can," she said.

"You'll do what you *can*? You were supposed to come by here with an official document, making me the dog's legal caretaker until the investigation is finished. Remember? A so-called dangerous dog has to be kenneled. And he *is*. With me."

"Yes, I remember. And it's an investigation that has a lot of angles I'm actively pursuing. I don't have time to deal with you and your dog troubles. But, as I said, I'll do what I can."

"Angles? What angles? A minute ago you told me the man died of a dog bite."

"Yes, that's the official position as of now, but we *are* pursuing other aspects. And, as I said, I've really had about enough of you and your attitude. I understand you've had years of experience with the NYPD, but this is Maine, buddy. Just let us do our job and everyone around here will be a lot happier."

"Sure, everyone but Roark. He'll be dead."

She hung up on me.

"I'll do what I can," she'd said. That certainly made me feel secure about Roark's future. I sat there for a moment, thinking things over, wondering how much time I had before Goodrich came back with a warrant or a court order.

I called Jamie but got her voice-mail. I left a message for her to call me as soon as possible, then went out to the kennel and got Roark out of his canine "hotel room"—the one with the lobster and sailboat motif.

I told Leon, D'Linda, and Sloan—who was back from her study session—that I was going out and wouldn't be back until five.

"If you need me for anything important," I said, picking

out a new collar for Roark—his old one had too many tags with identifying characteristics on it—"call me on my cell phone."

They were stunned. "You're actually going to use it?"

I shrugged, shook my head. "It's an emergency, okay?"

"But you said—"

"Never mind what I said. This goofball Goodrich is going to try and kill Roark—" we all looked down at the tawny-coated little monkey-faced boy, who was wagging his tiny stub of a tail, totally ignorant of the trouble and peril he was in "—and I've got to figure out a way to stop him."

"Yeah, but Jack," Leon said, "we don't even got the number."

It was true. No one but Jamie knew my cell phone number, since she was the one who'd given me the phone for Christmas. So I grudgingly gave them the number, then said, "Sloan, you're in charge of the kennel. D'Linda, you're responsible for the salon, but if Sloan needs your help and you're not too busy, you help her out and try not to antagonize one another. The same goes for the salon."

Leon raised his hand. "Yo, Jack, what's antagonize mean?"

To Sloan and D'Linda, I said, "That means you don't tell each other what to do, you ask each other nicely, okay? Does that answer your question, Leon?"

"Sure, but how come you gets to antagonize anybody you feel like, and we don't?"

"Leon, just shut up, okay?"

"See, this is zac'ly what I'm talkin' 'bout."

"You keep an eye on the beagles. They're in the laundry room in the house."

I hooked Roark up to his old collar and took him out to the car (the Suburban, that is—the ice storm had made me question the viability of using the woody ever again), and the little guy looked up at me excitedly. He had no idea what was going on. All he knew was that I was charged up emotionally, and those emotions had flowed into him. He liked that. That and the fact that we were doing something together, as a pack, and that it involved a car ride. Roark loves going for car rides.

Once I got out on the open road, the first call I made was to Otis Barnes at the *Camden Herald*.

"Otis? Jack Field."

"Hey, Jack, what's up?"

"How's your coverage of Judge Merton's murder going?"

"Murder? The State Police are saying he was attacked by his dog."

"His daughter's dog, actually, but I can tell you for a fact that he was murdered."

"No kidding. Can I quote you on that?"

"No, you may not. You know how I hate seeing my name in the papers. Unless it's related to dogs and dog training." (Otis had once written a nice profile of me and my training methods in *The Herald*—and I was glad that he did.)

"So, the usual veiled reference," he said. " 'Someone close to the investigation'? That sort of thing?"

"Exactly. But this tip isn't just for you, Otis." *The Herald* is a weekly, published on Thursdays. I wanted my info showing up on the local radio and television within the hour, if possible. "I'm hoping you can get me hooked into the AP or UPI. You think you can arrange it?" I reached the bottom of the mountain, turned off the gravel road that runs between Hope and Perseverance, then headed north toward Rockport and Camden.

He sighed. "You know, Jack, for a smart guy you ask some pretty stupid questions sometimes."

"Such as?"

I passed the Perseverance grange hall and, as I did, in my rearview I saw Goodrich's Animal Control van and a Rockland County Sheriff's Jeep approaching the same intersection coming from the south. They turned onto the road that leads up to my kennel. The Jeep had its red lights on. It seems I'd gotten Roark out just in the nick of time.

There was a sudden silence on the phone, and I thought for a minute I'd lost the signal, but I just hadn't been paying attention. Otis had finished saying something that I hadn't heard and was waiting for my reply.

"I'm sorry, Otis. You there? I wasn't listening."

He chortled. "You are such a jackass. I was just explaining that I run a respectable newspaper, so obviously, yes, I can contact the AP or UPI. You know, I really should explain to you sometime how the world of journalism works."

"Hah. Explain it to some of the cable news networks, sometime."

He laughed. "I'm talking about how journalism *actually* works, not how it's *supposed* to work. And as far as the cable outlets are concerned, that's a lost cause, I'm afraid. Except for CNN."

"CNN? That's a laugh. You know what I saw on CNN the other night? A news alert. I mean, they even had it Chyroned onto the television screen: 'News Alert.' You know what it was? A Hollywood couple is getting divorced. That's a news alert?"

"No, you're right. I didn't realize that CNN had stooped to that level. So, what's the pro quo here, Jack?"

"Sorry?" I tapped the brakes, thinking I saw a squirrel run in front of the car. Roark lost his balance, then shot me a questioning look from his position by the side window.

"You know, quid pro quo? You may have just given me a pretty hot tip. What do you want in return?"

"Well, I'd like to find out how this Goodrich character knew the dog was at my kennel. Was my name on the hot sheet?"

(In New York City, the hot sheet is a synopsis of the day's activities of the various city bureaus and departments—police department, fire department, sanitation department, etc.—which the mayor's press secretary hands out or faxes to the media.)

"I don't have it in front of me, but I think if I'd seen your name on it I would've remembered."

"Okay. Can you check the wire services and local news outlets to see if anyone's been using my name?"

"Shit, no. I could maybe get a copyboy to do it, if I had a copyboy. But there *are* two hot sheets, you know."

"There are?" Roark got tired of the cold wind in his face and started circling around on the seat, attempting to lie down.

Otis sighed. "I really do need to sit you down sometime and explain to you how all of this works, don't I?"

Roark curled up in a ball. I thought a moment. "Oh, I know. There's the day's police reports, that are faxed from the local precincts to the mayor's press secretary—"

"In this case, it's the Governor's press secretary."

"Right," I said, "and then there's the hot sheet that the Governor's press secretary hands out to reporters."

Otis said, "So since the State Police know you have the dog staying at your kennel, the day's police reports would reflect that, but the Governor's hot sheet probably wouldn't. And since Goodrich works in the Governor's Office—"

"—he would have access to the fax room, and could have seen my name there on the initial police reports. That makes sense. Thanks, Otis. It's been a pleasure, as always."

"You're welcome. And you're sure the old man was murdered?"

"I saw the body and the air bag. His throat was slashed yet there was no blood spatter on the air bag, in fact no blood at all, which means he had to have been dead at least half an hour before the crash. So, there's no way the dog could have ripped his throat to shreds while he was driving."

Next I called Jill Krempetz's cell phone. It was Saturday

and I figured she wouldn't be at the office, and I couldn't remember her home number off the top of my head.

"Hello?"

"Hey, Jill. I need to ask you something . . ."

"What? Who is this?"

"Oh, sorry. It's Jack Field. Look, I need to know—what's the deal on attorney-client privilege when the client has committed, or is in the process of committing, a felony?"

"Oh, boy. I really need this on a Saturday morning . . ."

"Jill, it's one-thirty in the afternoon."

"Whatever. Just shows you I need more coffee. So what are you up to, Jack? Sorry, my mistake—don't answer that. You say you're in the process of committing a felony?"

"Not me. You *do* need more coffee. No, I'm talking about a hypothetical third party." A car horn sounded to my right. Roark looked up from his fetal position and snuffled. I looked around. I'd apparently gone right through a four-way without stopping. This is why driving and cell phones don't mix.

"Where *are* you?" Jill said.

"In my car."

Amazed, she said, "You're using a *cell* phone?"

I grunted. "Jamie bought it for me for Christmas. I should say she bought it for herself. She hates not being able to talk to me anytime she feels like—"

"Jack, stick to the subject. Attorney-client privilege while a felony is in progress, remember?"

"Exactly." I was coming to another four-way. This time I stopped.

"Technically," she sighed, "at least as far as this narrowly defined aspect of privilege is concerned—"

It was my turn at the intersection. I took it.

"—technically, privilege is always attached unless the client reveals plans for a future crime. If those plans seem credible, it's incumbent upon the attorney to report the matter to the proper authorities. Does that help?"

"I think so. I guess I won't tell you what I'm up to, and we can figure out how to fix it all later, is that it?"

"Something like that."

"Good. Whoops—there's my other line. Can you meet me at your office in half an hour?"

"Sadly, yes," she sighed. "I'm already at the office. Apparently I have no life."

"Good. I mean, I'm sorry, but I'll see you in a bit. Oh, and it would be nice if you could get Tim to come over too."

"Shouldn't be a problem. He has less of a life than I do at this point."

Tim was Tim Berry, a waiter and a former prelaw student at Bowdoin College, who'd got into a bit of a jam by firing a gun at a Camden police officer back in December. He was out now, on bail, awaiting trial. Jill was his attorney. And, as a favor to me, she had also hired him, part-time, to be her legal assistant. (I felt attached to the kid because I'd trained his dog, a tricolor basset hound named Thurston.)

I clicked over to the other line. It was Jamie, who was worried sick that something terrible had happened to me. Why else, after all, would I be using my cell phone all of a sudden? Then, after I'd explained, at least partially, what was going on, she was quite pleased and happy that I'd finally gotten around to using her Christmas present.

"Gee, Jack, does this mean that you might actually break down one day and buy a CD player, or sign up for AOL?"

I suggested that she not get her hopes up.

"So, why the urgent phone call? Did you miss me that bad?"

"Of course I missed you. The only time I *don't* miss you is when we're actually together."

"Or when we've had a fight?"

"No, actually, then I miss you even more." I turned right into the parking lot of the West Rockport Animal Clinic.

"I don't understand. Why do you miss me when we fight?"

"Because when we fight my mind won't let itself rest until we can resolve our differences and get back together. Or don't you feel that way?" I parked the car.

There was a pause. "Sort of. Except *my* mind won't rest until you apologize and admit that you were wrong."

I laughed—that's my Jamie, I thought; just like a woman. "You know, I think I've apologized enough for that already."

"Oh, really?"

"Yes, really. Let me put you on speaker." I switched over to the speaker phone and began taking off Roark's collar, the one with all the tags. As I did, I explained, at least partially, what was going on. I put on the new collar—a virgin, orange nylon affair, with a Velcro clasp—and asked Jamie if there was anything *she* could do to help rein Goodrich in.

"I don't have that kind of authority, Jack."

"I know, honey. But you know people who *do*. Dr. Reiner, for instance. Or your uncle Horace."

"I suppose, but I don't know what you're so worried about. All Goodrich can do is take the dog to an animal control facility. At this point he has the legal right to do that."

"No, he doesn't. Besides, I've known guys like him. He might think Roark looked at him the wrong way and kill him on the spot, just to be safe."

"Now you're just imagining things."

"Maybe so, but that exact kind of thing has happened before, trust me."

"Well, I don't know, Jack, it still seems to me that if Goodrich did something like that, I mean without just cause, he would be in serious legal trouble."

I snorted. "No he wouldn't. Did you know that killing a dog is only a misdemeanor? And besides, no matter how steep the fine, Roark would still be dead."

I could hear her thinking it over. “I hate it when you’re right,” she said. “Okay, I’ll make some calls.”

“Thanks. Where are you, by the way?”

“In my car on my way home to get some sleep. I was up all night, doing the prelim.” She yawned. “Dr. Reiner just started the actual autopsy.”

“Wait a minute, you’re talking to me while you’re driving? That’s dangerous, isn’t it?”

“Shut up,” she laughed. “I’ve got some calls to make. Remember?”

I took Roark in to the reception desk, but ran into a bit of a snag when Mary—an Ogonquit girl, about twenty or so, with black eyes and black hair, wearing the blue scrubs that vet techs wear—recognized the dog.

"This is Goose," I said. "He belongs to a client of mine named Tim Berry."

"No, he doesn't," she said. Her voice was flat and empty of emotion, though she smiled briefly at Roark. "That's Roark. He belongs to the Stevens family."

"I know he looks like Roark, but it isn't him. This dog's name is Goose."

"Um, Mr. Field? He doesn't *look* like Roark. He *is* Roark." She looked down at the dog. "Aren't you, boy?"

Roark wagged his stub.

"I'm telling you, this isn't Roark."

She gave me a look, shook her head, and pushed a clipboard and a pen across the reception desk. "Fill this out. I'll get the doctor."

I filled out the form, using Tim Berry's name and address, still attempting go through with my little ruse. When I was done with that, I killed some time under the fluorescent lights, looking at the flyers on the bulletin board and flipping through the brochures in the rack, noticing that they were low in my Dog Hill Kennel brochures and making a mental note to bring some by when I came to pick up Roark the next day or the day after.

Then I noticed the poster. It was advertising a concert being put on by the Maine Barbershop Quartet Society, and featured a black-and-white photograph of a typical barbershop group—four silly-looking gentlemen in late nineteenth century attire, with their arms raised, as if singing. One of them looked familiar. He had an absurdly large handlebar mustache. It was Grant Goodrich. There was a blurb under the photo, which read: "The Olde Timey Boyz, last on the bill, will round out an evening of good old-fashioned American fun!" The concert was being held in Belfast, on Saturday, February 22.

Finally Mary came back in with Dr. Stanhope—medium height and build, early sixties, with white hair, and drooping blue eyes that always seem like they should be brown for some reason.

"Hello, Jack," he said, and we shook hands and exchanged the usual pleasantries. He looked down at Roark. "So, who's this skinny young fella? Or is it a girl?" He checked out Roark's undercarriage. "Nope, a male, it is."

"His name is Goose," I said, with a look at Mary.

"No, it isn't." She crossed her arms. "That's Roark."

"Is that you, Roark?" Dr. Stanhope said. Roark wiggled his butt and bowed his head, hoping for an ear scratch.

"I told you. Mr. Field is pretending it isn't Roark."

The doctor looked at me, a little more serious. "Is there a reason why we're pretending this isn't Roark?"

I explained what was going on with Grant Goodrich. As soon as I mentioned his name, their demeanors changed. They both seemed angry and upset. Then, almost in unison, they looked down at the dog and said, "Hello, Goose."

"I thought it was Roark," said Mary. "Guess I was wrong."

I pointed to the poster of the Olde Timey Boyz. "You know, it's kind of funny that you know Goodrich is an ass, but you still put up his poster in your office."

They didn't know what I was talking about, so I pointed to the photo and said, "That's him, right there."

Without saying a word, Mary came around the front desk, took the poster down, ripped it in two and put it in the trash.

I smiled, then, to the doc, I said, "Can you do a complete physical, and check his left ear. He seems to be favoring it."

"Can do."

"And the ME's Office wants us to save his fecal matter for evidence purposes."

"That's fine. And don't worry. He'll be safe with us." He looked down at the boxer boy. "Won't you, Goose?"

My next stop was Jill Krempetz's office. On the way over the cell phone rang. It was D'Linda calling to tell me that Goodrich and a Rockland County sheriff deputy had just left. They had been there looking for Roark. Goodrich was so pissed that the dog wasn't there that he threatened to take every dog on the premises into custody. The deputy tried to calm him down, then got a radio call from the sheriff. (No doubt Jamie had talked to her uncle Horace, as I'd asked her to do.)

"What did Flynn say to the deputy?"

"I don't know, but right after he got off the radio with the sheriff, he escorted that freak off the premises and warned him not to come back without a court order."

"Good for Flynn."

"Where are you, Jack? Is Roark okay?"

"He's a little stressed out, but he'll be all right."

To someone off the phone, she said. "I'm going to tell him right now." Then to me, she said, "Leon's having problems with the beagles."

I told her to put him on.

"Yo, Jack, these dogs is trippin', yo."

"What are they doing, exactly?"

"Barkin' and howlin' and shit, tryin' to climb over the gate, and like that."

"Have you taken them to the play yard and played fetch?"

"Nah, man. There's ten of these little monsters!"

"How many times have I told you, Leon, dogs need to get their ya-yas out. Grab some tennis balls and take them out to play. You might even enjoy yourself."

"Yeah, right. It's like a hockey rink out there. I'll prob'ly bust my ass."

"Just do it. And play tug-of-war with them individually, or in groups of two, and make sure—"

"I know," he said, as if he could recite it in his sleep, "to always let them win and praise them for winning."

"That's right. Twenty minutes ought to do it."

"What about Maggie, though? She tries to bite some of the other dogs."

"Take her out separately. She needs special attention."

"Aw, man, I just know I'm gonna bust my ass. I'm tellin' you, that place needs a Zamboni."

"Yeah, you said that." I found a parking space right in front of Jill's office, which occupies part of the second floor of a brick two-story on Main. "I gotta go."

Jill's building, which is just a shout or two away from the harbor, has some nice stone ornamentation around the doors and windows and is probably a hundred years old. As I got out, I noticed how much colder it was, being this close to the water, but reminded myself that in the summertime, driving and parking downtown was a full-time job. It could take you an hour or more to find a space, and usually it was at least five or six blocks away from where you wanted to end up. It seems like everybody in the world, or at least everybody from New York to Montreal, loves Camden in the summertime.

I got upstairs and found her office empty, though the door

was standing half open. Then I heard the sound of retching coming from the bathroom down the hall. I went to investigate and knocked on the door.

"Jill? Is that you?"

"Go away." My first thought was that she was having a bad reaction to the chemotherapy for her breast cancer. She'd had a mastectomy a few months earlier, and the chemo was to make sure the cancer didn't spread.

"Jack, go wait in my office," she tried to say, but was unable to articulate the word "office" and hurl at the same time.

I felt so bad for her. "Is there anything I can do?"

"Yeah, you idiot, I just told you what you can do—you can go wait in my office."

I started to say something but did as she asked.

I sat in her office feeling helpless and lonely, the way I used to do, I guess, when my kid sister Annabelle and I would come home from school and find our mother locked in her bedroom with a "sick headache." It affected Annie more than me, I think, but at least she had me to lean on.

I was thinking this over when Tim Berry appeared in the doorway. Short, with anxious, rat-brown eyes and dust-brown hair, clipped short—he just sort of stood half in, and half out of the door—he said, "So hey, Jack, what's going on?"

"I'll tell you when Jill's finished what she's doing."

He cast a sad glance down the hall then came in and sat down, nervously tapping on the arms of his chair until I gave him a look. Then we talked a bit about his upcoming trial, and the fact that he was no longer wearing his nose ring.

"Jill's idea," he said. "She wants me to look more respectable for the judge, or the jury, if it goes that far."

We sat in silence for a while, not wanting to talk about what was most present in our minds. Then we heard the bathroom door open and close and Jill appeared.

"That was fun," she said, her voice a little hoarse. "Who's got a mint?"

Berry jumped up and said, "I've got some gum." He dug into his pants pocket.

"Good." She sat down behind her desk and put a hand out. "Gimmee."

Tim did as he was told. I noticed, as Jill focused on unwrapping, first the paper, then the silver foil, that her usually frizzy red hair was tucked up under a yellow ski hat, or more likely, that it had begun to come out in clumps as a side effect of the cancer medicine, and the hat was there to hide the way she looked. I also saw that her skin was extremely pale, except around the eyes, where it had a brownish tinge.

She popped the gum in her mouth and caught me looking at her. "Shove it, Jack. How many times have I told you I don't want you coming around here with a sad face, fucking up my already crummy mood?" She looked at Berry. "And that goes for you too, you little sad sack."

"Sorry," I said. "But I don't think either one of us has ever seen you this bad before, Jill."

"Actually?" she cracked a smile. "I have your pal Farrell Woods to thank for that. The funny thing is, I'm getting better, week by week, in an overall sense, but that dog buddy of yours has disappeared on me. He doesn't answer his phone, he won't return my pages . . . So I'm all out of my usual medicine."

I knew that Woods had been supplying Jill with grass to ameliorate the negative side effects of the chemo. "Well, he's not actually a friend of mine, Jill. And I've got my own share of troubles with his disappearance." I filled her in on the fight Woods had had outside the bar with Tulips, the gunshots, the possible Eddie Cole connection, Cole's threats against Jamie, and the fact that I had a laundry room full of semiorphaned beagles and no idea when their owner was coming back to get them. "When was the last time you spoke to him?" I asked.

"I was supposed to get a delivery last night and he never showed. I suppose the fight outside Gilbert's explains the reason for that. Or part of it. So didn't you have something else you wanted to discuss? Involving some sort of felony?"

I explained about Roark and that Tim Berry was now the proud new owner of a boxer named Goose. I looked at Tim. "Unless you'd rather I didn't use your name to keep this dog safe for a few days." Tim said he didn't mind. It suddenly occurred to me that, being of college age, he might know where to score some weed. So I asked him if he did.

Jill shook her head. "You've already got him mixed up in your little dognapping scheme without asking—"

"He owes me."

Tim sadly shrugged and nodded his head.

Jill said, "Well, that's true. But I don't want him getting arrested for possession before his trial."

"I didn't say he had to pick it up for you. *I* could do that."

"Yeah, so could *I*, you jerk. I wish you'd try to remember that I'm not helpless." She looked at Tim.

He shrugged. "The only person I know of is Kurt Pfleger."

I sighed. "Captain of the high school wrestling team?"

He shrugged again. "But I'm pretty sure he gets his stuff from Farrell Woods."

"Can we stop talking about this, please?"

"No. Look, Jill, if you've got a headache, you buy a bottle of Tylenol. If you've got indigestion—"

"Yeah, yeah, you buy some Pepto Bismol, or whatever. And if you're getting chemotherapy treatments, you smoke grass. I know, okay? I *know*. Now, if there's nothing else you need in the way of legal advice, let's get this over with, okay? If the autopsy shows the dog didn't do it, then Goodrich won't have a leg to stand on. If necessary, we can still slow him down with an injunction, which I won't be able to file until Monday. So, that's two hundred bucks for the surprise Saturday visit, and another three if I have to file the injunction. That okay?"

I sighed, stood up. "Fine."

"And, Jack? I'm okay, really."

After I left, I drove into Rockland to see Sheriff Flynn. It wasn't on my original agenda, but something new had come up.

He was on the phone when I arrived. He shot me a dirty look, then grudgingly waved me in and nodded his chin at a wooden chair. I sat down and waited for him to finish his call.

When he hung up, I thanked him for handling the Goodrich situation, then explained I needed another favor.

"What am I, suddenly your personal favor machine?"

I shrugged. "The first one wasn't really for me, it was for a boxer dog named Roark. And the second one is for my attorney." I explained Jill's situation and wondered if there might be a Baggie or two lying around an evidence locker somewhere that hadn't been weighed in yet or wouldn't be missed.

He stared at me hotly for half a second, then sighed. "You got a lot of nerve, you know that?"

I smiled. "It's my only flaw."

He snorted, twitched his mustache a couple of times, and said, "Yeah, along with about a million other only flaws."

He heaved himself from behind the desk, went to the door, stopped and, over his shoulder, said, "Just one thing. I want you to take back that crack you made last night about this being an election year. Fact is, it isn't. Fact is, I'm not sure I'm gonna run again when it *is*. And you need to get it through your head that the people of this county rely on me to take care of things. They feel safer when they see my picture in the paper or watch me on the news. I'm not sure *why*, but they do. I don't do it out of ego but because it's part of my job."

"I'm sorry, Sheriff. Looking back I can see that that was an unkind and thoughtless remark on my part."

"It was a cheap shot."

"And a cheap shot. So, what'll you do?"

"Sorry?"

"If you decide not to run again."

He scratched the back of his neck. "I been thinkin' of takin' early retirement, like you. Maybe movin' to Buffalo."

He left me there, and I was reminded of the fact that his wife was a patient in a mental hospital just outside Buffalo, New York, and he flew up there twice a month to be with her. She had been, and still was, I guess, the love of his life.

A few minutes later he came back with a paper lunch sack in his hand, which he placed on the edge of his desk.

"Crazy world, huh?" I agreed. "Here, my nephew screws up his marriage to the best girl in the world—"

"She is that."

"Shut up—'cause of illegal drugs, and here I am, doing you this fucking favor, you the guy who took Jamie away from him. Don't forget your lunch on your way out."

I had a hot, momentary impulse to ask Flynn about Eddie Cole—to get more info about who he was and why Jamie was so afraid of him—but she'd told me not to mention him to Flynn or anybody else, so I didn't. It wasn't until I got outside that I looked into the bag, but I could tell by the heft of it that it was chock full of weed. The blustering old softie—as Jamie liked to call him—had even thrown in a brand new package of rolling papers.

12

That night, Jamie and I drove to Portland. To kill time until Jamie's flight to Boston to visit her father, we took in a movie, a suspense thriller about murder in Washington. It was dark out and the streetlights were lit when we came out of the theater.

"So? Did you like it?" Jamie asked.

"Yeah, it was good," I said. "I like Clint Eastwood a lot. And I've always loved Laura Linney."

"Oh, really?" She looked at me. "Which one was she?"

"She was his daughter."

"Oh, her." She looked at me. "I never heard of her before. And personally, I don't think she's all that pretty."

"No, I don't mean like that, though I think she *is* pretty. She's got nice hair and beautiful eyes and cute dimples. No, I meant, I think she's a great actress. She used to live in my neighborhood in New York, and her golden retriever used to play with Frankie at the dog run sometimes."

"Yeah?" She took my arm. "So did you ever ask her out?"

I laughed. "No, it wasn't like that. I just think she's a really good actress. I mean, if I run into Meryl Streep at the dog run, I'm not gonna ask *her* out."

"Why not?"

"First of all, she's not my type."

"So you *do* have a type. And what makes you such an expert on acting?"

"Well, I had to take some electives in college, and being a psych major, I thought it would, you know, be interesting to—"

She hit me. "You took an acting class?"

A little defensively, I said, "What's wrong with that?"

She started to giggle. "I can't believe it. Jack Field in an acting class! I bet there was a girl involved, wasn't there? Some actress whose butt looked good in tight blue jeans?"

"Okay, so what? Although, they weren't that tight. Her blue jeans, I mean."

"You are such an idiot. Don't you know how easy those theater majors are? You didn't have to take an acting class to get into her pants, Jack. All you have to do with those girls is pour them a beer, tell them they're pretty, or that they have talent, and they'll immediately take all their clothes off and have sex with you right there on the spot. Let's go in here."

She pushed me into a Starbucks, and while she visited the ladies' room, I glanced at a copy of the Portland paper. This was on the front page:

JUDGE MERTON'S BODY FOUND
STATE POLICE TAKE BOXER DOG INTO CUSTODY

ROCKLAND COUNTY—The body of former State Supreme Court Justice, Thayer Merton, was found in his car, a Cadillac Deville, late Friday night near the village of Union by Rockland County Sheriff's deputies, State Police say. Judge Merton, who was sixty-one at the time of his death, had homes in Augusta and South Bristol. He had been missing for several days, and was the subject of an intense, statewide search.

Rockland County Sheriff, Horace Flynn, said the judge had been apparently mauled by a vicious boxer dog, while he was driving, though Maine State Police lead investigator, Sgt. Heidi Loudermilk, said she isn't ruling out the possibility of foul play by humans as well. The dog was inside the car with the respected jurist when his body was found.

Justice Merton disappeared while traveling from his home in Augusta, on Wednesday, to spend a few days with his daughter, Beth Stevens, in Camden. Mrs. Stevens is the wife of Camden Hills Regional High School wrestling coach Ron Stevens. It was Mrs. Stevens who first reported her father missing. She and her husband are the owners of the dog in question.

Sheriff Flynn said that when his deputies found the car, the dog was out of control, attacking the two officers. The vicious animal was later subdued by a local animal trainer, and is now being held for observation at his kennel until Dr. Reiner, the State Medical Examiner, can complete the autopsy.

One source, close to the investigation, however, has stated that the dog was clearly not to blame, noting that the car's air bag had inflated, but that there was no blood spatter on the bag, indicating that the judge was already dead before the car went off the road. This also indicates, the source said, the distinct possibility that the judge was, in fact, the victim of foul play.

The rest was the typical stuff about Judge Merton's past: how he led a "long life of service dedicated to his fellow man," etc. There was also a quote from my pal Grant Goodrich, who made the absurd claim that the dog was "obviously guilty, because all boxers are a well-known member of the pit-bull family," which was not only untrue, but ungrammatical as well.

"I just realized something," Jamie said as she came back from the ladies' room. "It was Kristin Downey! That's who you took the acting class with! Your wonderful ex-girlfriend Kristin Downey, who you're still in love with, is a total slut/acting major from college!"

I shook my head. "There are so many things wrong with what you just said. First of all, Kristin Downey wasn't an acting major, she wanted to be a set and costume designer. Secondly, I'm *not* still in love with her. I'm in love with you. And finally, she wasn't a slut."

"I bet you slept with some of those acting majors, though, didn't you?"

"Not really. They were all too self-absorbed for my liking. Besides—"

"But it was Kristin Downey you took the class for."

I nodded. "Okay, score one for you."

"And I'll bet you slept with those other girls too."

"Okay. A few, but only until I got tired of them being 'on' all the time." I gave her a long look. "So who are *you* ashamed of sleeping with back when you were in college?"

She looked over toward the menu board behind the counter. "Do you want to order something?"

I began to laugh. "Oh, no. One of your professors?"

"No," she said defensively. "Well, okay, yes."

"Not your literature professor—those guys are the worst."

Her ears turned red.

"Oh! It *was* your literature professor. And I bet he quoted Keats and Shelley to get into your pants. 'She walks in beauty like the night of cloudless climes and starry skies.' "

"I feel like having an espresso. How about you?"

"I don't think so. Too much caffeine for you, baby. And I bet he wore a tweed jacket with suede elbow patches and smoked a pipe and had sideburns and long, curly hair."

"Shut up. And it was Gerard Manley Hopkins, not Keats and Shelley. And he wore corduroy."

"Gerard Manley Hopkins? Never heard of him." I took her hand in mine. "This was your freshman year, right?"

She was stunned. "How did you know?"

"Hey, they likes 'em young, those lit perfessers."

She sighed. "Can we change the subject?"

"You brought it up."

"No, I didn't, *you* did. With your fascination for what's-her-name, Laura Somebody at the dog run in New York."

"Laura Linney. And I love you so much."

"Then why don't you act like it?"

"Can't. I failed that acting class. Have you seen the Portland paper?" I handed it to her. She glanced through it.

"Nice, Jack," she said after she'd scanned the article. "How did you arrange it? Otis Barnes?"

"You know me so well."

I ordered a cappuccino, and insisted Jamie get a decaf.

"You don't mind if I try some of your cappuccino, do you?"

"Yes, I do. Your father just had heart surgery. That means you're genetically susceptible to heart disease."

She changed the subject. "So, how's Roark doing?"

"He's okay. He's still in hiding. I thought he had an ear infection because he kept favoring his ear, but Dr. Stanhope says he has a hairline fracture over his left eye. You're a medical examiner. Can you tell me what that means?"

She smiled. "Of course. Someone right-handed hit him really hard. Or maybe they used a blunt object of some—"

"No, honey. Think. If they'd used a blunt object, Roark's injury would have been more serious than a hairline fracture."

She thought it over, smiled. "You're really good at this."

"Yes, I am."

"Know-it-all."

"It's my only flaw."

"Well, maybe he was injured in the crash?"

I shook my head. "I don't think the car was going fast enough. Besides, the passenger side air bag had inflated."

"Well," she thought it out, "maybe he was in the back seat

when it happened, and hit his head on something back there."

"On what? There's nothing in the back seat with a hard enough edge to fracture his skull. Besides, most cars, and definitely Cadillacs, have sensors to determine if someone is sitting in front of an air bag. So the passenger side air bag wouldn't have inflated if Roark weren't in the front seat."

She thought it over, nodded. "But then again, Roark didn't have a seat belt on, right? So he could've been thrown against a sharp object in the front part of the car."

I shook my head. "The rearview mirror is the only sharp object in the front, not protected by an air bag. The stereo knobs, the console, the gear shift lever—all are covered by air bags when there's a crash. And if Roark had injured himself on the rearview mirror, the glass would have been broken, or the mirror itself would've been knocked loose, or set at a crazy angle. It wasn't. It was perfectly in place."

She smiled. "You *are* really good at this. So, I guess you must have got a really good look inside the car."

"I took a quick glance. And I have a good memory."

"I guess that's why you think there was no blood spatter."

"Was there?"

She shrugged. "No, you're right. There wasn't a single drop of blood anywhere." She looked at my cappuccino. "Just one sip? Please?"

"No, you need to cut down on caffeine. Drink your decaf."

She draped her arm over my shoulder. "Yes, master."

"Anyway, I'll bet you anything that whoever hit Roark is the same person who killed the judge. Roark is innocent."

"Oh," she huffed, "you're always on the side of the dog. I don't know—maybe he snapped. Dogs sometimes do that, don't they?" She stared longingly at my coffee cup.

"Oh, for crying out—go ahead and have a sip." She took the cup and had a sip. "And no," I said, "dogs don't snap. That's a myth. They're not postal employees. They don't have the complex emotional equipment necessary to suppress their feelings the way people do. But the fact remains, how can a dog kill a man inside a car without leaving blood everywhere?"

"You have a point. Several, in fact." She played with the hair on my neck. "Are you going to solve this murder the way you did the Allison DeMarco case, my handsome hero?"

I laughed. "Don't you mean 'hotshot' hero?' " I sighed. "Look, all I want to do is just make sure Roark isn't locked up in a cage the rest of his life or get put to sleep for something he didn't do. Do *you* have any evidence to prove he *did* do it?"

She shrugged. "The blood on his jaws matches the judge's blood type."

A young couple left the register carrying two cups of latte and a paper plate covered with biscotti. They came over, smiled a hello, and sat down next to us.

"That doesn't prove anything," I said. "Remember when I got shot by the Camden PD?" She un-huh'd. The young couple glanced over. "And remember how the dogs kept trying to lick the blood dripping down my hand? Hey, save some for me . . ."

She took another sip, then nodded. "It *could* have happened that way. The dog might've licked the judge's wounds after someone else in*flicted* them." She licked the foam off her lips. "But my preliminary exam shows what appeared to be bite marks on the judge's throat."

The couple looked over, then made faces at one another.

"Bite marks? Dog or human?"

She shrugged. "You'd have to ask a forensic odontologist. Oh, and then there's the corneal petechia."

"What? You didn't tell me that."

"Yep. Both eyes were as red as a cherry."

"See? That *proves* Roark didn't do it. The victim had to have been either strangled or asphyxiated."

Jamie said, "Or hung. But it could also be argued that the dog's jaws put enough pressure on the carotid artery to rupture the capillaries in the subscleral tissue."

The young couple got up and moved a few stools away. I guess our casual chatter about bloody murder didn't sit too well with their chocolate biscotti and whipped-cream-covered coffee.

"Except that when a man is attacked by a dog—especially, a so-called 'vicious' dog, like they say here in the paper, *twice*, when there's no such thing—there isn't enough time for the blood pressure to build to the point where it could rupture the scleral capillaries and cause corneal petechia. If he was choked or hung it *would*. Do you know how long it takes—"

"—to asphyxiate a man? Yes, dear, about two minutes. Less than that to strangle him." The young couple got up and headed for the door, leaving their lattes and biscotti behind. Jamie leaned over—she's very tall—and took one of their cookies. "And what do you mean there's no such thing as a vicious dog?"

"Vicious denotes evil intent. A dog *can't* be evil. It's one of those hot-button words that idiots like this Grant Goodrich use to scare people and serve their political agendas. All I'm saying is it takes time for the blood pressure to build. And when a dog goes for the jugular, you get zero blood pressure almost immediately."

"It's possible." She took another sip of cappuccino. "God, this is good. What do they put *in* it? Heroin?"

"No, but it's almost as bad. At least for *you* it is."

"Oh, by the way," she took another sip, "the 'bites' on Judge Merton's throat were put there to cover up bruises made by someone's hands. The main tissue damage was done postmortem."

"Handprints? So he was strangled."

"Mm-hmm. By someone with very large hands, as far as I

could tell. Which is why there was no blood in the car. Oh, and his hyoid bone was broken. Did I mention that?"

I shook my head, sighed. "You really got a big kick out of watching me go through my paces, didn't you?" She just smiled sweetly. "You could have told me all this *before*, you know."

"You could have told me you were playing me left-handed at pool." She drank some more of my cappuccino.

I hung my head. "I can't wait till you get over that. So he was definitely strangled."

"Mm-hmm. I think you were also right about something else you said last night. What did you call it? A sexual—"

"An unconscious sexual dialectic. And don't give me any credit for that idea. Blame Freud, or Jacques Lacan."

"Well, I'm starting to think maybe there *is* a power struggle going on between us. I think I like it too."

"You do?"

"Yes, it's like the balance of power between us is shifting back and forth. It keeps things interesting. It's also kind of exciting, in a way. Sometimes I like the feeling of being more powerful than you. Sometimes I like it when you're in control."

"Don't you see, honey? That's why I played you left-handed at pool. To give you the pleasure of winning."

She shook her head. "I don't think that's why you did it, Jack. You just did it to make the game more interesting. Not for me, but for yourself. But even if you *had* done it for me—which is fine, I suppose, and very generous, I must say—the mistake you made was not keeping that information to yourself. You don't do something to make someone feel good about themselves and then just take that feeling away when you feel like it. That isn't cricket. What's so funny?"

"Nothing. I was just amused by your use of the word cricket. I thought you were going to say 'kosher.' "

She took a sip of my cappuccino. "So, Jack, in your 'acting days,' " she did the air quotes with her fingers and even overdramatized the phrase, "did you ever do those silly exercises where you cluck around like a chicken, or roar like a lion, or bark like a dog?"

"The animal exercises? Sure. We all did."

She started to laugh. "What did you do, purr like a kitty cat or slither across the stage like a snake?"

"Close. I did a very well-realized, very creative lizard."

She laughed. "I would have loved to have seen that."

"It was quite good, actually. One of the two best lizards ever. In fact, to this day, some in the business say that my lizard rivaled that of Robert DeNiro, whose entire performance in *Taxi Driver*, by the way, was based solely on a lizard he did at The Actor's Studio in the late sixties."

"Oh, really? I didn't know that." She laughed some more.

"Yes. And to this day, Dustin Hoffman's only regret as an actor is that he was never able to match the lizard *I* did at my little acting class at Columbia. In fact, every year he goes back to The Actor's Studio and tries, yet again, to do a lizard to match mine, and every year he fails, the poor little bastard."

She was nearly falling off the chair.

"On the other hand, Al Pacino's lizard—which he used to great effect in that movie he did with Keanu Reeves, which I forget the name of—was a blatant rip-off of mine, and he's even admitted as much in several print and television interviews. 'My lizard,' Pacino once stated on *Good Morning America*, 'was stolen outright from an acting student at Columbia by the name of Jack Field, who I believe'—dramatic pause—'is now one of the top thirteen dog trainers in the United States.' "

By now she was laughing so hard I thought some of the cappuccino foam would come out her nose.

"Then there's Jack Nicholson, of course. Every performance he's ever done since *The Shining*, but not including *Terms of Endearment*, well, I don't need to tell you: *my* lizard."

She was in tears, helpless.

I didn't let her off the hook yet, though. I stared at her for a long moment, then began twitching my neck and jaw muscles—not in an obvious way, just enough to give my lizard impression a little flair. Then I began to dart my tongue out of my mouth and let it flick at imaginary flies, and she just lost it.

She fell off the stool and nearly peed her pants.

13

Sunday morning I took Leon, Frankie, and Scully and Mulder up US 1 to Searsport, to see if I could find an armoire—or something for Jamie to use for closet space—at one of the antique shops along the highway. Most of them were closed for the winter. I finally found an old wooden medicine cabinet, painted light green, at a shop just north of Belfast. I could hang it on the wall of my bathroom so Jamie could at least keep some of her makeup and sundries at my place. We loaded it in the back of the Suburban then drove home, where Leon helped me carry it up the stairs.

"So, things is gettin' serious with you and Jamie, huh?"

"It looks like it," I said. "Careful. Watch that end."

When I was done hanging it on the bathroom wall, I left Leon and Sloan in charge of the dogs then took Frankie and Maggie across the road to see how Mrs. Murtaugh was feeling. I figured she was home because her car was parked in the driveway. I let the dogs play in the ice and snow while I went up the front steps and knocked on the door.

I waited. There was no answer. I knocked again, then called out. Mrs. Murtaugh has lived alone ever since her husband Wally died about ten years ago. The fellow I bought the kennel from insisted she had to be part of the deal he made with me or he wouldn't sell. I had no reason to argue with him at the time, and I've had no reason to regret it since then. Alice Murtaugh keeps the place together in more ways than one.

"Maybe I should've called first," I said to Frankie.

He looked up at me then went back to digging a hole in the ice, which he subsequently peed into. Maggie barked at me.

The glass storm door was unlocked. So was the wooden door behind it. I went inside and looked around. I called out again but there was no answer. The place was tidy and smelled of cat litter, but no one was home. I went back outside, then took Frankie and Maggie back across the road.

Before going up to my house, I stood in the driveway awhile, looking down at the play yard, which I use for training sessions and for exercising the dogs that board with me. It was currently unusable, for *any* purpose, though that would change once the ice melted and the ground dried out. Still, I stood there, creating a mental image of how to fix it. It involved something close to what Dorianne Elliot had done, leveling the whole area, putting in a storm drain, cementing it over, then covering it with either sand, soft pebbled gravel, or some kind of rubberized asphalt; I couldn't decide which. I'd have to talk it over with her. While I was at it, I thought, I might as well put in a basketball court next to Leon's cottage so we wouldn't have to go into town so often to play. Being a black kid from New York, everyone at Camden Hills High assumed he'd go out for the basketball team next year, and he really wasn't that good. I had the (frankly) overoptimistic feeling that if he had a place to practice every day, he might develop enough skills to make the team, which would do wonders for his confidence and self-esteem.

"Kinda silly, huh?" I said to the dogs, who looked up, hoping to hear the words "bone," "ball," or "dinner." When they didn't, they went back to sniffing around. "After all," I said, "Family Court hasn't even decided if Leon can stay with me or if he has to go to another foster home."

I went inside to make some calls to see what I could find out about Mrs. Murtaugh, but Leon needed help with his math homework. An hour into the ordeal he slammed his book closed and said, "Man! Why do I gotta learn this stupid a'gebra for, anyway?" It was the same question I'd asked *my* parents when I was Leon's age, and I told him so. Then I said:

"I don't know. The only reason I can think of is that if you don't at least get a C or a D in it, you won't graduate."

"That sucks. Wha'd *you* git on this shit when you was—"

"Watch your mouth," I said, then told him I'd gotten A's. "But don't go by me. I got straight A's in everything." He pushed his pencil and textbook away and sat back in his chair, discouraged and depressed. "Hey, I was kidding," I lied. "I almost flunked my math classes. And look how *I* turned out."

He smiled. "Yeah, but if you think I wanna turn out to be like *you*, you're crazy." The sparkle was back in his eye, though, and he pulled the textbook toward him again.

Ed Murtaugh called and told me his mother was at Rockland Memorial, recovering from an emergency gallbladder operation. She was fine—just a little weak from the surgery. I asked if I could come see her, and he said no, visiting hours were over for the day, but that she'd love for me to come by tomorrow. I said I'd be there first thing in the morning.

Frankie, Maggie, and I were just settling into bed—Frankie and Maggie each with a vanilla-flavored rawhide, and me trying to decide between a book of essays by Melanie Klein or an old Armistead Maupin novel I hadn't read in years—when the phone rang.

It was Jamie. We chatted briefly and caught each other up on the day's events. She'd spent *her* day driving her father and his new wife, Laurie, up to Christmas Cove from Boston. Now that the weather—and the roads—had improved, Jonas wanted to spend his days by the ocean. He said it would help him convalesce. Plus he could keep an eye on his various enterprises.

After she was done relating what she'd been doing, she said: "I probably shouldn't be telling you this—"

"Then don't." I put away the Maupin novel. Klein would put me to sleep faster. (Whenever I read Maupin I can't wait to get to the next page, which sometimes keeps me up all night.)

"Shut up. I shouldn't even know about it myself, since it might influence my opinion at the autopsy, but get this: the police found out that Judge Merton withdrew a hundred thousand dollars in cash from a bank in Augusta on Wednesday afternoon. Then, according to one of the bank employees, he put it all in a brushed-metal briefcase; you know the kind. *And* . . . he had Roark with him! He said he needed the dog for protection!"

"Un-huh," I said.

"Jack, *listen*! The police just now found his briefcase—empty—in a trash barrel behind the Union General Store."

"Sure, I see; it all makes sense now. Roark killed him, stole his money, hid the briefcase, then came back and locked himself in the car. *Gee*, they're smart, them boxer dogs . . ."

"Idiot. What are you doing tomorrow?"

"I don't know. The usual Monday routine. I'm taking Frankie to the hospital to wreak havoc in the pediatric ward—"

"Those kids love that dog."

"I know. Then I'm visiting Mrs. Murtaugh, and after that I'm picking up Roark from the vet."

"Well, I don't know, would you like to meet me for lunch?"

"Sure. Where?"

"In Augusta. You can pick me up at the morgue."

"That's fine. I'm seeing Annie later in the afternoon."

"Annie Deloit?"

"Mm-hmm. Henry has been biting her, she says."

"Her pug? I didn't realize he was still alive. Is it even possible to train a fifteen-year-old pug?"

"He's only twelve. Besides, I'm a training genius. Didn't you know that?"

"Oh, shut up and go to bed."

"I miss you too, honey."

14

Mrs. Murtaugh's room was on the second floor, down at the end of a long, fluorescent-lit, hospital-smelling hall. It was a double room, partitioned off by a white, nylon curtain. There was a large window which gave out on a view of another wing of the hospital. As Frankie and I came in, Ed Murtaugh jumped out of a chair and made a grab for my flowers. "Here, let me take those," he said. His fat belly jiggled underneath an orange and green rugby shirt. He wrinkled his bald forehead.

"Go lie down," I told Frankie, and he went to the spot on the floor I was pointing to and he did his Sphinx imitation.

"Sit down, Edward," Mrs. Murtaugh said, "you're making me nervous," Mrs. Murtaugh said. Edward sat back down. "Or better yet, go out to the nurses' station and see if they have a vase you can put them in. Hello, Jack. Hello, Frankie." Frankie wagged his tail.

Ed Murtaugh got back up and shuffled out of the room as quietly as he could in his frayed leather deck shoes.

"Hello, Alice. So, now we finally know what those back pains were all about," I said.

She nodded. "Gallstones. Forty-seven of them."

"Must be a record." I put the flowers on the bed.

"Oh, they're lovely, Jack. Wherever did you get them?"

A soft moan came from behind the nylon curtain. We

both looked over. "The hospital flower shop," I said. "Is she . . . ?"

She looked sadly toward the curtain. "The nurses say . . ." She sighed, then looked at the flowers. "Well, they're just lovely." She put her head back against the pillows. "Did you hear? Audrey is in town. With Ginger."

"Really? I'd love to see them."

"They're probably at the house now."

Audrey Stafford was Mrs. Murtaugh's granddaughter. Ginger was Audrey's Airedale, who had belonged to Allison DeMarco before she died.

"Leon wanted to come with me," I sat down, "but he's got school. He'll come by this afternoon if that's okay." She said that would be nice, and I said, "Sloan and D'Linda are gonna come by later too, if they can. Though probably not together."

"Probably not, those two."

"How do you manage them? They're usually so well-behaved when you're around . . ."

"Well, the main thing is, I don't let them listen to music when I'm there, otherwise they argue about what stations to put on. You know, D'Linda likes the rap music and Sloan prefers the country western. I tell them it hurts my ears."

"Very smart."

"Of course, when *you're* there, they get into a competition over your attention."

"Oh, come on."

"It's true. They're two young girls from a small town in Maine, and you're a handsome, big city detective from New York." I made a skeptical sound with my throat. "You should hear them talk about you when you're not around."

"I think I'll pass."

Another moan came from the curtain, followed by a liquid, gurgling cough. We looked over again. After a moment, all was still. "Maybe you should get a single room."

"Oh, I can't afford that. Besides . . ."

I nodded and said, "Speaking of detectives; Jamie wanted to come but she's assisting on the autopsy of that missing judge."

"Judge Merton? They found him?"

I took a seat and told her the gist of the latest news.

"I'll bet the wife did it," she said.

"Why do you say that?"

"If he had been my husband, he would have driven *me* to murder him, that's for sure."

It was odd to hear this gentle woman talk like this. "I didn't realize you knew him that well."

"I didn't. I just know that . . . well, let's just say he was not a very nice man, and leave it at that." She sighed and then apologized for letting me and the kennel down. She said she'd be back to work as soon as I wanted her.

"We can manage for a while without you, Alice," I assured her. "It won't be easy, but we'll struggle through. You just concentrate on feeling better. How long are you—"

"How's this?" Ed came back in with a vase. He held it up for his mother's approval.

"That's fine, thank you, Eddie." She picked up the flowers and held them out for him. "Just fill it half full and put it over by the window where I can see it."

Ed did as he was told.

There was another liquid cough from behind the curtain. We glanced over. Then, after we heard normal breathing again, we breathed a little easier ourselves. Mrs. Murtaugh began smoothing some nonexistent creases in her sheets.

Under his breath, Eddie looked toward the curtain and said, "She's terminal," then gave a slight, involuntary shudder.

"Poor dear," said Alice. "Hasn't any family to come visit her?" Eddie gave her a look. "May I ask you something, Jack?" I said she could. She looked at Eddie. He was holding the vase full of flowers away from his body, letting it drip over the tiny hospital sink. "Oh, you overfilled it, Eddie."

"Sorry, Mom."

"Oh, that's okay. Just put it by the window." He did as he was told. Alice looked at me, her gray eyes a little moist with fear. "You wouldn't replace me, would you, Jack?"

I got up, went over to the bed, and took her hand. Frankie got up and followed me. (That was all right—I hadn't told him to stay, just to lie down. Besides, I thought, his therapy dog instincts were coming into play.)

"I couldn't run the place without you, Alice, and that's a fact." Frankie put his head on the edge of the bed, near Mrs. Murtaugh's hand, and she reflexively took it from mine and stroked his fur. He wagged his feathered tail. "But if you're that anxious to get back to work, we'll bring all the poodles, Pomeranians, and Persians down here so you can keep your hand in."

She laughed, but not very hard. It was too painful.

"Oh, my stitches," she said. She stopped laughing, looked at Frankie. "What a good boy," she said, and Frankie's eyes seemed to sparkle. Maybe it was just me.

I told her I had to go, but that I'd try to come by again later. She thanked me a half-dozen more times for the flowers, then Frankie and I went out to the nurses' station and told them I wanted Mrs. Murtaugh moved immediately to a private room with a nice, sunny view.

They were happy to do it. I put it on my credit card.

15

I picked up Roark from the vet and took him and Frankie back to the kennel. Audrey Stafford, a lovely champagne blonde with a freckled face, and her Airedale Ginger were waiting inside.

"Hey, it's nice to see you," I said. "You're really coming along!"

"Thanks." She rubbed her belly. "The baby's due in July."

Ginger came running over to see Frankie. They started tussling and wrestling in their doggie fashion, so I opened the door and let them take the fun outside. Roark looked up at me. It seemed like he wanted in on the action . . . *maybe*. He wasn't too sure about Ginger. She was a wild thing.

"Sorry, Roark. The doctor says no play time for you."

"What's wrong with Roark? And are they okay out there?"

"It's just a hairline fracture," I said. "He has to take it easy for a few weeks. And don't worry, Frankie will stay close to the house, and Ginger is not about to leave his side."

Then she caught me up on what was going on with her and her husband Tom. She'd come back from Boston to help take care of her grandmother while she was recuperating. I asked her if she'd like to earn a little extra money working at the kennel while she was in town. She said that would be great, as long as it didn't interfere with her granddaughterly duties.

We let the dogs play for a while, then Audrey said she had to go across the street to take care of some things at the house, so she took Ginger over there. I put Roark in his kennel, left Frankie in the house, then took off for Augusta.

I got to the morgue around twelve-thirty, but Jamie said our lunch date would have to wait. The jury had just come back in a murder case, and she wanted to hear the verdict. Would I mind? It would only take a few minutes. I told her I was starving, but if that's what she wanted to do, it was fine by me. She kissed me and then dragged me across the street to the courthouse.

We had just slipped into the back row and were taking off our gloves and things when Judge Fleming, a balding, owlish, sweaty little man, with large, black, dark-rimmed glasses and—at least to my mind—a noticeable lack of compassion in his watery gray eyes, opened the slip of paper handed him by the bailiff, yawned and said, "Madame Foreperson, has the jury reached a verdict?"

A slim, middle-aged woman with a nervous smile smoothed the creases in her maroon dress, stood up a little straighter than she had been, and said, "We have, your honor."

"The defendant will please rise."

A tall blond man and a fat brunet both stood up.

I leaned over to Jamie. "Speaking of murder, I could *kill* a grilled cheese sandwich just about now."

"Ssshh," Jamie said. "Just listen."

The judge said to the forewoman, "In the matter of The State of Maine versus Dennis Seabow, on the first count of the indictment, Driving While Under the Influence, what say you?"

The forewoman looked down at her own slip of paper, looked up at the judge and said, "We find the defendant, Dennis Evan Seabow, guilty."

I said, "Or a tuna melt, with real cheddar cheese—you

know, on whole-wheat? I mean—why did you drag me here?"

"Not now, Jack," she said. "I want to hear this."

"On the second count of the indictment," the judge said, "Vehicular Manslaughter, how do you find?"

"Manslaughter?" I said. "I thought you told me this was a *murder* trial."

"It *is*. Now please shut up and let me listen."

Again the slim woman looked down at her slip of paper as if she couldn't remember what she and the jury had just spent the last two days deciding. "We find the defendant guilty."

The judge yawned again and said, "As to the last count of the indictment, Murder in the Second Degree, how do you find?"

"What? Murder Two? Are you kidding me?" I suddenly forgot about grilled cheese sandwiches, tuna melts, catsup-sodden fries, and (hopefully, later) stolen kisses with Jamie in the back halls of the morgue. "For a drunk driving accident?"

"*Now* do you see why I dragged you here?"

"Not exactly, but I'm starting to get an idea. And I don't think I like it." This was aimed at Jamie, not the judge.

"We find the defendant, Dennis Evan Seabow, guilty."

There was a gasp from the crowd. Seabow's shoulders sagged; his long, limp, yellow hair fell around his face. His attorney put a fat, comforting hand on his shoulder.

"What the hell is going on here?" I said to Jamie. "The DA went for Murder Two and the judge let him?"

"That's what I've been trying to tell you, Jack. Something fishy is going on here, and I'd like to find out what it is. But we're going to need your help."

"We? Who's we?"

She pointed to the fat brunet in the Brooks Brothers suit. "Well, me and my friend Barry Porter. He's Seabow's attorney."

"I knew you were up to something. I *knew* it."

The judge said, "The defendant is remanded into custody pending a sentencing hearing. Court is dismissed. Members of the jury you are free to go. Thank you for your service."

Everyone got up. I kissed Jamie's neck, whispered in her ear, "This is a rotten trick to pull on me, kiddo. I'm already up to my eyeballs with that other little case of yours, not to mention having a house full of beagles, and now you want my help in this fiasco?"

"It may be a rotten trick to pull on *you*, Jack, but it's not as rotten as the trick being pulled on Dennis Seabow."

I hated to admit it, but she was right.

16

"We're going to appeal, of course," said Barry Porter over burgers and fries at the local diner—the kind of place that Tom Waits used to write songs about. Jamie had wanted sushi, and Porter said he was in the mood for Italian, but hey, if they wanted to waste my time by trying to get me involved in some lost cause, I thought, the least they could do is eat the same greasy food I was in the mood for (though I insisted that Jamie have the soup). "But," Porter went on, "we need your help."

"*My* help?" I dipped a big french fry into a bowl of catsup. "What do you expect *me* to do? I'm just a dog trainer. Didn't Jamie tell you that?"

He looked at her. She shrugged. "Well," said Porter, "she told me a number of things. Including the fact that you were one of the most successful homicide detectives in New York."

"Pure hyperbole," I said, dipping another french fry. "I was just a working detective. Besides, I gave all that up to run a boarding kennel and to play with—"

"Jack, will you just shut up and listen?"

"You know, honey," I waved a fry at her, "you've been saying that an awful lot this afternoon, and I'm starting to—"

"Well, then just *do* it, okay? For once?"

Just then the waitress came by, took a pad out of the

pocket in her apron, tapped a pencil against it and said, "So? Anybody want pie?" She was smiling at me when she said it. It was a nice, big smile. She had cute blue eyes and long lashes.

I looked at Jamie. She looked at Porter. We all looked at the waitress.

"No thanks," I said. "We're fine."

She shrugged, tore off the bill, set it next to me, and said, "Well then, thank you and have a nice day," winked at me and left.

I watched her go. Her buns moved nicely beneath her shiny black pants. Jamie hit me with the back of her hand.

"What?" I said.

"Like you don't know?" She kicked me under the table.

"Ow," I said. "Honey!"

Porter smiled at our antics, took a last sip of coffee, closed a fat file folder which sat on the table in front of him, pushed it toward me and said, "Will you at least take a look at the case file before you decide what to do?"

"No," I said, pushing the file back to him. I glanced over at Jamie. "Look, honey, I'm sorry, but I can't afford to waste my time on this. I have dogs to take care of. I mean, I know that twenty-five to life is a bit stiff for a drunk driving rap, but after all—he did *kill* the girl, didn't he?"

Jamie sighed and shrugged an apology at Porter.

"Yes, but what if he *didn't* kill her?" Porter said.

"Yeah right," I said. "From what Jamie told me earlier, he was found passed out behind the wheel of his car with this girl—what's her name again?"

"Marti MacKenzie," Jamie said.

"Marti MacKenzie? Wait a second, Dorianne Elliot was telling me about this case. She's the daughter of Moon MacKenzie, right?"

"That's right."

"Huh. What do you know? Well, anyway, she was found

pinned against a tree by his front bumper. The State Police *found* him passed out behind the wheel, right? I mean—smoking gun. So, how is he not guilty?"

Porter said, "Well he's sure as hell not guilty of Murder Two!"

"Hey, that's your fault, not mine. You should've gotten your client to take a plea on the Manslaughter charge."

He sighed. "I tried to, but the DA wouldn't settle. He said he wanted to set an example."

I munched a fry, thought that over. "Set an example?"

"Yeah. Come down hard on a drunk driver to impress the voters."

"Okay, sure, that makes sense, I guess."

I eyed the waitress. She came back over. "Need anything?"

"Yeah," I said, "I need a double bourbon and Coke. Badly. Oh, and a small vacation."

She picked up the check and gave me a coy smile. "A small vacation? Is that the name of a new drink or an invitation?" She fluttered her eyelashes.

I swung my legs sideways, so as to get out of Jamie's reach. "Sorry, peaches, I'm with *her*." I got out of the way just in time. Jamie got my chair this time instead of my leg.

"He'll have a *single* bourbon and Coke. He's driving."

I looked up at the waitress. "I'll have a single bourbon and Coke. I'm driving."

Peaches looked at me, shrugged, then went to get my drink.

" 'Peaches,' " Jamie said, glaring at me.

Porter said, "*You* think the DA is simply overreaching on this. *We* think maybe something fishy is going on."

"It could be just bad lawyering on your part."

Porter sighed. "Dennis Seabow is a political activist, trying to get marijuana legalized, housing for the homeless, among other things. He's also a pot smoker and's been arrested on a DUI three times—but for marijuana, not booze."

"But aren't prior bad acts inadmissible in front of a jury? Why didn't you make a motion to have them excluded?"

"I did, but they were central to the DA's theory of Murder Two. He argued that his priors showed that my client had a depraved indifference to human life. The judge agreed."

I laughed. "I get it. He outmaneuvered you."

Jamie hit me. "Jack."

To Porter, I said, "Why didn't *you* argue that the priors show he's an addict and therefore had diminished capacity?"

"I tried, but the judge ruled against me."

The waitress brought my bourbon, made a point not to look directly at me, dropped the check and left—very quickly.

"I'm not a lawyer," I said, taking a sip of the drink, "but it sounds to me like you've got reversible error. Just appeal the case and you'll probably get the Murder Two rap dropped and we can all go home." I felt a little guilty on Jamie's behalf, so—just to smooth things over a little—I said, "Of course, if a dog were somehow involved in the case, then I might give a damn." I took another long sip of my drink and handed Porter the check, indicating that the meeting was over.

He looked at it and said, "Well, there *is* a dog involved, at least tangentially. Ten of them, actually."

"Nice try," I said.

"No, really. We have a witness who saw something at the scene of the accident. Or I should say, he was with Seabow shortly before it happened. Someone who, apparently, had a history with Dennis Seabow. An unfriendly history."

"Okay, so where do the dogs come in?"

He took a fat brown wallet from his jacket, took out three twenties and lay them next to the check, smoothed his tie and said, "Do you know a man named Farrell Woods?"

Surprised, Jamie and I both said, "He's the witness?"

"Mm-hmm. Apparently he was at the scene shortly before

the accident, or very nearby, and he claims that Seabow wasn't drunk, and in fact was set up. He didn't even drive the car. He couldn't have, so Woods says."

The waitress came back and picked up the money. Porter said, "Keep the change." She seemed a little disappointed that it was the fat guy, not me, who had given her such a big tip.

I tried not to look at her so Jamie wouldn't kick me again. I said, "So what exactly did Woods see that night?"

He sighed. "We don't know for sure. He won't talk to us. And he was afraid to testify in court."

I took a long moment. My eyes started to feel funny.

Jamie said, "Jack, what is it? Are you crying?"

I shook my head. "Nah. It's just that from what I know, Farrell Woods may be a pothead and a drug dealer, but he's not a coward. He even won a couple of medals during the war in Vietnam for risking his life to save the lives of half a dozen dogs and soldiers—the Purple Heart and the Bronze Star."

Farrell Woods had told me about the medals one fine October afternoon while his ten beagles and Frankie were all running around the play field—which sits about thirty yards down the hill from my kennel building—all having doggie fun in the fall air. After Woods told me his version of what happened, I did a little research, asked around, and—yes—even had Leon log on to the Internet to help me piece together the following story:

"During Vietnam," I told Jamie and Porter, "the K-9 Corps had a group of dogs that were sent out to locate minefields."

Shocked, Jamie said, "Oh, my god. They wouldn't!"

"What? No, honey, they didn't let the dogs go out in the minefields and get blown up. They were trained to detect the smell of a mine before anyone got close enough.

"So, Wood's company was out on reconnaissance one day, walking through a grassy valley next to a canal, which led from the Mekong River past a low hill and into a rice paddy. Woods and his German shepherd, Champ, were on point. Suddenly, Champ lay down in the tall grass. This was how he'd been trained to signal that there was danger ahead. Woods signaled the others, and as soon as he did, machine-gun fire filled the valley.

"Woods got shot first, in the arm. Champ saw this, leaped up to protect Woods. This made him a perfect target. A bullet hit him in the chest. Woods and Champ fell to earth together. One still alive, one dying. The rest of the company ran for cover and got pinned down behind a mound of earth on the other side of the canal. One of the other dogs was wounded.

"Woods lay still for a while—he wasn't sure for how long—trying to deal with the shock of Champ's death. The machine guns were still spattering gunfire across the valley but all Woods could think about was saving the other half-dozen dogs who were still pinned down behind the canal. So without even being aware of what he was doing, he scrambled through the tall grass toward the hill, got to the bottom and charged up the side, blasting away with his M-16. He got two of the snipers before his weapon jammed." (The M-16 wasn't built for combat in humid climates—one reason we lost the damn war.) "He was shot five times by the third and last sniper before getting close enough to plunge his bayonet through the man's heart."

The three of us sat there, taking a moment to absorb the story I'd just told. I took a sip of bourbon and Coke, went on:

"When it was over, the silence in the valley was as overpowering as the moisture in the air. Then, the other members of the company heard a strange, rhythmic sound coming from the top of the hill. They approached cautiously, and when they got there, they found Farrell Woods, jabbing his bayonet into the last sniper's dead body, over and over and over. He said he couldn't stop until he knew that all the dogs were safe.

"Now, the brass thought he had charged the hill to save his fellow *soldiers*, but when he told *me* the story, he said he'd just done it to avenge Champ and to save the other dogs. He hadn't even been thinking about his buddies at all." I got a little choked up. "I mean, I know he sells pot and some of it ends up going to teenage kids, and I can't condone him for it. But how can you not *love* a guy like that? A guy who risks his neck just to keep a couple of dogs from being killed?"

There was a silence. Porter pretended to look out the window at the cars going by. Jamie took my hand and stroked my shoulder. "Sorry," I said to Porter. "That story always gets to me a little."

"Quite all right," he said, but I could tell that it had had no effect on him whatsoever.

I took the case file from him anyway. "So, since they're both pot lovers, I guess Seabow and Woods know each other?"

He nodded. "Yes. In fact, they used to be good friends. Until this case, that is. Needless to say, my client is not too happy with the fact that Woods wouldn't testify on his behalf."

I shook my head. "Well, I don't know if you're on the right track with this or not, but I *do* know one thing: after what happened to him in Vietnam, my feeling is that if Farrell Woods is that much afraid of testifying, his life must really be on the line. Which Jamie and I can testify to, since we both saw him get shot at the other night."

"Someone tried to kill him?"

I nodded. "Or tried to scare him."

"So, maybe he really *does* know something."

"Maybe." I got up to go. "The main thing is, I hate to think about those beautiful beagles of his ending up without a home." I finished my drink and said, "You coming, James?"

She shook her head. "Barry and I have some things to talk over. I'll call you later."

As I walked away I heard Porter say, "So, Jamie—is that the kind of guy you go for? The sensitive, weepy type?"

I stopped, looked back at him, ready to throw his goddamn case file on the floor and show him how sensitive his fat face would be when it came up against my bare knuckles. It didn't bother me so much that he was putting me down, but the way he said it was, I thought, extremely disrespectful to *her*.

Meanwhile, Jamie—knowing me as she does—stopped me with a smile. While gazing at me, she said to Porter, "He's only sensitive about some things, Barry. Dogs, mostly. And kids. Oh, and me, of course." She looked back up at me and her eyes got a little moist. "His only problem is that sometimes he cares a little too much. Oh, sure he's arrogant and oafish and a little bossy sometimes, but a guy who gets choked up over some dogs he doesn't even know, who died thirty years ago?—I mean, come on, how can you *not* love a guy like that?"

Porter mumbled some sort of halfhearted apology, but I wasn't really listening. I was looking at Jamie's smile.

"Thanks, brown eyes," I said. "I'll see you later."

"You sure will," she said.

17

My nerves were a little on edge on the drive over to see Annie Deloit and her pug, Henry. I thought when I first noticed my hands shaking that maybe Jamie had been right to tell me to order a single bourbon and Coke instead of a double, then realized it wasn't the bourbon that had my nerves on edge, it was the sugar in the Coke. I don't usually eat (or drink) much sugar, and when I do, I always get a little wobbly.

I was glad, though, to be on my way to a training session. It would take my mind off the world of murder, mystery, and double-dealing in the criminal justice system, and put it back in the world of doggies, where it belongs. My mind, that is.

I arrived on the tenth floor of the co-op apartment building where Darryl and Annie lived, walked on the beige carpet down the beige hall and knocked on a dark brown door, with a brass marker which said 10E. Immediately, a dog started barking inside. I had to laugh. He sounded so serious, though I could tell he wasn't. It's like when a little kid tells you he's going to kill you, or like when Leon says he's gonna kick my ass when I tease him too hard. It always makes me chuckle.

After a few more barks, Annie opened the door, shook my hand and invited me inside.

I came inside.

Henry, her formerly black pug (now, at age twelve, he's

more silver than anything), stopped barking and came over to sniff my pants. I let him.

"Hello, Henry. How are ya?"

He wagged his corkscrew tail and jumped up to my knee.

"No, Henry! Off!"

He ignored her. She gave me a somewhat nervous smile. I could tell it wasn't me she was nervous about. It was the dog, and whether or not I could solve her problem. She was wearing neatly creased khakis, and a chocolate wool turtleneck sweater with maroon bands of color around the wrists and neck.

I took a step back from Henry, said, "Okay, Henry! Off!" and he jumped down.

The apartment was spacious, though large moving boxes were scattered everywhere. We went into the living room, which was mostly beige and tan—carpet, furniture, walls, etc.—though the ceiling and the window blinds were white. The only real color came from a blue, red, and tan Oriental rug, which lay beneath a glass and chrome coffee table, covered with arty magazines, and some wooden folk-art objects from Africa and Asia.

"Are you moving?"

"Yes. We're buying a house in Rockport. Didn't Jamie tell you? Come on into the living room and sit down. The house has a one bedroom apartment upstairs, and she's thinking of renting it. Would you like something to drink?"

There was a glass of white wine, smeared with lipstick, on the coffee table, along with a half-empty bottle.

"No thanks," I said, taking a seat on the couch. "She never mentioned the move to me, though she *did* say she's tired of living with her mom."

She nodded, then sat across from me in a matching chair, picked up the wineglass and took a long sip, finishing the glass, then picked another bottle up off the floor.

Henry jumped up next to me and rolled over, hoping for a tummy rub. I gave him one.

"How's the case going?" she asked, opening the bottle.

"Which one?" I said. She gave me a puzzled look, so I explained: "Jamie just dragged me into another investigation." I told her about Barry Porter and the Seabow case.

Her green eyes crinkled in a smile. "She's really got you whipped, doesn't she?"

"I'm not 'whipped,' " I said.

"Yes, you are."

"Not the way you mean. I may be 'Jamie-whipped,' but not the other thing."

"Whatever you say, Jack." She poured herself another glass of wine. "Are you sure you don't want some?"

"So, about Henry," I changed the subject, or rather, got down to it. "You say he's been acting aggressive?"

"Yes." She took a sip, then set down her glass. "It's always been a problem but it got worse recently, to the point where he won't even let me leave the apartment."

"Won't let you leave the apartment? What do you mean?"

"Well," she sighed, and squeezed her hands, "as soon I put on my coat and grab my keys, he runs to the door, starts growling, bares his teeth, and just stands there and won't let me leave. If I try to go past him, he snaps and nips at me."

I continued giving Henry his tummy rub.

"We had this behaviorist come out and he said he's doing it because he wants to be alpha."

I laughed, pointing to Henry. "This dog really looks like he wants to be alpha, doesn't he?" Henry had his head in my lap, his wide pug mouth open in a happy if somewhat noisy smile, all four of his paws sticking straight up in the air. "No, I think he's doing it because he's sad. He has certain natural instincts that aren't being nurtured and satisfied by his packmates, you and Darryl."

She put her arms up in the air. "Well, I don't know! What am I supposed to do? The behaviorist prescribed phenobarbital, which Darryl, being a doctor, would not agree to. Henry's really Darryl's dog, you know. So if he's not being alpha, what is it and what do we do?"

I didn't have time to explain that the pack is not a "top down" system, ruled by the alpha male, but rather a "bottom up" one, ruled by how the choices each individual member of the pack makes creates a pattern of behavior. This gives the illusion of a pack leader whom everyone else follows, when they're really just following their own individual urges and impulses.

Nor did I explain that the alpha theory has grown top-heavy in the past twenty years, to the point where they're now telling us that there is not just *one* alpha wolf but several, each of whom becomes "pack leader" under different circumstances. A better explanation of this is phase transition, one of the rules of emergent systems. This is where under certain conditions the structure of a self-emergent system changes dramatically. The clearest examples of phase transition in the canine pack happen during mating season and in the presence of large prey.

You see, instead of being in constant conflict, the pack is actually always either *in* harmony, or striving to *attain* harmony. As a result, each phase of the pack's life—hunting, mating, playing, and so on—transitions into another phase when conditions are right, creating a harmonic shift between pack members, and thus in the organization of the pack. It's this harmonic shift which explains why there is seemingly more than one pack leader under specialized conditions.

What did all this have to do with Henry? Simple. I was going to show Annie how to put *her* pack into phase transition, and thereby create a harmonic shift between her and the dog, using a tennis ball. It was also (though I didn't know it at the time) the way I was going to solve the Dennis Seabow case.

I didn't tell her any of this, I just said, "Don't worry, it'll be all right. I've handled plenty of cases like this before. Does Henry like to play fetch and tug-of-war?"

"Yes, but the behaviorist told us—"

"—not to, I know." I sighed. (They spend all this time studying dogs, and end up not knowing the first thing about them.) "Well, he was wrong about that, but never mind. Maybe you should just show me the behavior."

"Are you sure?"

"Don't worry. I know what I'm doing."

"Okay." She got up, as did Henry and I. She put her arms out. "But you'd better hope I don't get bit."

She went to the hall closet and got her keys and purse. Henry began to growl. He ran over, blocked the door, and began barking like Cujo.

"Now, watch," I said, taking a tennis ball out of my down vest. I came over and showed it to Henry. His ears pricked up slightly, though he was still growling. "Hey, Henry! Good boy! Nice tennis ball!" I bounced it on the floor, caught it with one hand, then threw it backhanded into the living room.

Henry went racing after it.

Annie stood there, perplexed. Henry came back to me with the ball in his mouth and dropped it at my feet, panting and wagging his corkscrew tail, happy as hell. No more growling. No more barking.

I picked up the ball and gave it to Annie. Henry wagged his tail and jumped up on her, asking her to throw the ball. He was a totally different dog.

"That was amazing," she said.

"Now throw the ball for him."

She did, and Henry raced after it, then brought it back to her. She took off her coat, we decamped to the living room, and I told Annie to keep playing fetch while we talked.

We sat down and Annie began to throw the ball for Henry. "Okay," she said, "but explain what just happened."

I said nothing about phase transition or the harmonic shift, I just said, "Well, basically I just redirected his urge to bite you into a safer and more satisfying urge."

"And that's it? I just do that when I leave every day?"

"Either that, or try throwing some slices of chicken into the kitchen. He'll probably go after those too. Use whatever works best."

"But how did he change so completely in just a heartbeat?"

"I don't know exactly how to put it. I repolarized his urge to bite you into the ball? I don't know. Again, he's not acting this way because he's aggressive, or mean, or he wants to be alpha. He's doing it because he's sad and he doesn't know what else to do to make himself feel happy."

"I wish you wouldn't keep saying how sad he is."

"Well, it's true. Though I wouldn't worry about it too much. It's not like Henry is lying around all day, *thinking* about how sad he is. Dogs are not self-reflective, so he has no ability to *know* that he's sad, he just feels it."

"So how do I make him feel happy?"

Henry brought the tennis ball to her, dropped it, backed off, and panted and wagged his tail.

I said, "He sure looks happy now, don't he?"

She laughed and threw the tennis ball. "So that's it?"

"No, but it's a start." I gave her a list of things to do that would change Henry's relationship with her, if not with Darryl. "First of all, *you* need to become the dog's primary caretaker. Meaning, you feed him all his meals, you take him on all his walks, you go with him to the park and play fetch every day. Is he well enough to be that active at his age?"

She threw the ball and Henry went scampering after it, happy as could be. She poured another glass of wine, took a long sip and said, "What do you think?"

"Fine, then. And one other thing, and this is the most important of all: play tug-of-war with him every day, always let him win, and always praise him for winning."

She was appalled. "Tug-of-war? That is probably the worst advice I've ever heard."

"No, the worst advice you've ever heard is the one about putting him on phenobarbital."

She laughed. "But still, tug-of-war makes a dog *more* aggressive, doesn't it? That's what I've always heard."

"Me too. Then I tried it on an aggressive dog one day, and in three days the dog's aggression disappeared. The truth is, tug is a *release* for aggression. *Not* playing tug, or playing but never letting a dog *win*, increases aggression."

She shook her head. "You have some strange ideas."

"Just try it and see how it goes. And another thing, it might not be a bad idea for you to try to stop drinking."

Her neck went back. Her cheeks got hot. "What the hell does that have to do with the dog?"

"Not a damn thing. It's just that I think you're drinking too much and I worry about you. So does Jamie."

She took a deep breath. She grabbed the top of the wine bottle and tilted it. It was almost empty. She looked across the room toward the wine rack in the dining room.

"I know," I said. "My saying that makes you want to drink even more right now, doesn't it?"

She let out another hot, bitter breath. "I think you'd better leave."

I went to the door, followed by Annie and Henry.

Henry looked up at us questioningly. I thought we were playing fetch?

I paused and said, "As soon as I leave you're going to open another bottle, right?"

"Just go," she said. Her cheeks were still hot but her chin was quivering and her eyes were filling up with tears.

I went through the door and heard it close behind me. I wondered if I had done the right thing. Way to go, Jack, I thought, you really put your foot in it this time.

18

Later that evening Jamie said, "I have something to confess to you, Jack."

We were sitting in the whirlpool at the Samoset after three games of racquetball. I'd won all three: 11-0, 21-5, and 21-10. Somewhere toward the end of the third game, Jamie had resigned herself to being beaten. After it was over, not only did she forgive me for what I'd done at Gilbert's, she actually seemed pleased that I had beaten her. It was a primal thing, I think—I was a man and she was a woman, and that's the way things oughta be. (I'm glad I stifled the impulse to tell her that Kristin Downey used to beat me at racquetball all the time. And not just me—she beat nearly every guy at Columbia: they used to line up outside the courts after school, hoping for a chance to play one game against her.)

As we left the court, Jamie had said, "You know, I bet if I practiced more I could even beat you once in a while. I was ahead of you by two points during that last game."

"Yeah? How do you know I wasn't playing left-handed?"

She snorted. "You idiot. Like I wasn't checking you out the whole time?"

Now—as we were relaxing in the hot swirling water, and inhaling the chlorine fumes—she had that little girl look on her face again (a look I adore, by the way), and was about to confess to some terrible crime she'd committed.

"What is it?" I asked. "Tell me."

"I want to. I'm just worried you won't forgive me."

"Of course I'll forgive you. That's what friends are for."

She looked at me and smiled. "We *are* friends, aren't we? I mean, not just lovers, but friends too."

"That's how *I* feel about us. No relationship can last without friendship."

"That's how I feel, too. But that's what makes it hard."

"Jamie, just tell me, okay? Before we turn into a couple of prunes here?"

She hung her head. "Okay. I lied about getting back together with Oren. I mean, when I said I told Sheriff Flynn that I'd think about it. What I actually told him was that it was completely out of the question. That I was completely in love with you, and that Oren and I were over forever." I think my heart skipped a few beats when she said that. "Do you forgive me? I only lied about it because I was jealous."

"Of Kristin Downey?" She nodded. "Of course I forgive you, honey. If anything, this only makes me love you more."

She was taken aback. "But why? I mean it was just an awful thing to do. I've been feeling so terrible about it, it was so dishonest and stupid and manip—"

"Yeah, and childish. But it shows me how much I mean to you. And that's irreplaceable, just like *you're* irreplaceable. Plus, we're best friends, which you and Oren never were."

"That's so true." She shook her head and smiled. "You see, this is what I love about you. I go and do something really awful and treat you really badly and you automatically forgive me." She hung her head. "You know, to be honest, I think I do it on purpose to test you, to see if you really *do* love me."

I brought her chin up. "Well, I hope you know by now that I do. And I've been meaning to confess something to *you*."

"What?"

"I know you sometimes feel that I'm ambivalent about our relationship, and in a way that's true—I *am*."

She pulled back. "Jack—"

"Wait, let me finish. However, I am totally *un*ambivalent about my *feelings* for you. In fact, I'm absolutely certain that you and I will spend the rest of our lives together. We will always be in love. We will always be best friends, unless I do something to screw things up, of course."

She leaned into me again. "Which you probably will."

"Probably. But what I mean is, sometimes I feel guilty that we're seeing each other at all because you're still married, you know? Sleeping with someone's wife—even if she *has* filed for divorce—well, that just isn't done. So I just wanted you to know that I'll pop the question, but not until after your divorce from Oren is final."

"Really? That's good to know." She thought a moment. "So what exactly do you call that—what you just said? A preproposal proposal?"

"No, it's just a heads-up."

"A 'heads-up,'" she scoffed, and hit me. "You're right, though. I feel guilty about it too. Though Oren and I *are* legally separated, so it's almost like being divorced. In fact, a wife who's legally separated can testify against her husband in court. Did you know that?"

I said I did not. We held hands.

"How'd it go with Henry today?"

I sighed. "It went fine with the dog, but I may have done something I shouldn't have."

"Oh, no. What?"

"Well, I told Annie I thought she had a drinking problem."

She thought this over for a moment. "How did she take it?"

"Not well. She was mad at first, if that's the right word. Furious would be better. Then, as I was leaving, I think she started to cry. I was kind of direct about it."

"What did you say to her?"

"I don't remember. I just kind of blurted it out."

She chuckled. "Yeah, you do have a tendency to blurt things out, don't you." She sighed too. "Well," she squeezed my hand, "at least you were up front about it. No one else has had the courage to say anything to her, including me."

"Maybe it's because I'm not as close to her as you are."

"Maybe."

We sat there awhile thinking about our friend.

"By the way," I said, "I got you your own medicine cabinet for the bathroom so you can keep your makeup and whatnot at my place. I couldn't find a wardrobe or armoire for your clothes, but I'll keep looking."

"Really? That's very sweet. Why did you suddenly decide to start . . . ?"

I shrugged. "I have the feeling that my boyish charm is beginning to wear off a little, so I figured it's time to start wooing you with fancy gifts and extravagant gestures instead."

"That's really nice, Jack," she said, and smiled. Then her free hand went under the water.

I felt myself blush. A guy was doing laps in the swimming pool. A spa employee, carrying a stack of towels, walked by.

"Honey, don't do that here. There are people around—"

"It's under the water. No one can see." She had that look on her face, that fierce, determined smile, with the half-closed eyes, she always gets when she wants to make love.

"Can't you wait until we get home?"

She leaned closer and whispered in my ear, "Yeah, I'll wait. But just until we get to the car. Then you are going to get a special treat on the ride home."

"I don't think that's very safe, do you?"

"You can handle it. You studied stunt driving at the Police Academy, remember? Besides, I can't wait to reward you for being so wonderful and forgiving."

I smiled. "Ah-hah. So you agree with me that everything

is like dog training." She gave me a questioning look. "Well, whether it's a liver treat or . . ." I whispered something in her ear. ". . . it's all positive reinforcement."

She hit me, then started laughing and fell into my arms.

19

Farrell Woods showed up later that night. Jamie was upstairs asleep. I was in the living room, tending the embers of a dying fire, enjoying the smell of the burning wood, and watching Letterman. I find it relaxing to have a good laugh at the end of the day, and to me, Dave is always funny. (The only time Leno is funny is when he's stealing Dave's material.)

There was a knock at the door and I got up to see who it was. It was Woods, standing on the front porch, grinning under his navy blue woolen watch cap, his long reddish-brown hair tucked behind his ears and falling over the shoulders of his camouflage field jacket. I opened the door.

He said, "Hey, Jackie boy, how are my babies?"

Jackie boy. Other than my father, he was the only person who ever called me that. Somehow, I always let him.

"They're a pain in the ass," I griped, but held the door open for him to come inside. Frankie came over and sniffed his trouser leg. "You come to pick them up? I hope?"

"No, not part of the detail tonight, buddy. Sorry. You know, I'm still flying under the radar out there. Trying to put out a few fires. But, uh, I heard you wanted to see me about something. I hope nothing's wrong with the dogs."

"They're fine, though they tend to be a little—" Before I could say "loud," the dogs did it for me. Several of them began to howl. Woods's voice must have roused them. "See what I mean? And you know what? I've got a lovely lady upstairs who's trying to sleep!"

"Aw, man, I'm sorry. I shouldn't have come."

"Nah, it's all right," I said, leading him into the living room, then through the kitchen and back to the laundry room. There was quite a ruckus when we got there. Even Frankie started in. "They already know you're here. And, hey, you know, if you miss your dogs, then I guess you gotta see your dogs."

When the dogs actually *saw* Woods, they really went nuts (if they weren't totally nuts already), some twisting around in frantic circles, others rising up as tall as they could get on their back legs, others running toward the gate, then running back to the washer and dryer, then running toward the gate again. Not a single quiet one in the bunch. I just had to laugh. When I did, Frankie jumped up and licked my face.

It's a wonder that I was able to hear Jamie's voice coming from the top of the stairs. "Jack! JACK!"

Woods climbed over the gate and let the puppies jump all over him and lick him and nip his boots and trousers. While he did this, Frankie and I went back to the living room, where I looked up at Jamie, standing there, fuming. "What the hell is going on?" She looked lovely in my terry-cloth robe, even though she was frowning and had a pillow crease down her left cheek.

"Farrell Woods came to see his dogs," I said as quietly as I could while still being heard over the beagle racket. "Go put something on. We'll interrogate him about the case."

"Oh," she sighed, ran her fingers through her hair, and came down the stairs. "I don't feel like getting dressed." She came down to the couch, picked up the remote, sat down, and—since I was standing there like an idiot, thinking about checking back in with Farrell and his dogs—she patted a place next to her for me to sit so she could use me as a pillow. I sat down and she cuddled up sideways next to me, her head on my chest, both knees pulled up in the fetal position. She clicked around for a while, then yawned and handed me the remote.

"Were you watching Dave?"

"Mm-hmm. He's got Stupid Pet Tricks on tonight."

She lifted her head and looked toward the kitchen. "Speaking of which . . ."

Woods came in, followed by the ten beagles. Frankie joined the parade, though when he did, Maggie, the one with the white patch on her back, launched herself at his closest ear. He quickly, and wisely, turned his head and retreated.

"Hey, Jackie, okay if I take them out for a quick pee?"

"Be my guest. Frankie, you can go too." He stood there, looking at me, wagging his tail. "Go on, go for a walk!" He turned and happily followed Woods and the beagles to the front door, and they all went out into the cold.

While they were busy, Jamie and I watched The Top Ten List. It was a clever idea in theory, though it went over the head of the studio audience. Maybe they couldn't see the visuals as well as we could. It was The Top Ten Worst Movie Titles When Seen on a Theater Marquee, with actual photos of actual theater marquees for each one of the ten titles.

Dave explained, "If you run a studio and you're releasing a film, these are the worst things you can call your movie, as far as people, you know, just seeing the title up on the theater marquee while driving past. Doesn't matter if you have Julia Roberts or George Clooney in it. People are not gonna come."

Paul said, "Because when they see the title up in lights, they'll what?"

"They—" Dave shrugged, "—they just won't, you know, they just won't buy a ticket. Ready?"

There was a drum roll.

I won't give you the whole list but it started with "Undergoing Renovations," again with the title as seen on an actual marquee, then went on to "We Serve Infected Popcorn," "Blind Projectionist on Duty," "Closed for the Holidays," "Sticky Seats, Half Price," "Free Autopsy with Giant Nachos," "Unbalanced Ushers, Armed with Knives," "All Winos Watch Free," and ended with the kicker, "Starring Pauly Shore."

I thought it was hilarious but Jamie didn't get it. "Who would name a movie 'Infected Popcorn'?"

"It's a joke."

"No, it isn't. A joke is supposed to be funny."

"You mean like *my* jokes?"

She touched my cheek gently. "Like *some* of your jokes, honey. Got any new ones?"

"Yeah, but you won't like it. How many dyslexics does it take to screw in a bulb light?"

"How many?"

"No, that's the whole joke. Bulb light, not lightbulb."

She thought it over, then laughed. "That *is* pretty good, but only in retrospect. Got any more?"

"Sure. How many alcoholics does it take to, I love you, man, did I ever tell you that?"

Jamie laughed.

"Okay, How many paranoids does it take to . . . what are you looking at?"

Jamie laughed, involuntarily.

"Oh, you think this is funny?"

She laughed again.

"Oh, I'm a joke to you now, is that right?"

She said, "Next . . ."

"Okay. How many thesaurus writers does it take to screw in, twist into position, or otherwise replace—" She chuckled. "—a glass-enclosed, vacuum-packed incandescent light-producing filament, in exchange for a nonfunctioning, ineffective, or otherwise dead globe of the same type, sort, kind, or variety?"

She cracked up. After a moment she wiped her eyes and said, "You realize that you've just invented deconstructionist humor?"

I laughed. "I hadn't thought about it but I think you're probably right."

At this point Woods came back in with the doggies. He asked to use the rest room, and I pointed to a door between the mud room and the kitchen. He went inside and the dogs came over to warm up by what was left of the fire. Petey and Wampus came sniffing around me and Jamie, as did Maggie, followed by Townes Van Zandt, who seemed enamored of her. Jamie said hello and pet their heads. Frankie attempted to lie down in his favorite spot, just left of the hearth, but he had to go past me to get there and Maggie didn't like that. She launched herself at him, whining and squealing. B.B. and Smokey turned their heads to watch as Frankie retreated to the staircase.

"What's with her?" Jamie said, patting the couch for Wampus and Petey to jump up next to us. Wampus jumped up and immediately rolled over between us, hoping for a tummy rub.

"Maggie?" I said. "She thinks she's alpha."

"I thought you didn't believe in that." She scratched Wampus. I reached down for Townes Van Zandt and pulled him up.

"It was a joke. Does she look confident and secure when she does that? No, she whines and seems anxious. Not very alpha-type behavior. What she's actually doing is resource guarding. Also, she's a beagle, which means she naturally has an independent temperament, but she's been made to feel like she has to be the center of attention at all times, which is a dependent feeling state. The two things are totally in conflict, and as a result, so is she. The truth is, she just needs more to do. I've been teaching her to use her tracking skills, and—"

We heard the toilet flush, and Woods came out of the guest bathroom, thanked us and apologized and made as if to leave.

"Don't go yet. Come sit by the fire for a while."

"Well, thanks, Jackie boy, but I've got a lotta shit to take care of—"

"Like I don't? Namely your dogs, for one thing. And whatever mess you're out there creating for all of us?"

"Hey, that ain't fair. I've never done anything to hurt you or anybody else, but now there are some very powerful people out there trying their best to screw me good. And I mean I am being screwed, glued, and tattooed."

Jamie sat up, brushed her hair back. "Okay. Sit down, right now, and tell us about it. Barry Porter says Dennis Seabow was your friend and that you've got evidence that could overturn his murder conviction. Farrell, don't stand there staring at the door. He got twenty-five years for something he didn't do! Talk about being screwed, glued, and tattooed!"

"Ahhh, okay," he said.

"And don't worry. You won't get screwed and glued here." She pointed to an overstuffed leather armchair to the right of the fireplace. Some of the beagles—Janis, Grace, and Lucy, I think—followed him over there and tried to climb into his lap. Janis and Grace made it. Lucy gave up and lay at his feet.

"Though you might get tattooed," I said, making a fist. He cracked a smile. "So, what's the story? What's going on?"

20

"Okay, but most of this has gotta stay just between the three of us."

"You mean the fourteen of us," I said, referring to Frankie and the ten—by now, snoring—beagles.

"Yeah, real funny, Jack, but this is serious as a fucking heart attack." To Jamie, he said, "You're a doctor, right?"

She nodded.

"Well, I've been under a lot of stress lately, and if I could just discuss it with you, maybe I might feel better . . ."

"Fine. I'm your doctor, talk to me."

"Okay, the background is me and Seabow had a falling out recently because he's been ratting me out to the DEA. Well, not me, but some of my private growers. There's this new nark sniffing around, causing trouble. So, I saw Seabow that night to try and straighten things out. And he wasn't drunk. I know that for a fact because I . . . well, I slipped him a rufie."

"Rhohypnol," Jamie nodded, "I *thought* that's what it was."

"What do you mean you thought that's what—"

"I'll explain later. Right now I want to hear how and when Seabow got drugged."

Woods nodded. "Right. Well, we met at a little diner, about half a mile from where the so-called accident took place. I slipped it in the fucker's beer while he was yakkin' about hooking up with Eddie Cole and makin' some kind of big score."

I looked at Jamie. "So, it's Cole you're afraid of?"

He snorted. "That little prick? He couldn't fart his way out of a paper bag."

Jamie gave *me* a look. "I told you he's just a bigmouth, Jack, with nothing to back it up."

"Well," Woods said, "he *does* like to push women around." He looked Jamie over. In my white terry-cloth robe, she was quite something to look over. "Though you've got a good four or five inches on him, so I wouldn't worry too much." I wasn't sure if he meant that the inches were in relation to her height or to her chest measurements, though either way . . .

"Okay," I said, scratching Townes Van Zandt, "so he's not involved, let's get back to the night of the accident."

"Well, the thing is, he *is* involved—I mean, Cole, that is. See, he was blackmailing Terry Merton."

"Terry Merton?"

"Yeah, that's what everybody called him back in school. We both went to high school in Belfast."

"Wait a minute," I said, not liking where this was going, "you don't mean Judge Merton, the guy that was just murdered?

He gave me a "well, *duh*" look. "Why do you think I pulled a Judge Crater when they found his body the other night?"

It was Jamie's turn to look puzzled. "Judge Crater?"

"It's an old expression," I explained. "It means to disappear, after this famous case where a judge from New York was supposed to meet his wife up in Maine back in the 1880s—not too far from where we're talking right now, as a matter of fact—but he disappeared and was never heard from again."

She patted my hand. "Well, Jack, he probably just ran off to Venezuela with his legal secretary, didn't he?"

I laughed. "Good one, Jamie." To Woods, I said, "So, let me just get a couple of things straight: Judge Merton was being blackmailed by Eddie Cole, and you think that's why this girl was murdered? First, what was he being blackmailed about, and what does it have to do with Marti MacKenzie?"

He chewed his lower lip. "Okay, you know Tulips, right?" We said we did. He explained that she was half Vietnamese, born in Saigon to a fourteen-year-old prostitute. She came to America when she was three and a few years later was adopted by a family in Washington State. About four or five years ago she decided to look for her biological father, a former U.S. Army lieutenant from Maine named Terry Merton.

"She was Judge Merton's daughter?"

"She thought so. And so did he. Now, the thing you need to know about Terry Merton is, he was the kind of guy who never excelled at anything except that he was always able to rise to the highest levels of mediocrity. The only truly smart thing he ever did was marry Penelope Goodrich, the ugliest rich girl along the Maine coast."

I said, "Don't tell me she's related to Grant Goodrich?"

"Yeah, I heard you had a run-in with him. He's her cousin, on one of the wrong branches of the family tree."

"What does that mean?"

"He's not as rich or connected as the rest of the clan. In fact, before he got this gig with the Governor's Office, he was an auto mechanic and a car salesman. In fact, I think he still sells cars on weekends."

"When he's not singing in a barbershop quartet."

He got an "Ah-hah" look on his face. "So that explains the mustache." He thought a minute. "But wait—do people actually still do that—sing barbershop?"

I shrugged, and he went on with his story: the Goodrich family was not only rich and connected, they were also a very uptight and morally hidebound clan. "No hanky-panky," he said, "without spanky spanky. That's the family motto."

"Yeah," I said, "that one used to be very popular on some of the old Puritan wall samplers." Jamie hit me.

Woods shook his head, then went on with his story.

Terry Merton and Penelope Goodrich got married, right out of prep school for her, Belfast High for him. He goes to Boston College, excels at his usual minimalist level, enrolls in ROTC (Woods pronounced it "Rotsey"), and after graduation joins the army as—what Woods called—an "asswipe lieutenant."

"From what I heard from some of the guys in some of the units he was in charge of, he was the type of officer who's lucky he doesn't get fragged his first day in-country."

"I'm sorry," Jamie said, "what's 'fragged' mean?"

Woods explained. "If an officer is too by-the-book, in a way that puts his men in danger, or if he's an idiot, or a coward and calls a retreat while some of his men are still outside the perimeter, essentially leaving them to fend for themselves, he might accidentally get shot by some of the men. We called it fragging."

Jamie scoffed. "Sounds to me like a military version of an urban legend," she said, "something soldiers talked about, but that never really happened."

Woods grinned. "You're right in a way. The guys? We had more of a tendency to talk about it than to actually do it. You had to be pretty hard-core to toast an officer. But if you're a seasoned noncom or just a grunt and you see your guys ending up in body bags over and over because of a green lieutenant's stupid mistakes, the choice is pretty easy. And the idea wasn't necessarily to outright kill the guy. Any injury that keeps the turd out of combat was considered a righteous fragging too."

"So, was Merton ever fragged?" I asked.

Woods smiled, then laughed outright. "Oh, yeah. From

what I heard, he got fragged pretty good. It coulda just been an accident," he shrugged, "but then that was the beauty of it. He got his foot run over 'accidentally' by a fuel supply truck at the airfield in Da Nang. Put him right out of commission."

"And you know all this, how?"

He shrugged. "Word gets around. Guys transfer in and out. First thing anybody says to a new guy, once you know his name and unit, is, 'Where you from, soldier?' You kinda get lumped together with anyone else from your home state." He stopped. "Why am I telling you this again?"

"Eddie Cole was blackmailing Judge Merton."

"Right. So after he recovers from his injuries, only not enough to go back into the field, he gets stationed in Saigon and starts seeing this teenage prostitute there, using some of his family's money to keep her on full-time, which is how she's sure that Merton is the father after the baby comes along.

"A few years go by, the mother dies, and when she's six, Tulips is adopted by an American family living somewhere near Seattle. But she still remembers what her birth mother told her about her American father.

"So she comes looking for him some thirty years later. And when she does, well, if Merton had been married to anyone but a member of the Goodrich family, it might have been something that could have been swept under the rug, just a youthful wartime indiscretion, quickly forgotten and forgiven. But not only did he marry into a pretty unforgiving family, they'd started getting tired of him, because frankly, he turned about to be a sorry disappointment to the family in general, and Penelope in particular. I mean, they were ready to dump his ass, pull the plug on his judgeship, and take away any other perks that come from being a Goodrich."

"Wait a minute," I said. "This is all very interesting, Farrell, but how the hell do you *know* all this?"

He shrugged. "I get around, you know. Part of the job is to

hang with people and let them talk. And when they're high, they'll talk about anything. Mannnn, I could tell you a lotta things about a lotta people in this county.

"So, Merton's in a real jam if the family finds out. The mother was a teenage prostitute, the girl is a junkie—"

"Tulips is a junkie?"

"Yeah," he sighed, "it's a damn shame too." For some reason, I got the impression that Woods was hopelessly in love with her. "She's a smart girl too," he said. "College education, master's degrees in theoretical math and computer logic. But, yeah, she's a junkie and a fool, which is where Eddie Cole comes in. Thanks to her, he's got Merton on the hook as his own personal 'get-out-of-jail-free card,' and in the meantime he keeps her off of Merton's back by giving her a free, daily supply of H."

Jamie said, "I'm having trouble following this. What's a 'get-out-of-jail-free card'? Outside of Monopoly, I mean."

"My poor, tired baby." I stroked her back. "Don't you see? Cole wasn't blackmailing the judge for money, but to make sure any case the cops had against him got fixed from the inside."

"But what about the $100,000 Judge Merton withdrew from his bank account, the day before he disappeared? Remember? The police found the empty briefcase at the Union General Store?"

I shrugged. "Maybe the judge was backing out of the deal and Cole said fine, then clean out your bank account. Or it could have been someone else. But wait a second, I kind of need more of a fix on Eddie Cole. Who is he? What's his deal?"

Woods shrugged. "He's a drug dealer and a pimp, what can I tell you? He's cornered the market on rock and smack and pills, and, I guess, hot young college girls around the county."

"And he's dangerous?"

Woods laughed. "No, not especially. Though he *does* have this saying, 'Bitches who snitches ends up in ditches.' "

"Like Marti MacKenzie, maybe?" I thought of something. "So how does he deal his way into Judge Merton's bank account?"

Woods said, "It's an interesting question, isn't it?"

I looked over at him. "Huh. You're saying that since the judge was already on a tight leash with the family, and by extension, on a tight leash with the family's money, and since your typical judge doesn't usually have discretionary access to that kind of dough, how was he able to glom onto a hundred Gs?"

"Could be a story there," Woods agreed.

"So, maybe," I said, "someone from the Goodrich family was in on it. Of course, he *could* have forged his wife's signature on a check or some kind of document, but that seems unlikely."

"Why?" Jamie yawned.

"Well, forgers are, you know, forgers, not judges. Not usually. Anyway, we can't know anything for sure until we check his financial records and find out where that money really came from. It could've been the wife, covering up for the straying husband, or it could have been this cousin, Mr. Mustache."

"Ah, yes. The car salesman turned dog killer."

"Here's another thing—who did he pay it *to*? I mean, look, if the judge had manipulated the system often enough to keep Cole out of jail, someone else might have gotten suspicious. That would explain the large cash payment. So, who else knew about the blackmail besides Cole, the judge, and Tulips?"

Jamie yawned, tapped my arm. "That's where Marti MacKenzie comes in. She was temping as his law clerk when she was killed. She was studying prelaw at Bates College."

"So if Marti knew about the blackmail, and threatened to expose the judge *and* Cole, they'd both have had a reason to want her dead. And what better way to do it than to make it seem like a drunk driving accident. Nobody would even look into the possibility that it was Cole or the judge who'd killed her. But how does Seabow come into it? And who got that hundred grand the day the judge was killed?"

A few sparks flew over the fireplace screen.

Jamie yawned again and said, "Don't ask me, Jack. Do I have to do all your work for you?"

"Yeah, right," I grunted.

"I don't know either," Woods said. "Last I saw of Seabow, he was passed out in the parking lot of that diner I told you about. I took his keys, opened the trunk, got out all the grass he'd stolen from me, then put the keys back in the ignition and split. I have no idea what happened after that."

We sat in silence for a bit. Then I remembered something I wanted to ask. "So, who took a shot at you the other night?"

"I don't know. Probably whoever framed Seabow. If I knew who *that* was, we'd all be sitting pretty."

"Instead of being screwed, glued, and tattooed," I said.

While we were talking, Frankie had sneaked over by the fire. A log cracked, and he got up and started to turn around. Maggie, who was lying between my left hip and arm, growled and whined. I grabbed her collar and said softly, "Good girl." She stopped growling and looked up at me, confused. "Yeah!" I said. "Who's a good girl?" She wagged her tail, then remembered she had to kill Frankie. She got up and growled at him again. I said, "Maggie, down!" in the same happy tone I'd just used. She lay down and I quickly said, "Stay!" again with the same happy tone. She obeyed both commands. "Good girl." She lay staring at Frankie, who was keeping his head turned away. I praised her again and she groaned, sighed, then draped her neck over my arm.

Woods said, "That's it? You just praise her for growling at him and she stops?"

"I wasn't praising her. Not in the traditional sense. When I said 'Good girl,' my voice held a much softer tone and a feeling of me encouraging her to actually *be* a good girl. Plus, I was giving her positive attention, and Maggie is a girl who likes lots of attention."

"You got that right. But I still don't get why you tell her she's a good girl when she's clearly not."

"Because praise sets the emotional tone, it tells her how to feel. And feelings—that is to say, emotions—create behavior."

"I kind of see where you're going with this, although I'm not sure I understand completely." His eyes lost their focus. He stared up at the ceiling and out of nowhere said, "You know, sometimes I think I'm the last goddamn hippie on the planet."

I shrugged and said, "Not necessarily a bad thing to be."

He looked surprised. "How so?"

"Well, never mind the fact that there are thousands of hippies still living in northern California, Taos, New Mexico, and, I don't know, Asheville, North Carolina, and all over Utah, not to mention certain parts of Oregon, where they seem to have a monopoly on the subject . . . I'm sorry, what was I saying?"

Jamie said, "You said it's not a bad thing to be."

"Right. I mean, being the only one of *any*thing is a good thing to be as far as I'm concerned. You know, one of a kind?"

"Sort of like Maggie?"

I laughed. "You got that right. Of all the beagles in the world, she is the absolutely only one of her particular ilk."

"She sure is."

"Well," I said, "I've found it's the dogs who give us the most trouble that we end up loving the most in the end."

Jamie clapped her hands on her thighs, threw her arms up into the air and said, "Thank you, God. Now at last I understand my entire dilemma with this man!"

I began to laugh.

After a moment Woods said, "What did you mean about a dog's emotions controlling their behavior?"

"Well," I said, "the simple fact is that dogs pay far more attention to our emotions than they do to our words. After all, they have no ability to understand or use language, because they don't have the cognitive architecture necessary to do so."

"Okay," Jamie sat up, "here we go. When Jack starts making the cognitive architecture speech, I'm out of here." She kissed me. "I love you, honey, but I get enough of this with my—"

"—dad, I know." I said to Woods, "He's a brain surgeon. And he agrees with me, that since dogs have no Broca's center—"

"Oh, Jack, no!" she whined. "Not the Broca's center speech too! I'm *tired*!" She got up and walked over to the stairs. "Let me know when you've solved the case."

I snorted. "Which one?"

She turned her back and waved her hand over her shoulder. "Either one, Columbo. Either one. And save me some of that infected popcorn."

I laughed. In fact, I nearly doubled over.

With that, she went up the stairs. Frankie got up quickly and followed her.

Maggie raised her head and growled at him. I praised her softly, saying, "Good girl, good girl," and she sighed, tucked her head down, and fell back asleep next to Townes Van Zandt.

21

"I like her," Woods said.

"Thanks. Where were we?"

"I mean it. I like her a lot. Though I don't get that infected popcorn line."

I chuckled again.

"And I don't know how she puts up with you."

"Yeah, the same goes for the rest of Rockland County. So who else is in the picture besides Cole and Tulips?"

He sighed, gave Janis a scratch under the ear. "Well, like I said, there's this new nark in town, name of Gary Bermeosolo. There's been a big increase in illegal drugs in Maine the past few years. They have these pie charts? And guess which drug has the smallest piece and is the same damn size as it was ten years ago? And guess who they're targeting first? Grass.

"Now, you know how these assholes work. They terrorize the little fish, hoping they'll be scared enough to make a deal and roll over on the big fish." He stopped. "Am I being too direct for you, Jack? You ever work narcotics, and come down hard on some small-time pot dealer, just to get him to roll over?"

I shook my head, looked him in the eye. "I'd be very surprised, after your performance here tonight, if you didn't know every precinct house I worked at, and every case I ever worked on. You want something to drink?"

"No thanks. You're right, though. I know you never worked narcotics. I even know what you did for Jill Krempetz the other day too, so I guess I know a little about where you stand."

I had no comment on that. I got up, poured myself a glass of single malt and said, "Go on."

"Well, in my opinion, if they're gonna go after pot dealers at *all*, they should at least start with the Koreans."

"The Koreans? They've moved down from Canada?"

"Well, I wouldn't put it that way, exactly. No, they're still at it up there, the original group. They've just been expanding. They've got some new hydro houses now in Portland, Bangor, and Portsmouth."

Back in the nineties a group of enterprising young Koreans began growing marijuana in British Columbia, using an ingenious technique. They would rent a couple of houses in a suburban neighborhood, put hydroponic tanks in every room, being very careful to move the tanks and lighting equipment in late at night, in small boxes, over a period of a week or two. The only thing they hadn't considered was the enormous electric bills. It wasn't long before the authorities knew what was going on. A lot of the crew got busted, but not all of them. They regrouped and figured out ways to fool the power company, tapping into different power lines at different times of day, and they became wildly successful. The plants were huge, the Grow Lights were on 24/7, which meant that the normal growing time for each bush was cut almost in half, from three months to less than two. Something about the hydroponic gardening also made the plants extremely potent, with highly concentrated levels of THC. Now, the Koreans were in Maine.

I took a sip of scotch. It was good—smooth and peaty and warm. I sighed, letting the "angels' share," as they call the fumes in Scotland, flow out through my mouth and nostrils.

That was good too. "So are you pissed because they're running you out of business or you just don't like 'gooks'?"

"Fuck you, man. I could give a shit what nationality or race they are. And me? I don't worry about the competition, I only sell the stuff so I can pay for gas and groceries and keep myself in herb. I'm just saying, the DEA shouldn't be going after *any* pot dealers at *all*, but if they *are*—" He stopped himself, then said, "You don't like me very much, do you, Jack?"

I laughed a little. "Actually, I *do* like you. And I don't mind the fact that you sell pot. Not really. What I *really* don't like is the fact that you sell it to high school kids."

"Like hell I do!" He was indignant. "I have never supplied so much as a single bud to anyone under the age—"

"What about Kurt Pfleger?"

He shook his head. "I sell stuff to his older brother, Brent, who's in college. Now, if he gives some of it to his—"

"Which he wouldn't be able to *do* if you didn't sell to his brother in the first place. Look, I don't want to argue with—"

"Cannabis is totally natural, nonaddictive—"

"Hah!"

"Well, if it *is* addictive, it's not *physically* addictive like other things out there, like beer, cigarettes, and coffee. And scotch!"

"Keep your voice down."

"Sorry, man."

"Look, I already know all the arguments. Some of them are valid. Most of them aren't. The point is—"

"This is why you won't give me a job, isn't it?"

"Honestly? Yeah. If you were a recreational user, I'd probably hire you in a second. But that ain't the case."

"No, it ain't."

The fire was dying down. The smell of smoke was starting to be replaced by the smell of ashes. There was a long silence. "Maybe we should put your dogs to bed and call it a night."

He made no move to get up. In fact, he scratched Janis under the chin, then draped her ears over the top of her head, always a fun thing to do with a sleeping beagle. "No, man. Not yet. I want to explain something else that's been goin' on. Now, it may be important, it may not. The thing is, I don't want you thinkin' I'm only tellin' you this to justify what I do. But we're a lot a like, you and me—in the fact that like you I don't give a rat's ass what anyone else thinks about me."

I took another sip of scotch. "Fine. What is it?"

He let go of Janis's ears. "Narks, man, like I said: they terrorize the little fish in order to get them to roll over on the big fish. I'm no big fish, but that's what's been goin' the past couple of weeks. They been scarin' the shit out of my people."

"Your people?"

"Yeah, my growers, man. They're basically just a string of mom-and-pop types, spread out all over the county. They don't even know one another. They grow a plant or two in the basement, or in a planting shed out back. I mean, they're just trying to make ends meet, man. Like this one grower I've got—her husband left her, she's got three kids, a minimum wage job, and if it weren't for the weed she grows for me, there'd be no food on the table for those kids, man. Of course, some of these people use the product, some don't. Most of what I get goes to rich college kids. Point is, my people are the real serious, hard-core type of desperadoes our government should be chasing down and trying to put away for twenty years, don't you think?"

I said nothing, just nursed my scotch.

"So, recently, one of 'em's got a suspicious-looking van parked across the street from her house. Another found someone going through her garbage at six A.M. The way things are going, it's only a matter of time before one of 'em gets busted."

"And you're afraid they're going to roll over on you?"

"Hell, yeah, man. I don't want to go to jail, do you? But I don't want any of my people going to jail either. So, I've been in contact with them and told them to do exactly what I did—which is eliminate every last trace of the stuff in my house, clothes, car, yard, whatever, down to the smallest seed and stem. Now, I've got some money stashed away for a rainy day and I've promised every one of them that I'll reimburse them for everything they have to destroy, including their Grow Lights, potting soil, and plant food."

Wow, I thought, there are a lot of corporate CEOs who could learn a thing or two from this low-life pot dealer.

He must have seen something in my eyes or body language, because he said, "Ah, it's nothing. Just another Vietnam vet cliché. 'No man gets left behind.' In fact, the worst thing an officer could do was to call a retreat while some of the men were still pinned down and unable to get out. That was the most fraggable offense of all, especially if it was clear that his motive for calling the retreat was to save his own ass."

It was getting cold. The fire was out. I hated what I was about to say: "Which is exactly what you're doing to Dennis Seabow. Hanging him out to dry to save your own ass."

He smiled broadly. "That would be a good point if he was one of my people. Which he isn't. He's more like the enemy."

I nodded. "Fine, but does he deserve to spend twenty-five years in prison for something *you say* he didn't do?"

"Of course not. But maybe that's one of the reasons I dropped by here tonight. To make sure you had enough ammunition to get him off the hook."

I laughed. "Me? So I'm part of your outfit now?"

He grinned. "Would that be so bad?"

I shook my head, got up. "Let's get your dogs to bed."

He picked up Janis and Grace, stood up, and gave a low whistle. The other dogs began to rouse themselves in a kind of slow-motion chain reaction. We led them to the laundry room and they trotted obediently behind us. He put Grace and Janis down and we got them settled inside, and they all lay on their beds, some cuddled up with a pack mate, others curled into a solitary beagle ball. They were all sound asleep again in about ten seconds. All except Maggie, who grunted unhappily a few times before laying her head down and finally closing her eyes.

Woods and I stood on either side of the door. Woods was staring fondly at his little canine platoon. Without looking at me, he said, "I heard you told Barry Porter about my service record."

"I might have mentioned you got a couple of medals for taking out some snipers."

He shook his head and sighed. "The military." He made it sound like a dirty word. "They got it all wrong, man." He looked up at me. "I wasn't being a hero. They killed my dog and I just lost it. I just lost it, man. Something came over me and I ran up that hill in a blind rage. I wasn't thinking about saving the lives of the men in my unit. I mean, they were soldiers, man. They had weapons, and ammo, and combat training, and experience under fire." He looked down at the sleeping beagles. Their little chests were rising and falling almost imperceptibly with each breath. "But those dogs, man, they were defenseless. Who was gonna protect them, if I didn't?" He started to cry and turned his head away. "Sorry, man."

"That's okay," I said, a little misty-eyed myself.

"I tried to tell them I didn't want the medals, that I didn't do it for the men, I did it for the dogs. I never would have charged that hill if it weren't for those damn dogs."

He sniffled a bit. I had to work a little to keep myself from sniffling too. A moment passed.

"When the Medivac chopper came," he started to smile, "every man in that unit—of course, *they* all knew why I'd done it—every man in that unit refused to get on board unless the dogs got on first." He sort of laughed and cried at the same time. "I remember Sergeant Tucker even insisted that we take Champ's body with us so we could give him a proper soldier's burial. So the medics put him on a stretcher and we took him with us."

"That's good to know."

He looked at me with his sad brown eyes. "They were just doing their job, man. Those snipers. We were the enemy, and their job was to take us out any way they could. The funny thing is, about ten months later, when the U.S. was pulling out of 'Nam, all the dog handlers wanted to take their dogs home with them, you know? I had a new dog by then, Rufus, and I just loved that character. He almost made me forget about Champ. So we all asked if we could keep our dogs, and the brass said no. There were health code problems or something, they said. The dogs would have to stay behind. They'd be well cared for in their own kennel, they said. We found out later it was all a lie. There were no health regulations. It was just too expensive to take them home so they killed them all."

"What?" I couldn't believe my ears.

"That's right. To the military, they were no different than some old broken-down Jeeps or some spent shell casings. Those dogs—who saved I couldn't even begin to tell you how many lives—were no different to them than military surplus."

"I can't believe it," I said, knowing all too well that it was probably true—those bastards.

He smiled through his tears. "So who are the real villains

in this story, Jackie boy? Those snipers, who were just doing their jobs? I don't think so. So who are the real bad guys?"

I went to the kitchen counter to grab him a paper towel. He blew his nose and dried his eyes. The dogs were all asleep now, so we walked to the front door. As we walked, Woods said, "I just hope there's some kind of canine karma for whatever soulless bureaucrat made that fucking decision, you know?"

We stopped at the front door and I said, "Well, if it helps you any, I like to believe that anyone who mistreats dogs in this life will be reincarnated as a fire hydrant in dog heaven. Does that help?"

"Yeah, it does." He laughed and sniffled. "That's a good one. I'll have to remember that—a fire hydrant in dog heaven."

We shook hands and Woods settled accounts, paying me in cash for two weeks boarding for each of the ten dogs, then he started to leave, saying, "Take good care of my babies."

"I will," I said. "And listen, just one more thing." I looked upstairs. "I know she says she's not scared of Eddie Cole, but he *did* threaten to kill her."

He shook his head. "I wouldn't worry about Cole."

"Yeah, but where does this asshole hang his hat?"

"I told you, I don't rat. Not even on rats like Cole."

"Yeah, but what if I was in the mood for a hooker, or an eight-ball. Or a hooker *and* an eight-ball?"

He laughed and gave me his prepaid cell number, to call him in case Cole got serious with his threats. We shook hands again, he left, and I trudged upstairs and got undressed.

Jamie was sound asleep. Frankie, who was lying next to her, lifted his head to look at me, then lay back down again. I crawled under the covers, with Frankie between me and Jamie. That's all right. This way we could all *three* cuddle up.

I just lay there, not wanting to close my eyes yet. I was so tired I knew I'd fall asleep instantly if I did, and there was something I wanted to remember come morning. Some important concept that Woods's story had distilled for me. But I couldn't quite wrap my mind around how to put it into words.

I heard a few birds start to sing and realized the sky would be growing light soon and in a few hours the sun would come up. I remembered a line from a poem I'd read years ago in college. I think it was Kristin Downey who made me read it:

The distance is damp with the promise of spring.
Deep in the dark woods cold birds sing.

Maybe it was the whisky and the lack of sleep, but I felt, somehow, that this was exactly what I wanted to remember, what I wanted to take away from Woods's sad tale. It was just two lines from an otherwise forgettable bit of verse, but it seemed to crystallize everything that was going on; the murder case (or cases), the mess that Woods was in, the mess that drugs made of people's lives (like Tulips's), and the terrible tragedies that all wars leave in their wake. Even Maggie's need to kill Frankie seemed to be encapsulated somehow in those two lines.

Jamie made a soft, sleepy noise in her throat. Trying to talk, perhaps? To tell me something? Like, "Shut off your brain, you lunkhead, and go to sleep. That stupid poem isn't going to solve a damn thing and you know it." She was right. It wasn't the poem that would solve things. But the poem was showing me that *I* could, that I *would.*

The distance is damp with the promise of spring.
Deep in the dark woods cold birds sing.

Again, it could have been the whisky, but it seemed to me that those two lines were showing me that I *would* solve the case (or cases), that I *would* teach Maggie how to feel good around Frankie, that I *would* keep Roark safe from Goodrich, and that I might even be able to get some of Jamie's friends to like me (not that I cared, but Jamie *did*—and if it was important to her, then it ought to damn well be important to me). Those two lines were the turning point. I knew I would be able to solve everything and take care of everything that needed taking care of. I just didn't know how to do it. Not yet.

Finally, I closed my eyes, and those lines from that poem began to circle around in my brain again:

> *The distance is damp with the promise of spring.*
> *Deep in the dark woods . . .*

And I fell asleep.

22

The temperature hit sixty the next day. Everything was thawing and melting. It was the beginning of, or at least a coming attraction for, what in Maine is called "mud season." It's what they get up here instead of spring. They have a saying: "This has been the most severe winter since last year." That kind of sums it up.

Anyway, the next day was spent trying to keep Leon's carriage house and the kennel from flooding due to the melt-off. The house itself was safe. It has a stone foundation that's at least two feet above ground level, depending on where you stand. The carriage house and the kennel, which started life as a barn, weren't so carefully constructed.

I was able to dig a kind of channel from the side of the hill behind the kennel, around it and down to the gravel driveway and parking area. There's a slight drop-off past these, down to the play yard, which was fast becoming a swimming hole.

Meanwhile, the power was back on throughout most parts of the county that had been affected by the ice storms. This meant that a lot of people who had brought their dogs to stay at my kennel were now showing up to retrieve their lonesome, though safe and warm, pooches. It also meant that I had a place besides my laundry room to keep the ten beagles. (Though, to tell you the truth, I *did* let Maggie and Townes Van Zandt stay in the house with me and Frankie.)

Audrey was a big help. Still, the only time that I had to go over the trial transcript and police report on Dennis Seabow's case was during bathroom breaks and at mealtime.

I did find *one* thing interesting, since, according to Woods, the two murders were connected: Heidi Loudermilk had not only been the first officer to arrive when Judge Merton's body was found, she'd also been the first officer at the scene of Seabow's "drunk driving accident." But then I remembered that Quentin Peck, not Loudermilk, was the one who found Judge Merton's car, and that both locations—Dennis Seabow's supposed drunk driving accident, and the final resting place of Judge Merton's Cadillac—were on Loudermilk's usual route. So maybe her being at both scenes *wasn't* important. Still, it was something to keep in mind.

The police report showed that someone had called 911 the night of the accident, complaining about a drunk driver heading toward the junction of US 1 and State 3, where Marti MacKenzie was found dead. A few minutes later Heidi Loudermilk got a radio call to be on the lookout for a possible DUI in a white Honda. There were transcripts of both calls. Something in them didn't gibe, but I couldn't quite put my finger on what it was.

Transcript of 911 Call

911 Operator: 911, how can I help you?
Muffled Voice: There's a . . . there's a white Honda.
911 Operator: Sir, can you speak up, please?
Muffled Voice: There's a crazy drunk in a white Honda. I think it's a Honda, I don't know.
911 Operator: Sir, can you tell me your location?
Muffled Voice: I'm . . . yes, I'm on State 3, near Belmont Corners . . . I just saw a car go east, a white Honda—
911 Operator: What is your emergency?
Muffled Voice: Well, I don't know. I just saw a car go

past and he was . . . my god, he must have been going eighty, you know, weaving all over the road. He's gonna kill someone. He's gonna kill himself. You've got to send—
911 Operator: Who is, sir? Who's going to kill—
Muffled Voice: The driver! The driver of the car! My god, he must be drunk out of his mind, he's going to kill—
911 Operator: You said a white Honda?
Muffled Voice: I don't know what to say, what else to say.
911 Operator: Sir? Sir? Are you there? (To another operator:) Report of a drunk driver on State 3.
Background Voice: Did you trace the—
911 Operator: No, prepaid cell. Who's out near there?
Background Voice: Um, car 247, I think.

Transcript of police radio call

Dispatch: 247, 247, come in?
Loudermilk: This is 247.
Dispatch: 247, what's your twenty?
Loudermilk: Dispatch, I'm heading north on US 1, near Belfast Airport.
Dispatch: Copy. We've got a report of a white Honda, headed east from Belmont Corners on State 3. Possible DUI.
Loudermilk: Copy that. I'm coming to State 3 now. I think he's near here, I can hear, I heard his tires squealing. (brief pause) Now heading west on . . . oh my god. Oh my god. Station, we're going to need an ambulance. (sound of car door being opened, muffled sound of officer getting out of vehicle, footsteps leading away from vehicle—pause—footsteps coming back to vehicle) Oh my god, she's dead. (into radio)

Dispatch, we, uh, we have a situation here. Uh, one dead, one unconscious. Repeat, pedestrian dead, driver unconscious. White Honda Civic, he just ran off the road. Near the junction of US 1 and State 3. Looks like a drunk driving accident. Send an ambulance and an ME.

Dispatch: Copy that, 247.

Loudermilk: He just, he must've just ran off the road, and, uh, and killed her. This is 247, out.

One of the other things I did, or had to do, just to keep things straight in my head, was to make a rough timeline of all the pertinent facts about the two murders.

Four or five years ago: Tulips comes to Maine, looking for her father, Judge Merton. Shortly thereafter, Eddie Cole begins blackmailing the judge.

(four or five years pass)

October 18, last year: Farrell Woods slips Dennis Seabow a rufie outside a diner, near Belfast. A few minutes later Marti MacKenzie is killed in what looks like a drunk driving accident with Seabow at the wheel.

(three months pass)

February 11: Judge Merton withdraws $100,000 from his bank and then disappears. He has Roark with him.

February 15: The judge's car is found. He and the dog are both inside, the judge is dead, his throat cut.

February 17: Seabow is convicted of second-degree murder in the death of Marti MacKenzie. Barry Porter asks me to talk to Farrell Woods about the case.

While I reviewed these facts, Jamie had been keeping busy at the hospital in Glen Cove and at the ME's office in Augusta. We checked in with each other several times; at least, we tried to. She was not only busy with work, she was looking at apartments. Like Annie said, she'd decided it would be easier to live near Glen Cove or Augusta, rather than at her mother's place in New Hope. As for moving in with me, it didn't feel right. She was a semipublic official who was still married, technically speaking, to another man. I think she wanted me to *ask* her to move in, which she would have loved to do on one level—to keep an eye on Kristin Downey, when she arrived—but it just wasn't in the cards at the moment.

She was also shopping for a new car. She called me late Tuesday night, when I was dead tired and about to go to sleep, and told me she wanted to trade in her Jaguar for an SUV. I tried to talk her out of it.

"They're not safe, honey. They tip over."

"*You've* got an SUV," she griped.

"No, the Suburban is actually a truck, and it has a much wider wheel base than most SUVs. Which—did I mention?—are not *safe*!"

"You don't need to yell. Besides, they're safer than my stupid Jagwire when the roads are flooded. What are you laughing at?"

"The way you pronounce the name of your car. It's pronounced Jag-wahr, honey, not Jag-wire. And no car is safe when the roads are flooded. When the roads are flooded you're not supposed to drive on them. In fact, you *can't*—"

"Okay, but at least SUVs don't get stuck in the mud like my Jag-wahr does. You know, in England they say Jag-yoo-wahr."

I laughed. "That's true. But in England they also say pu-tah-to, when we say potato. Do Eve Arden have a boyfriend?"

"Which one?"

"Either one. I was thinking—"

"Their names are Evelyn and Ardyth, you know."

"I know. So, do either of them have a boyfriend?"

"Not right now." There was a pause. "Why?"

"Well, you said you wanted us to have more of a social life with some of your friends, but that none of them liked me. So I thought maybe you and I, and either Evelyn or Ardyth, could go on a double date, if one of them had a boyfriend, that is."

"I don't quite know what to say. I mean, that's very sweet of you, Jack, but don't give yourself an aneurysm."

"What's that supposed to mean?"

"I'm just saying that if you want to socialize with some of my friends, that's terrific. It's just that you should probably start with someone who might, realistically, someday actually *like* you. Not Eve Arden. They *hate* you."

"I know that. Still, you don't think I could get them to like me? I can be very charming, you know."

I could hear her smiling. "That's true. You've charmed the pants off of me—literally speaking—on a number of occasions. However, it's not the same thing, now, is it?"

"No, it's not. Well, how about Flynn?"

There was a pause. "Oh, I don't know about that."

"Come on, it'll be perfect. He's going to Buffalo this weekend to see his wife Joan, right? We can go car shopping in Rockland on Sunday afternoon, then take him out to dinner when he gets back from the airport on Sunday night."

Another pause. "Are you sure about this?"

"Yes. Come on, you know how sad and lonesome he'll be when he gets back from seeing her. We could cheer him up."

"Maybe he won't feel like having company." She let out a long, deep breath. "You really want to do this?"

"If it were just me? No. But how can I be happy if I'm sitting across the table from you, while we're out together, you know, just the two of us, at some romantic restaurant, all the time knowing that there's something you feel is missing in your life, something I could give you, like the two of us spending time with Flynn or Eve Arden or any of your friends?"

"I—I—I'm flummoxed. I don't even know what to say. This is quite a turnaround. I mean, it's not like you, Jack, to—"

"—try to make you happy? To give you what you want? By the way, what did you think of Farrell Woods?"

"Well, that's going a little far. Besides, he's one of *your* friends, not mine."

"He's not my friend. And I wasn't talking about adding him to our social Rolodex. I meant, what do you make of him?"

"Oh." She thought a moment. "Well, I hate to say it, but I actually kind of like him. Though I probably shouldn't. And what the hell does screwed, glued, and tattooed mean?"

I laughed. "I have no idea. Although, now that I think about it, it sounds to me a little like what a carpenter might do when making a cabinet. You glue the pieces together, then screw them tight, and tap them with a rubber mallet."

"Okay. But where does the 'tattooed' part come in?"

"One of the definitions of the word tattoo is a rhythmic tapping sound. I don't know. It's just a wild guess. And as for liking Woods but feeling you shouldn't? I know what you mean. In fact, I hate to admit it, but in some ways, I actually admire the guy." I told her some of the things that went on after she'd gone to bed. She was as impressed as I was with his commitment to taking care of his "people."

She said, "Not the kind of thing you'd expect from a drug dealer, is it? In fact, it's almost noble, in a way."

"Don't let Woods hear you say that. To him it's just a matter of being practical, though I think you're right. I think there is an element of duty, or honor, or something involved."

She sighed. "Well, that makes it even finer then, doesn't it? There aren't many like him left."

"I can think of one, which is why I'd like us to take him out to dinner Sunday night." I told her what Flynn had done for Jill Krempetz, though I asked her not to mention it to him.

She sighed again. "Well then, that makes two of you, doesn't it. You both went out of your way to help someone who—"

"Don't give me that. It was just something that had to be done, that's all. And all I'm saying about Flynn is, yeah, he rubs me the wrong way, and vice versa, but there's something really decent about the guy. Why are you laughing?"

"You idiot, haven't I been trying to get that fact through your thick skull for the past—"

"Well, you finally succeeded."

"Well, good. Just don't tell me you're going to get all gooey and sentimental on me, Jack."

I laughed. "Hardly. I am a total realist."

It was her turn to laugh—a little too loud, if you ask me.

"I'm serious. I mean, sure maybe I love dogs a little too much, but I hate those crappy, sentimental, soft-focus puppy pictures you see on calendars and greeting cards."

"It always comes back to dogs with you, doesn't it?"

"May I finish what I was saying? The truth is, puppies are a huge pain in the ass. They're always chewing on something they shouldn't. They're always eating something they shouldn't. They're always peeing on something they shouldn't."

"Jack, can you, just for once—"

"But do you ever see cute pictures of puppies eating out of the litter box, or peeing on a $5,000 Oriental rug? No. It gives people who don't know what it takes to raise a puppy the wrong impression. No offense, Frankie."

He wagged his tail.

"Can we get back to Sunday night? Are you really sure you want to do this? And will you promise to be nice to Flynn?"

"Of course I am, and of course I will. Besides, we may need Flynn's help solving the case, or cases."

She paused. "Have you had a chance to look over the trial transcripts and the police report?"

I told her I had and asked if she could get me taped copies of the two calls I was interested in.

"Well, I can have Barry request them from the prosecutor. I don't want anyone at the ME's Office knowing what I'm up to."

"Why, what are you up to?"

"Well, I'm basically reviewing an investigation that was closed before I was ever hired as part-time ME. It puts me in kind of an awkward spot." I remembered that Jamie hadn't been offered her position at the ME's Office until late December. And that Marti MacKenzie was killed a few months earlier, in October. Then Jamie told me she'd been reviewing the death certificate, and that there had been no autopsy.

"No autopsy?" I asked, more than a little surprised.

"No, it seemed like an open-and-shut case, so it was written up as a death by misadventure and then—"

"Meaning, it was an accident."

"That's right."

(There are four legal categories for the *manner* of death: homicide, suicide, misadventure—or accident—and natural causes. The *cause* of death is always expressed in medical terms, heart failure being the most common: victim bled to death from multiple gunshot wounds, cause of death, heart failure; victim was poisoned, cause of death, heart failure, etc.)

I asked, "So, who was the volunteer ME that night?"

"Hang on, let me check."

While she was checking, I remembered that Maine has only two full-time medical examiners, Dr. Howard Reiner, the head honcho, and Dr. Phyllis Feeney, his assistant. (Dr. Jamie only works part-time.) But, as you can imagine, there are more deaths in the state during any given week than can be handled by only three people, so the state has a system of volunteer MEs. These are local doctors who are paid a small fee to come to the scene of an accident, for example, and examine a body, usually in cases where there doesn't appear to be any foul play. Dr. Reiner then reviews the volunteer ME's findings and determines whether or not further examination, such as an autopsy, is necessary. Of course, when weapons are involved, such as guns, knives, even an accidental shooting by a bow and arrow, or a cracked skull from a baseball bat, the ME's office *always* does an autopsy, and in most cases, they also examine the body at the scene, even if a volunteer ME has already been there. Now, if the death seems at all suspicious—as happened in the Allison DeMarco case—they'll also perform an autopsy. In the Seabow case—seemingly a simple drunk driving accident—they didn't.

Jamie said, "It was, uh, Dr. Kevin Osborn. He runs a family practice in Bangor."

"I doubt if he has any connection to Judge Merton or Eddie Cole, though I should probably look into it, just to be sure."

She said, "You think Eddie Cole killed her?"

"Do I like him for it? I don't know. He might've killed her, I guess, but I'll be damned if I know how he, or anyone else, could have staged it to look like an auto accident. He sure as hell couldn't have pulled off a cover-up without *some* kind of help. Still, if he was blackmailing the judge, maybe he had something on someone else inside the system. Who knows? Besides, the first thing we need to know is whether Marti MacKenzie knew about the blackmail. If she didn't, then neither Merton nor Cole makes a good suspect.

"Meanwhile," I said, "I've got Kelso checking WestLaw and Carl Staub pulling the LUDs for Merton, MacMillan, and Cole."

"Sounds like the name—"

"—of a law firm, I know. I'm also going to try and talk to

anyone who knew her. How are you doing with the ME's report?"

"Well, without an autopsy, it's hard to tell if something's not right. There are photos of the body, of course. And there's something in them that makes me a little suspicious."

"Like what?"

"Like the placement of her pelvic fractures in proportion to the size of Seabow's front bumper. I need to take some measurements of his car, but again, I don't want anyone in the ME's office to know what I'm doing."

"So, how do you propose to—"

"Well, both Seabow's car and Judge Merton's car are being held at a salvage yard just south of Belfast."

"A salvage yard? There's no state impound lot?"

"Yes, but in some cases they just take the car to the nearest junkyard or car dealership and throw a tarp over the vehicle and wrap the whole thing up in yellow tape. So anyway, I was thinking we could case the joint and break in one night."

I laughed. "I love the way you think."

"Same here, honey. Only, I mean about Flynn and Sunday night. Though let's do it tomorrow night, can we? I don't think I can wait till Sunday. And I don't think I can tell you how much it means to me that you're willing to behave yourself and play nice for a change. I may even get grateful. And you know what happens when I get grateful . . ."

"You do that thing I like?"

"Mmmm-hmmm."

"I guess I need to work on making you feel grateful a lot more often. 'Cause I *likes* it when you do that thing I like."

"I know you do. I'll bet Kristin Downey never did it for you, did she?"

Actually, Kristin Downey used to do it all the time, but I didn't tell Jamie that. "Hah! Her? Are you kidding?"

"I thought so."

23

Lou Kelso called me the next morning from New York.

"How's the weather up there?" he said, in that low, throaty voice of his. It was a little after eight A.M.

"Everything's turning to mud. What's it like in New York?"

"Couldn't be better. I've got a few things for you . . ."

My old pal—bless him—had found some things on West-Law that I hadn't even asked for—and should have. Dori-anne Elliot had told me that Marti MacKenzie had filed a paternity suit against a local police officer. For some reason, I hadn't mentioned that fact to Kelso, but he found out about it on his own. This is why we'd made such great partners back when he was with the DA's office and I was a cop:

When she was seventeen, Marti MacKenzie had gotten pregnant. The father—or so she alleged in her paternity suit—was a Lewiston police officer named Randall Corliss. Corliss refused to take a blood test, so there was a hearing in family court. Corliss lost. The judge found substantial evidence that he was the father and ordered him to pay child support. Marti MacKenzie later filed a police report, claiming that Corliss was stalking her and had even threatened to kill her. A re-straining order was issued against him.

"Was he fired?"

"What, I've got to do all your work for you? I was checking WestLaw, not the Lewiston PD's employment records. Would you like me to do that for you too, you putz?"

I thought it over. "Yeah. How long would it take?"

He grunted. "I don't know, ten minutes?"

"Good. Let me hop in the shower and I'll call you back."

"Asshole."

Ten minutes later Kelso told me that the Lewiston PD had not, in fact, fired Randall Corliss. Legally, they couldn't, not based solely on an allegation of improper behavior. He *had* been reprimanded, though, and was suspended for two weeks, *with* pay. (The PBA is a strong and influential union.)

I thanked Kelso for the information then asked him if he could do one other thing for me.

"Oh sure, I've got nothing else to do all day but help you with your legwork."

"I did mention that I would pay you for this, didn't I?"

"Jack, I'm not going to take your money."

"Well, if you're not going to take my money, then for chrissake stop griping."

He laughed. "Good point. Okay, send me a check. What else do you need to know that you can't find out on your own?"

I told him about Bermeosolo picking on Woods's people instead of going after guys like the Koreans and Eddie Cole.

"What do you care what this DEA character does? And are you sticking up for pot dealers now?"

I told him about Jill Krempetz and how hard it was to get medical marijuana because of Bermeosolo.

He laughed. "You are such a sap."

"Hey, she's a friend, okay?"

"Okay. But I still say you're a sap." He grunted. "All right, I'll put a bug up someone's ass and get him off your 'best friend' the pot dealer's back."

I thanked him and hung up the phone, then Audrey and I

got the dogs exercised and fed and back in their kennels, or in Frankie's case, on his bed by my desk, by nine. When that was done, I called the Lewiston PD, told the desk operator who I was, and asked if I could speak to Randall Corliss.

"May I know what this is in regards to?"

"I'm sorry? I can barely hear you!"

"Yes, I know. What's all that racket?"

"Just some beagles howling." A pause. "What did you say?"

"I didn't say anything."

"No, I meant before the Beagle Tabernacle Choir started in. I didn't hear what you—" To the dogs I said, "Will you KNOCK IT OFF!" They shut up.

"Oh," the operator said, "I believe I said, 'May I know what this is in regards to?' "

"Oh, sure," I said. "This is in regards to me speaking to a detective named Randall Corliss."

"I'm sorry, but I'll need more information than that."

"Okay. It'll be a *telephone* conversation. How's that?"

"Nope," she laughed. "Still more."

I sighed. "Tell him I have some questions regarding the death of Marti MacKenzie."

"Oh, Jesus," she gasped. "He'll chew my head off if I mention her name. Maybe I'd better just put you through and *you* can explain what it's about." I resisted the impulse to point out that this had been my whole idea in the first place.

I finally got Corliss on the line and told him who I was.

"Jack Field? You're the ex-cop that's been bangin' that hot ME. What's her name?"

"You mean, Dr. Cutter?" I used, and emphasized, Jamie's medical title to try and get him to show a little more respect for her. It didn't work.

"Yeah, that's her." He made a few admiring, though crass and unwelcome, comments about certain parts of Jamie's anatomy. I felt the tops of my ears and the backs of my arms begin to burn. He said, "So, you lucky dog, what can I do you for?"

"Well, frankly, for starters, you could be a little more respectful when you talk about my lady friend."

He guffawed. "Or what? You gonna choose me off? Meet me behind the bleachers after study hall?" He cracked himself up.

"No, but if it comes down to it, I may have to wash your mouth out with soap." I felt a little foolish saying it.

He guffawed again. "I'd sure like to see you try. So, what's this I hear about you working for Dennis Seabow's attorney? I thought you were one of the good guys."

"I am. I just want to make sure they got the right guy behind bars, that's all."

"What? It was a drunk driving accident, cut and dried."

"Yeah, or else somebody wanted to make it look that way."

He laughed. "Are you fucking kidding me? How in the hell would someone pull off a frame like that?" He didn't sound skeptical of the idea as much as he was interested in learning the mechanics of how it might have been done. Then he said, "Hey, I hope you're not looking to jam *me* up on this."

"Not unless you did it. But in that case it wouldn't be jamming you up, exactly, would it? You'd just be guilty."

"Well, hell," he laughed, "*I* didn't do it. I'd like to know who did. Though I still think you're wasting your time. No way that was a frame job."

"You may be right. Then again, maybe somebody wanted her dead. You threatened to kill her yourself, didn't you?"

He huffed. "That's a fucking lie. She made that whole thing up. I never threatened her. I just told her I wished she would die. So then, I finally got my wish five months ago, and that bitch is still ruining my life from beyond the grave.

Jesus, never fuck a crazy person, Jack. That's my advice. Anyway, I got nothin' to hide. You wanna talk to me? Drop by the station house. You know how to get here?"

I said I did and that I'd see him at ten.

I parked on the Lisbon Street side and took the sidewalk up to the main entrance. It was a fairly new structure, kind of neo-deco, if there is such a thing. I went through the double doors to a wide spacious room, where a curved wooden reception desk stood invitingly a few yards away.

"I'm looking for Randall Corliss?" I told the female officer on duty.

"You mean Randy?" She pointed behind me. "There he is."

I turned and saw two plainclothes officers headed toward the front door. One was kind of nondescript, at least at first glance. The other was something else.

He was Mr. Handsome—six foot, solid, well-built, with deep brown eyes, dark, wavy hair, and a full, dark mustache. He was tan and had a complete set of choppers too. They had been bleached, toned, and buffed to their whitest. His wardrobe was an almost exact replica of what Regis Philbin wore on the *Millionaire* show—jacket, shirt, and tie all the same color, more or less, that color being a dark, brownish maroon, somewhere in the neighborhood of puce, but not quite so pretentious. His slacks were a shiny, dark olive green, and his shoes—a nicely polished pair of oxblood wing tips—were nearly the same damn color as his shirt and tie. He wore a gold and ruby pinky ring on his left hand, and what looked like a Tag Heuer on his wrist. The backs of his hands and fingers had a healthy fuzz of dark hair—not enough to make him seem freakish, like Robin Williams, just enough to show you how masculine he was. And he was *that*. I could almost smell his aftershave from across the room.

He caught sight of me, stopped in his tracks, gave me the

once-over (turnabout is fair play, I guess), then grinned (showing me his lovely set of choppers), then shot out his right arm, making a pistol with his thumb and index finger.

"Jack Field, am I right?"

I held out one arm in a gesture that said, "Who else?"

"You bring your soap, or was that just talk?"

I shook my head and rolled my eyes, as if to say, "You're nowhere near as funny as you think you are." Then I stated the obvious. "You look like you're on your way out."

"Yeah, we gotta pick up a perp." He and his partner came over to me. "We got a warrant on this kid from Salt Lick, Kentucky; Dirk Dillbeck—can you believe it?—who's holed up in an empty apartment downtown. Seems he was caught practicing his second amendment rights on his girlfriend's ass, then flew the jurisdiction. We got a tip on where he might be." He tilted his head toward his partner, a young, twenty-something kid with thin brown hair, maybe five-ten, and the eager air of a Mormon missionary, but without the plastic name tag.

Corliss introduced me to his partner—David Greene. Greene stuck out a slim, shiny hand, with long, slender fingers. His handshake was cold but firm, as was the way his eyes met mine, as if he were telling me he knew what an asshole his partner was but hoped I wouldn't hold it against him.

"It's a pleasure to meet you, Detective."

"Please, I run a kennel now. And call me Jack."

Corliss stuck out *his* paw, but I ignored him. He shrugged, looked at the kid and said, "He's still pissed over some cracks I made about his girlfriend."

Greene said, "Now, there's a surprise."

I liked the kid already. Maybe he'd been in the room when I'd called Corliss, and had heard his part of the conversation.

Corliss said, "So, Jack, you want to go on a ride-along?"

"Not especially."

"Look, dickhead, I ain't askin' you to go through a door

with me. Just to take a ride." He tapped me with the back of his hand, then put an index finger close enough to my face that I had to stifle an urge to grab it, just for fun, and see how far it would bend. "Thing is," he went on, "you got questions about Marti MacKenzie, right? Maybe I got answers. But only between here and downtown, which is where this perp is holed up, supposedly. You still call 'em perps in New York?"

"Depends." Skel, perp, twitch, dirtbag—there were a lot of words for criminals, each dependent upon the type of individual involved. Skel, for instance, referred to someone who might not necessarily be a criminal but was definitely a certified lowlife, living on the verge, yet still liable to know things helpful to an investigation. A twitch was someone who drove you nuts, trying to get a straight answer out of, on account of the fact that all he's really thinking about, while you're interrogating him, is his next score, or how to get his next half pint of Wolfschmidt. A perp, however (short for perpetrator), was a bona fide suspect or known criminal.

Meanwhile, the kid got his back up over Corliss's idea to have me ride along with them while they picked up Dillbeck—who, from what I could tell, was not only a perp, but a dirtbag too.

"Listen, Randy," he said, "it's against regs to—"

"Shut up, kid." To me, he said, "Greene here's a bear for regulations."

"Well, in this case, I happen to agree with him. Why don't I just wait here until—"

"Nope. We talk in the car or we don't talk at all."

With that, he went out through the double doors. The kid started after him, then turned back to me with a helpless gesture. "Shit," he said, "you might as well come along. He'll be impossible to put up with if you don't."

"Is he ever *not* impossible?"

The kid laughed. "I wouldn't know. I'm only around him during working hours."

We went out to the parking area. Corliss was already behind the wheel. The car's exhaust was blowing blue smoke.

Greene held the front door open for me. "You might as well take shotgun."

"That's all right," I said, "I don't mind sitting in back."

"Trust me. We'll all be a lot safer if you're in the front. If you're in back he'll spend the whole drive looking over his shoulder to see how impressed you are with him."

I laughed. "So, that's what this is all about?" I got in.

"Yeah." Before he closed the door he said, "The rest of it is, he's just a natural born asshole."

24

The drive shouldn't have taken long—the building was just ten blocks from the station house, but Corliss said he had to make one stop along the way. It was at an abandoned warehouse down by the Androscoggin River. A shiny, black Mercedes-Benz sat waiting in the morning sun. Corliss pulled up across the street, cracked opened his door, but left the engine running.

"Gotta talk to my CI," he said, over the car's warning beep. (CI is short for confidential informant.) "It'll only take a minute." He shut the door, the beeping stopped, he looked around, then went across the street and got in the limo.

"What's this?" I said to Greene. "Is he picking up his weekly take or something?"

"His weekly take?"

"You don't buy those kind of clothes on a cop's salary. Especially if you're also paying alimony and child support."

Greene shook his head. "He tells me he shops at the outlet stores in Freeport."

"Giorgio Armani has an outlet store? I don't think so. And he expects us to believe he's meeting a CI in a black Mercedes, outside an abandoned warehouse? Please."

"Look, I don't ask too many questions around this guy."

Probably a good idea, I thought, and let it sit for a moment or two, then said, "So how long have you and Regis been partners?"

It took him half a minute to stop laughing and coughing. Finally he said, "About eight months."

"So, how does a guy like him stay on the job? This town's got a pretty clean reputation, from what I hear." It was true. The Lewiston/Auburn PD is the second largest in the state, right after Portland, and they have a sterling reputation for honesty, integrity, and service—Detective Randy Corliss, notwithstanding.

Greene shrugged. "Union bullshit, as far as I'm concerned. Or politics. Take your pick. The thing is, he can't be fired unless he crosses the line, and he's too good at dancing right up to the edge and not getting caught."

I thought it over. "Well, maybe they should give him a female partner."

"Are you kidding? No woman could stand to work with him."

"Exactly. Two, maybe three weeks with a female partner, and he'd create a hostile work environment. Then comes mandatory sensitivity training; after that, it's automatic dismissal if he screws up again."

"The way you put it, it sounds like we couldn't lose."

"I don't see how." I sat a minute, putting my thoughts together. "Look, this is none of my business, but it seems to me that this guy simply doesn't belong on the job, you know? The sooner the job knows that, and the sooner they take care of it, the better. In my opinion."

"You're probably right."

"Well anyway. I'm a dog trainer now, not a cop. And certainly not IAB. It's just that—"

Mr. Handsome got out of the limo and was coming back to the unmarked radio car, where we sat. He got behind the wheel.

"Let's roll," he said, seeming a little more chipper and pepped up than he'd been before his trip to the Mercedes. Cocaine, was my first thought, but I had no real proof of the matter. I did take a look back at the Mercedes, though, and saw that the license plate read: EC1. Eddie Cole one?

We ended up back on Lisbon Street, heading into the downtown area, and as we drove I got an earful of Corliss's opinion of Marti MacKenzie. He'd met her when she was a student at Bates College. She was a freshman at the time (just seventeen, if you know what I mean), and she was working part-time off campus as a waitress at a coffee shop that Corliss and his then partner used to frequent. Corliss was in uniform then, working the night shift, and Marti MacKenzie apparently (at least it was apparent to me, though not necessarily to Corliss) had a Monica Lewinsky fixation on him. (There were a lot of teenage girls, sad to say, in the late 1990s, who, as they were experiencing their own burgeoning sexual drives, were heavily influenced by the constant media barrage of the Kenneth Starr report, etc., and who, as a result, identified with Monica, and in some cases, wanted to *be* her. Since President Clinton rarely came to Lewiston, Marti MacKenzie set her sights on another authority figure, a local cop, who was also Mr. Handsome.)

"I got a wife and kids at the time, and right away I tell her so, 'cause I can feel she's coming on to me. But one night she tells me she wants to come out to the squad car with me and 'polish my nightstick,' so I leave my partner in the coffee shop, and we drive to a parking lot, and she undoes my belt, and—"

"Yeah yeah yeah. You don't need to paint me a picture."

After that first night, his story played out along the usual lines: they start to see more of each other; she's willing to do things, sexually speaking, that his wife won't do—all for free; he thinks of it as just sex but eventually she gets too attached, wants him to leave his wife and starts making scenes when they're together; so in order to control her outbursts, he starts to get a little physical, meaning that there were some bruises, black eyes, and contusions, but no broken ribs, etc.

"And then," he says indignantly, "she gets herself pregnant!" He looked at me as if expecting fraternal sympathy.

I was all out. "Really? She got her*self* pregnant?"

"Yeah yeah, she stopped using birth control."

Of course, it's always the woman's fault. Though he was probably right, in a way. There have been cases where a woman has gotten pregnant deliberately, willfully, and intentionally, in order to trap a man. This didn't sound like such a case.

Finally, after all this crap, he got to the good stuff. Just as Kelso had said, after the baby was born (a six pound baby girl), Corliss denied her allegations of a relationship and refused to take a blood test, so there was a hearing in Family Court to determine if there was enough evidence to warrant a ruling in her favor. There was. Marti MacKenzie had kept a written record of every phone conversation, date, assignation, and romp in the hay she'd had with Randall Corliss. She had also kept artifacts—gifts, love notes, matchbooks from restaurants (where he had made reservations and paid with a credit card), and so on. The man's goose was basted, baked, and broiled. I mean, he was cooked.

"So, she kept a diary?" I asked.

"A diary? A diary!? Hell no. She had whole encyclopedias of information, all about this big (he indicated something the size of the book you're now reading), and she kept them all hidden too. I could never find them. She said she had me by the bull nose."

"What does that mean?"

"How the hell do I know? She made it sound like a secret place, but I got the impression that she meant she had me by the nose, the way a bull has a ring in its nose, you know?"

"What did she say, exactly?"

He shrugged. "She said, 'It's all in the bull nose. I've got your whole life hidden in the bull nose.' Of course, I looked and looked, but I could never find it."

"You broke into her house?"

He nodded. I shook my head in disgust. "Hey," he defended himself, "exigent circumstances."

I didn't bother explaining the Fourth Amendment to him.

We pulled onto a side street and ended up on a short block of squat apartment houses, a mom-and-pop store, and an Irish bar, the kind that opens at 9:00 A.M. and serves bourbon and eggs—hold the eggs. We ended up parking at the far end of the street, next to a paved parking lot, surrounded by a chain-link fence. Regis shut off the engine.

"Anyway, we're here. You want to wait in the car while we collar this perp?"

"Not especially, but since I need more information from you, I guess I've got no choice. So that's the building where this guy, Dillbeck, is holed up?"

I pointed to a five-story, 1920s era, brick apartment building with a gray stone facade.

"That's it. Apartment 4R."

There was a steel fire escape at the back (or rear) of the building, which led down to a couple of Dumpsters on the side of the parking lot we were facing.

I looked around the neighborhood. It was a quiet morning, there were no cars around, except for a black Ford Expedition parked across the street from the apartment building's entrance. A young Rasta man, either five-nine or seven feet tall, depending on whether you included his tricolor, Jiffy-Pop hat or not, got out of the Ford and crossed the street to the building's entrance. He pressed a buzzer and was immediately let inside. A drunk came out of the Irish bar and puked into the gutter. Another glorious American morning.

Corliss switched off the engine and started to open his car door.

"Hold it," I said. "Aren't you going to wait for backup?"

He snorted. "Backup? Backup!? We don't need no stinkin' backup!"

I grunted. "I didn't know you were a fan of John Huston movies. But you know, you should really try to do your impression with a Mexican accent—"

"What the fuck are you talking about? John Huston? I haven't seen any of his pictures since *Pretty in Pink*, which was a piece of shit, if you ask me."

I laughed. "Not John Hughes, John Huston—the director of *The Maltese Falcon*, and *The Dead*, and a little thing called *The Treasure of the Sierra Madre*, in which a couple of Mexican banditos, claiming to be Federales, tell Humphrey Bogart that they don't need no stinkin' badges."

"What the fuck is wrong with you? Humphrey Bogart? I guess it must get pretty lonely up on that mountain with nothing but dogs to keep you company."

"Screw you, Corliss. And just take a good look at that fire escape. Apartment 4R, meaning it's in the rear of the building? If you're not gonna wait for backup, one of you's got to plant himself outside that window on the fourth floor."

Greene said, "He's right, Randy. I could go up there and—"

"—let me go through that killer's door by myself? Some partner you are."

"Okay, then we should call for backup."

"Screw that. We'll be inside the apartment and on this guy's ass before he knew what hit him." He got out of the car and started off toward the front of the building. "Let's go," he barked at Greene over his shoulder.

I sighed, shook my head, and watched them go to the front of the building and ring a buzzer. They waited. Nothing happened. Corliss buzzed again, putting his back into it this time. Nothing happened again. A white-haired, red-faced old coot came out of the bourbon-and-eggs joint across the street and shouted something to Corliss and Greene. They crossed the street to talk to him, pulling out their badges. The guy had skinny legs and arms, but the rest of him was all belly.

They showed him their stinking badges and he pulled a very large key ring out of his pocket.

The Rasta guy came back out of the building just in time to see them flashing their badges. He walked quickly toward the black Ford Expedition. The old white-haired drunk ushered the two cops into the building, using his key ring like a magic wand. As soon as they got inside he headed back to the bar and the Rasta boy flipped a cell phone open, dialed a number, began gesticulating wildly, and said something apparently urgent to whoever was on the line. Conversation over, he flipped his cell phone closed, got into the Ford, and drove away.

I looked up at the fire escape. A window opened on the fourth floor, in the back of the building. A young white guy with rock band hair was climbing out the window. He had a shotgun with him. I looked down at the car seat and opened the folder Corliss had taken with him to the scene. I looked at the photo in the suspect's sheet. Yep, that was Dirk Dillbeck up there on the fire escape. I looked back up in time to see him fire his shotgun back inside the apartment through the window.

I got on the radio, gave them my twenty, which I read off a street sign, and said, "Shots fired, possible officer down, Repeat, shots fired, possible officer down."

The operator said, "Who is this?"

"Jack Field. I'm with Corliss and Greene on the Dillbeck pickup. I'm a retired police officer on a ride-along."

"We'll send an ambulance and backup right away."

I rogered that and then got out of the car.

Dillbeck was scrambling down the fire escape. Corliss came through the window, followed by Greene. There was no blood flowing, as far as I could tell. Both men had their weapons—.38 police specials—drawn, but unlike what you often see in the movies, it's not a good idea to try and shoot someone through the metal rails and stair steps of a fire escape. In fact, it's a stupid, stuntman move. That's because of a little property of physics called Newton's law of motion, which in ballistic terms is translated as the ricochet effect. Randall Corliss thought he was smarter than Sir Isaac, though, and began firing at the fleeing suspect. All he got for it was cut on his left cheek, thanks to a bullet fragment that ricocheted past from part of the fire escape, and a broken car window in a Camaro down in the parking lot, which also set off a car alarm.

I wasn't that much smarter than Corliss at this point, I'm afraid, because I walked toward the parking lot, intent on stopping Dillbeck from escaping. Not my job, I know, and with Corliss's cowboy act, it *could've* been my ass.

However, I caught a break. Dillbeck's only avenues of escape were into another apartment or down the last piece of fire escape and then out the open chain-link gate of the parking lot, which was about twenty feet from where I stood.

He got to the second floor level, where the fire escape turned from stairs into an actual ladder down to street level. Corliss, meanwhile, decided to pull his second dumb stunt of the day—this is the one where you lean out as far as you can over the railing and try to get a shot off while hanging on with one arm: (a) it's hard to get off a good shot while dangling in space, (b) you still haven't done anything to cancel Newton's laws of motion, and (c) you've got another Newtonian law to deal with, namely gravity, which is what tripped Corliss up, so to speak. That and his penchant for fancy dress shoes.

So, while Dillbeck was trying to figure out how to negotiate the ladder while holding a shotgun, Corliss decided to do another stuntman move, which he wasn't qualified for. He leaned out as far as he could, hanging on with one arm and struggling for balance with his feet, which, unfortunately for him, were clad in nice dress shoes with slippery leather soles.

He went heels over head, but his left arm was still wedged into the steel railing. Basically he was upside down with his center of gravity focused solely on his left elbow. Something snapped, Corliss screamed, dropped his gun, which fell and scattered behind one of the Dumpsters. His arm came loose, and he tumbled over himself and fell to the ground in a squealing, screaming, cursing pile of bad cop.

Dillbeck saw all this, thought he was home free, and since he couldn't negotiate the ladder while holding his shotgun, he set the safety on, threw it down on the closed plastic top of one of the Dumpsters, and started down the ladder.

The shotgun didn't stay on top of the Dumpster, though. It bounced off and landed in the gravel about two feet from where I was standing, hidden behind the Dumpster. I strolled over, picked it up and shouted up to Greene, "Hold your fire!"

Dillbeck looked over at me, from halfway down the ladder, and saw I had his shotgun. I clicked the safety off, making sure he saw me do it. He shook his head, dropped to the ground and put his hands in the air.

Corliss was still screaming and moaning over by the Dumpster. I heard some sirens in the distance.

"Okay, asshole," I said to Dillbeck, "you know the routine. Facedown with your hands over your head. Both hands!"

He did as he was told. Greene quickly got down the last of the stairs, slid down the ladder—quite athletic of him, I thought—holstered his weapon and approached the perp.

"Pat him down before you put the cuffs on," I reminded him.

He did as I told him. Corliss, meanwhile, was now praying to Jesus Christ, although I don't recall our Lord and Savior having a middle name starting with the letter F, which was the manner in which Corliss was addressing him.

Greene got Dillbeck up on his feet, and Corliss called me over to him. "We collared this guy, not you. You got that?" He was going into shock, which meant he was getting past the pain. "That's the way you're gonna tell it."

I laughed in his face.

"I'm serious. They ask you how it went down, you tell—"

"Shut up, you asshole. You put people's lives in danger here today, you know that? In fact, you put people's lives in danger every time you go to work at a job you're just plain bad at. You are bad at your job, Corliss. Do you understand? In fact, you're so bad at it, you don't even know what the job is. The job is protecting people's lives, not putting them in danger. If you're an airline pilot, or a ship's captain, and you're bad at your job, you're putting people's lives in danger every time you punch in. Same with being a cop. You know, maybe you should get a job in an insurance office, or, since you like to look nice, as a TV anchorman. Hell, be a movie star for all I care. Look at Judd Nelson, or Steve Guttenberg. Neither one of them can act worth a damn, but they don't put people's lives in danger just because they can't produce believable human behavior on screen. That's you, Corliss. You're a bad cop and a bad actor and you should damn well find something else to do."

"I shoulda known you weren't a team player."

"Greene," I said, my face feeling a little numb, "you're gonna hafta drag me away from this piece of crap before I start testing my boots on his broken collarbone."

And all this just because I wanted to find out if Marti MacKenzie knew that Judge Merton was being blackmailed. I'd only learned two things that were useful. She'd kept a diary, and she kept it hidden in a place called the "bull nose."

25

I had to give my statement three times; once to a uniform, who was the first one to arrive at the scene, once again to the first detective to get there, and finally to a lieutenant back at the station house.

I didn't embellish anything about Corliss's ineptitude, nor did I go out of my way to paint him in a favorable light. It was just the facts, ma'am. That should have been enough to make him start thinking about his severance package, unemployment insurance, and maybe get him looking through the want ads.

It was noon by the time I finished my iterations and reiterations and, if there is such a thing, rereiterations. (That isn't a real word, I know, but I felt like it *should* be by the time I finally made it out to the car.)

The rest of the day was spent taking care of kennel business: writing payroll checks, taking inventory of dog food, chew toys, salon necessities, and the like. I even helped D'Linda with the grooming at one point—not the actual clipping, but running the dryer and toweling off a few wet doggies.

Late that afternoon, as the sun was being swallowed up by some dark, threatening clouds, I took the beagles out to the play yard and let them run around for about half an hour. I did nothing but watch them play, occasionally laugh myself silly, and from time to time think about the two murder investigations.

Even with the invigorating feeling that watching the dogs gave me, I still ended up dog tired, so I was glad when Jamie called to tell me that *she* hadn't felt like going to a bunch of different lots looking at cars on Sunday and had just gone to a dealership in Augusta on her lunch hour and traded up for a new Jagwire, with automatic transmission and all-wheel drive. She said she'd come by around six, show me the new car, and then we could drive down to Rockland for our dinner date with Sheriff Flynn.

"Can't we go to Señor Froggie's?" I said.

"No, Jack. I know you like Mexican food, but we're not driving all the way up to Ellsworth just to eat dinner. We're going to The Waterworks in Rockland. And you'll be happy to know it's not fancy, so you don't have to dress up."

"That's good, because, as I remember, you were *there* the night I fell off of Sam Kirby's roof and ruined my good tuxedo."

"I didn't mean *that* fancy. And you have a bad tuxedo?"

"I do now."

She laughed. "But, Jack, please don't say anything about Sam Kirby unless Uncle Horace brings it up."

Sam Kirby was Sheriff Flynn's illegitimate son with Joan Kirby, who was married at the time to Flynn's best friend, Camden Police Chief Walter Kirby. Flynn had been a captain at the time, but resigned once Walter Kirby found out. Years later, after she lost her mind and ended up in a mental hospital in Buffalo, Flynn married the woman. And even though half the county knows about Sam's paternity, *Sam* doesn't know about it, and Joan wants to keep it that way.

"How is Sam?"

"He's okay. He got a job as a fitness instructor at the Samoset. Which he seems to enjoy."

Sam Kirby had been one of Flynn's deputies but was forced to resign due to some shady goings-on during the investigation into Allison DeMarco's murder, especially after a certain ex-detective, now a dog trainer, found out that Sam Kirby and Allison DeMarco were related (don't ask). So I had two strikes against me as far as Flynn was concerned: I'd supposedly taken Jamie away from his nephew, Oren, and I'd also been responsible for his biological son, Sam, losing his job with the Sheriff's Department. I had to wonder how dinner would go, and how long a guy like Flynn would hold a grudge against a guy like me.

"Don't worry," I told Jamie, "I won't bring it up."

After I hopped in the shower and shaved my neck, I got a call from Beth Stevens, who wondered if I could keep Roark with me until after her father's funeral, which, she said, was being held on Friday morning. "I'll pay you, of course."

"That's not necessary. We like having Roark with us. And Beth . . ." I paused because I'd said what I was about to say so many times to so many family members of the victims of violent crimes during my years in New York, and I didn't want to rush through saying it now and have it come out sounding rote or clichéd. ". . . I'm sorry for your loss."

She sniffed a little and thanked me.

Jamie showed up a little while later, proud as hell of her new automobile, and rightly so. I spent so much time looking it over and made such admiring noises that I thought she might even let me drive it, but she didn't. Then, as we made the trip down to Rockland, enjoying the new car smell, I told her about my day's adventures with Regis.

"My god, Jack, you could have been killed!"

"No kidding. That's why I keep telling you I don't want to solve any more murder mysteries. I just want to run my kennel and train my dogs."

"Well," she said, "hopefully this will be the last one."

"Yeah, hopefully. This really *is* a nice car."

"Thanks."

Then we discussed what each of us had found out that day relating to the last case I would "hopefully" ever have to solve: me telling her about Marti MacKenzie's diaries, which were possibly hidden in something called a "bull nose," and she explaining to me the difference between a tib/fib, which is shorthand for the kind of fracture the girl would have suffered if she'd been hit by Seabow's Honda Civic (given her height), and a pelvic fracture, which is what the photos indicated. There was also what looked like a skull fracture just over the girl's left eye, or left orbit, as she called it. She couldn't tell for sure from the photos. She also said that the blood work showed evidence of liver failure as the cause of death.

"Can you get me a sample of her blood?"

"I suppose so. Why?"

"I'm not sure. Just an idea that's floating around in my brain. Something to do with a little beagle girl named Maggie."

We got to Rockland and Jamie found a parking space right on Lindsey Street. Once again, the Maine winters may be harsh, but at least you can always find a good place to park.

As we were walking toward the restaurant it started to snow and Jamie said, "Now, remember, you promised to be nice."

I laughed. "This whole thing was *my* idea, remember?"

"I know. But I had a hard time convincing him that you were being sincere. And I'm still not sure if he believes me."

"Well, that's *his* problem."

"See?" She stopped at the front door. "This is just exactly the kind of thing—"

I put my hands up. "You're right. I'll be nice."

We came through the entrance and found two large rooms: a loud, pub style area to the left, and a quieter and more elegant dining room to the right. We told the hostess we were meeting Sheriff Flynn for dinner and she directed us to the dining area where Flynn sat waiting for us at a booth near a tall, spacious window, where we could look outside and watch the snowfall. He had on an indigo sweater, and it was kind of shock to me to see him out of uniform like that.

Jamie came over and he stood up and kissed her cheek. I shook his big hand and we made the usual greeting noises, then we all sat down and began to involve ourselves in what seemed like long silent moments, contemplating the tableware, the snow falling outside, or the room's decor, followed by brief spurts of inconsequential conversation: "Have you ever eaten here before, Sheriff?" (me) "Isn't the snow pretty?" (Jamie) "I hear the meat loaf's really good." (Flynn) "I wonder where our waiter is?" (all three of us)

Finally we received our menus, got our drink orders out of the way (Flynn and I ordered scotch, Jamie wanted white wine), then were told the day's specials (corn chowder was the soup of the day, the entrée choices were penne à la vodka with chunks of grilled chicken breast, or stuffed pork tenderloin). Then we were given some water glasses, and some butter and breadsticks to play around with while we looked at our menus and waited for the alcohol to arrive.

While we waited there was more chitchat. "The meat loaf *does* sound good." (Jamie) "Doesn't it?" (Flynn) "I wonder if they serve malt vinegar with their fish and chips." (me)

"Malt vinegar?" says Jamie.

"That's right," says I. "That's how they eat fish and chips in England. The chips are actually these long, chunky french fries, which they salt, then douse with malt vinegar."

"You can always ask the waiter," says Flynn, looking over his shoulder. "If he ever comes back."

He did come back, with our drinks, which we set to immediately, and then ordered: two meat loaf dinners, one order of fish and chips (I was assured that they *had* malt vinegar).

Once the bottled spirits warmed *our* spirits, we began to loosen up and actually talk to each other. Jamie and I caught Flynn up on things with the murder cases, which wasn't much, just what Farrell Woods had told us about slipping Seabow a rufie the night of the so-called accident.

"Did the ME do a blood alcohol test?"

Jamie shrugged. "Of course. And it showed that he was legally drunk."

"Who drew the blood?" I asked.

"Well, he was passed out at the scene, so the EMTs took him to the hospital in Belfast. They drew it there, then it was hand delivered to the State Crime Lab in Augusta."

Flynn said, "Well then, either Woods is lying, or someone at the hospital, or at the crime lab, screwed up."

"Yeah," I said, "or someone who was in on the frame took the vial of Seabow's blood, which would have shown traces of Rhohypnol, and replaced it with the blood of someone who was legally drunk, and delivered *that* vial to the crime lab."

Flynn looked at Jamie. "Could someone do that?"

"Anything is possible, but it would be awfully hard to tamper with evidence that way."

He looked at me. "You trust Woods enough to believe him?"

"I don't know. His story has a ring of truth to it."

Just then our dinner came and the conversation took a more gustatory turn. Apparently, the meat loaf was good, and to my delight they really *did* have malt vinegar.

"This is exactly what I was hoping for," I said, with a mouthful of crisp, yet mushy (due to the vinegar) chips.

At some point between the time the dinner dishes were

taken away and the coffee and dessert was served, the conversation turned back to murder.

"So, let me ask you something," I said to Jamie, "how many vials of blood are usually drawn in a case like this?"

"Three. One for the lab test, and two for backup, all of which are kept at the crime lab. But the hospital would also have drawn blood as soon as he arrived at the ER. They would have done a cross-type, a tox screen, a chem panel, and a CBC. That's a complete blood count."

"Where are you going with this?" said Flynn to me.

"I'm just thinking. Don't most defense attorneys file a petition or a writ or whatever it's called to have a second test done—at an independent lab—on one of the backup vials?"

"Yes, something like that. The motion is usually made pro forma, especially if the defendant was found passed out behind the wheel of a car, the way Seabow was."

"Pro forma?" asked Flynn.

She shrugged. "It means the attorney doesn't really expect the second lab test to make a difference in the outcome of the trial. Then again, he might hope there'll be a minuscule discrepancy in the results. That way, even if there's less than a single percentage point difference between the two tests, he can argue to the jury that the results are inconclusive."

I said, "But Barry Porter didn't make such a petition, did he?"

Jamie shook her head.

Our coffee and dessert came.

Flynn dug into his chocolate ice cream and said, "You're really hepped up on this switching the vials thing, aren't you?" He shook his head in disgust. "You always gotta make it into some kind of kinky goings-on with law enforcement."

I could have pointed out that I was right on all counts in the Allison DeMarco case, which is what he was talking about, but I didn't. Although, I *did* flash Jamie a look to let her know what I was thinking, then said, "Maybe you're right, but what harm is it going to do to recheck the blood in the first vial against the vials at the hospital?"

Flynn looked at Jamie, who was having just coffee, no dessert. "Could you do that?"

"No. I wish I could."

"No?" I said. "Come on, honey, you can do anything."

She hit me. "No, I mean I couldn't do it *legally*. Not without a court order."

I jabbed at my carrot cake. "But if Barry Porter wanted it done, he could ask for a court order, right?"

"He could ask, but a judge isn't going to give it to him. Not after the trial is *over*, unless there are grounds for an appeal."

"Which isn't going to happen, now is it?" Flynn smiled. "Not unless your pal Woods comes forward and confesses to slipping the guy a rufie."

I shrugged, took a sip of coffee. It was good. "Well, I guess that's that, then, huh? By the way, Sheriff, you don't happen to know what a 'bull nose' is, do you?"

"No, should I?"

"It was just a thought."

Jamie got a gleam in her eye. She looked at me.

"What is it, honey?" I said.

"I just realized, I wouldn't have to test or retest any of the actual blood vials. All I would have to do is look at the tests that were done at the hospital and compare those with the blood-gas workup done by the crime lab."

"Of course," I said. "That's brilliant."

She smiled.

"Explain it to me," Flynn said.

Jamie said, "Everyone has different levels of substances in their blood; hormones, clotting factors, white cells, ketones, and on and on. Forget levels of Rhohypnol or alcohol, there might be two different blood types, or prescription medications in one and not in the other, any number of things."

"Yeah," Flynn said, "but would the crime lab have tested for these things?"

"It's not a matter of whether they had tested for them or not, Horace, it's only a matter of whether or not they looked at the results in the chromaspectragraph. It's like a chart with dozens of things to check off." She tried to demonstrate with her hands, holding a chart and checking things off. "The first thing they would check is the blood type, to make sure it was Seabow's blood they were testing. You know, whether he was O-negative, AB-positive, or whatever. Then they would look for his blood alcohol level and levels of illegal narcotics or prescription drugs that could have caused him to pass out. They wouldn't be checking his blood-sugar levels, or whether he was taking Imitrex for migraines or Tagamet for an ulcer."

"Can you compare the two blood tests?" Flynn asked.

"I certainly can. The spectragraph done by the crime lab is available from the DA's office, and if I can get Dennis Seabow to give me permission to look at his hospital records—"

"—which shouldn't be a problem—"

"—then I can get his hospital blood results and compare the two. Which I will try to do tomorrow. Now, if you boys will excuse me," she stood up, "I'm going to go powder my nose." She took her purse with her into the pub, where the ladies' room was located.

Flynn watched her go. He narrowed his eyes, shook his head, then said to me, "So, I guess this is the real deal, huh?"

I took another sip of coffee. "You mean me and Jamie?"

"No, I meant the fish and chips, you idiot. Of course I meant you and Jamie."

"Because, I have to tell you, they were very close to being

the real deal, malt vinegar and all. And I lived in England for six months when I was fifteen, so I should know."

"I can't tell you how uninteresting that is to me."

"I was an exchange student. Lived in Tunbridge Wells."

"And you just made it worse."

I spent a moment just trying to smile, then said, "Are we going to start getting along?"

He sighed. "I think we're going to have to."

"Because?"

"Because I think she really loves you." He played with his ice cream. "Are you planning to marry her?"

"If she'll have me. Yeah, as soon as her divorce becomes finalized."

"Then you'd better get ready to step up to the plate."

"Meaning . . ."

"Meaning from what I hear, that could happen any day now."

I hadn't expected this. "Wow."

"So, is that a happy wow or a nervous wow?"

"To be honest? A little of both. Mostly happy, I think, but I'm not sure. I guess I'll find out when the final decree is issued." I sat there for a bit saying nothing.

He sighed. "Me and you are a lot alike, Field."

I laughed. "That's what Jamie says. She calls us a couple of—" I stopped, too embarrassed to continue.

"A couple of what?"

"She says we're both a couple of 'blustering softies.'"

He took that in for a moment, then started to laugh too. "Well," he chuckled, "that's one way to put it. What *I* was going to say is, we're the type who like to help people; to try and make their lives better, if we can. With you it's dogs mostly, I guess, not people. With me, it's my constituents. Or whatever you call them when you're the sheriff. Jamie's the same way." He looked over my shoulder toward the pub. "Isn't she taking a little long back there, do you think?"

"Eh, she's probably okay."

He shrugged. "Anyway, that's how it was with her and Oren. I don't think she loved him as much as she wanted to . . . I don't know, help him become something he never could."

"Which is what?"

"None of your business. The thing is, unlike you, he's not a fool, just a weakling." He looked back over at the pub.

"You think I'm a fool?"

He chuckled. "You think you're not?"

I thought it over. "If I say no, that means in your mind I'm a bigger fool than I was to begin with, right?" He laughed. "So, tell me this, why do *you* think I'm a fool?"

He shook his head. "For one thing, who else but a fool would hop into a runabout and try to outrace someone in a cabin cruiser out on the open sea, all the while knowing nothing about how to operate the boat, knowing nothing about marine navigation, or even how to use the damn ship-to-shore radio?"

He was referring to an incident that took place near Monhegan Island, during my investigation into Allison DeMarco's murder. "Yeah, that *was* pretty stupid of me, wasn't it?"

"At least you've got guts. I know that about you."

"Well, thanks, I guess."

He looked at the pub again. "You sure she's all right?"

"Jeez, Sheriff, lighten up. She's going to the bathroom. You know how women are. Is he taking Naltrexone?"

"Who, Oren?" I nodded. "He *was*, back in Phoenix."

"Well, that's good."

"Why is that good, in your opinion?"

"It keeps the cocaine from having any effect, so there's no point in using it because you can't get high anymore."

He shook his head. "I don't see how taking a new drug is going to get him over the old one. Maybe that's just me." He looked over my shoulder again. "Maybe you should check on her."

I looked back. "She *has* been gone a long time."

"The thing is," he said, "I could've sworn I saw that little prick Eddie Cole go into the pub, just after she went back there."

My blood froze. My heart stopped. I couldn't breathe.

He said, "Take it easy. It might notta been him."

"Why the hell didn't you say anything about this before?"

"Sorry. You check on her, I'll grab my coat."

I stumbled to my feet and made my way to the back of the restaurant as best I could with two frozen legs. I knocked on the ladies' room door. "Jamie, honey? You're in there, right?"

The silence nearly killed me. I started to feel my eyes get wet but didn't allow it to happen. I knew I would find her. I went inside, just to be sure she was there, playing a joke.

She wasn't.

When I came outside, Flynn was there, putting his arms into a shearling coat with big pockets, which made him look kind of like McCloud, only fatter. He saw the look on my face. "Okay, let's ask around if anybody's seen her."

He went one way. I checked with the bartender.

"Uh, yeah," he said, throwing a bar towel over his shoulder. "I think I saw her go in. But it's kind of busy, and, where she went after that—hey, I don't know."

"Is there another way out of here?"

He pointed to a door in the back. "Through the storage room," he said. "It leads out to the parking lot."

I grabbed Flynn, told him about the back entrance, and, as we went toward the storage room door, a guy at the end of one of the long, wooden pub tables caught my eye and said, "Hey, you guys looking for someone?"

"Yeah, did you see her?"

"There was two of 'em," he burped. "A chick and a guy. I guess she dumped ya, huh, buddy."

"Pay the tab," Flynn said, "I'll check outside."

I went back and threw eighty dollars at the bartender, then, stumbling on rubber legs, followed Flynn out the back way.

"Shit," I said, looking around, "her car is gone too."

"Jack, breathe. We are going to find her, trust me."

"I—I—" I stammered. "I am going—" I lost my breath again.

"Breathe, Jack."

"I am going to . . . kill him."

"Jack, look at me. I am the sheriff of this county. Nothing bad is going to happen to her. I am going to take care of it, and you are going to get your shit together and help me. You got that?" I nodded. "Good." He flipped open his cell phone, speed-dialed a number, and said, "Trudy, it's Flynn. Dr. Jamie Cutter may have been carjacked. Hang on." He asked me to describe her new car. I did, and he repeated my description into the cell phone, then asked me if I knew her license number.

I shook my head. "New car. Brand new car. Augusta Motors, bought it this afternoon."

Into his cell phone he said, "Call Augusta Motors and find out the dealer's number on a car they sold to Dr. Jamie Cutter this afternoon, and get everybody from Wiscasset to Ellsworth out looking for that car. Copy?" Apparently, Trudy copied, because he flipped the cell phone shut.

"Call her," I said. "Call her on her cell phone."

"Now you're thinking." He dialed it, listened a long time, it seemed to me, then shook his head. "She doesn't answer."

"Shit. Okay, Sheriff, let's go find her."

"You know where that dirtbag Eddie Cole hangs out?"

"Somewhere in Lewiston, I think. I can find out exactly where if you let me use your phone. And thanks, Sheriff."

He handed me the cell phone as we walked over to his Sheriff's Jeep. "Thanks for what?"

I just shook my head, not knowing what to say.

"Well, you're welcome, I guess." He opened the car door.

"And you're right," I said. "We're going to find her. You *are* the sheriff. And I am the best fucking detective in the world. Well, one of the thirteen best."

26

I called Farrell Woods on the prepaid cell number he'd given me. It rang twice.

"Yeah?" he said, sounding a little guarded.

"Farrell, it's Jack Field. I've got an emergency."

"One of the dogs?"

"No, we think Jamie's just been kidnapped by Eddie Cole."

"Oh, god."

"Where would we find him?"

He took a breath. "I know of two places. One is the old mill, south of Waldoboro. The sheriff will know where it is."

"How did you know I'm with the sheriff?"

"Caller ID. The other is his place in Lewiston." He gave me the address.

"Thanks," I said.

Farrell sighed. "I hope he's in Lewiston."

"Why?"

"You don't want to find her at the old mill."

It sounded ominous. I didn't know what to ask, or if I even wanted to hear the answer.

"Let's just say Cole takes some of his girls there, from time to time, for a sort of . . . initiation ceremony."

"Ah, Jesus." I felt my arms grow weak.

"Well, the good news is it's thirty degrees out, so he's probably in Lewiston."

"All right. Thanks."

I told Flynn what I'd learned. There were a few expletives that flew around inside the car for a while, and after that there wasn't much conversation. We drove with the siren going and the police radio open. Flynn got us onto US 1, and I just sat and watched the towns blur by: Thomaston, South Warren, Warren, then Waldoboro, where we got off the highway and turned north onto 32. About half a mile up the road past Winslow's Mills there was a turnoff to the right, where I saw a small stream sparkling in the moonlight. A shadow up ahead described the silhouette of an old, abandoned mill building.

Flynn shut off the lights and pulled the Jeep to a stop. There were no cars parked nearby, there were no lights coming from inside. It was dark and lonely and spooky as hell. The snow had stopped falling.

"What do you think?" Flynn said.

"We could check inside, but I think we'd be wasting time. There aren't any cars here. Besides, it's too cold."

He gave me a look.

"No, not too cold for me. I just don't think he would take her here on a night like this. He'd take her home. Besides, I don't see any tire tracks in the snow, do you?"

"I hadn't thought of that. I guess we'll try Lewiston."

He backed the vehicle back down the road, turned it around and headed back onto 32. The towns blurred by again: Jefferson, Cooper's Mills, South Winston, and turning on 224 to Randolph, then Gardiner, where finally we got on the turnpike and started going south. Flynn was a good driver. I was better, I thought, but he knew the roads.

Once on the turnpike, he really cranked her up. In no time at all we were just south of Lewiston, where we got onto State 196 and headed toward the center of town. I had given Cole's address to Flynn earlier and he knew where he was going, even though I didn't. When we pulled up in front of a five-story apartment building downtown, I said, "Do you want to call for backup or just go upstairs?"

"You want to wait for backup at a time like this?"

I hesitated, thinking about what I'd told Corliss earlier. "Look, if he's got her in there, I don't want her getting killed."

"You think *I* do?"

"No, of course not. But the thing is, you're not in uniform, which would help, and we don't have any weapons."

"Don't we?" He pointed to the shotgun in the rifle rack, then said, "Plus I got a Colt .45 stuffed under the front seat. Both fully loaded. You want the Colt or the shotgun?"

I shook my head and took a deep breath. "You choose. It's been years since I was on the firing range."

"Okay, then you take the shotgun. You'll be less likely to miss with it." He gave me his key ring, telling me the key to the shotgun rack was the round one, then got out of the car, put one hand on the steering wheel, leaned back inside, reached under the front seat, and pulled out a blue-steel pistol. "And, by the way, Field, how many times have *you* gone through a door while wearing plainclothes?"

"You've got a point. There's one other thing to consider, though. This isn't Rockland County. You've got no jurisdiction here and I'm just a private citizen."

"Not tonight you're not. I've just deputized you. And jurisdiction doesn't matter when you're in hot pursuit. Cole has threatened to kill Jamie, the two of them were seen together, or if not together exactly, then in the same place at the same time. Shortly after that, she disappeared, and we're in hot pursuit of them. I'd say we're on solid legal ground."

"I guess you're right. You got any riot cuffs?"

He grabbed a dozen plastic handcuffs out of the glove box, handed me half. "Now, how do we get inside the building?"

I took a deep breath. "Watch this . . ."

We got out and walked up the steps to the front door. There was the typical buzzer with a brass button for each apartment. Cole's was easy to spot, even if I hadn't known he lived in 5C: there was no name next to the button—typical for a drug dealer. I leaned on it and let up.

"Who's there?" a man asked. He had a Jamaican accent.

"It's Corliss," I said, talking from the back of my throat.

"What? Who's dat?" We could hear loud music playing.

"Corliss, you stupid fuck. Randy Corliss."

"Dat don't sound like you, mon."

"Well, it *is* me," I croaked. "I'm just sick, that's all."

"Sick, eh?"

"Yeah. You heard what happened to me today? I broke my arm and ruined my best Armani suit. Fucking hospital would only give me Tylenol for the pain. Not even Tylenol 3."

"Okay, dat's you, mon. Come on up, we'll take care of it."

The buzzer sounded and we went through the front door.

"Nice job, Field."

"Hey, I once took an acting class in college."

"That so?" he said as we walked to the elevator.

"Yeah. You should ask Jamie about my lizard impression sometime. She loves it."

He shook his head. "I don't think so."

We got on the elevator. I pressed four *and* five, then held the door open so we could have a powwow.

"Are we going up or not?"

When you're about to break down someone's door, someone who might be armed and crazy enough to shoot you, you want to know that whoever is breaking that door down *with* you knows what to do. I'm sure Flynn had some experience in this sort of thing. He'd been a police captain before becoming sheriff. But even though he was ten to fifteen years older than I, I was more experienced than he was at going through doors. It's just a matter of statistics. There are more doors to go through in New York than in Rockland County. So I wanted to make sure we both knew what the other was going to do, under all possible scenarios.

"Yeah, we'll go in a sec," I said. "First I want to make sure we know how to work this thing out. Now, there are two possible things that can happen when we get off the elevator: someone could be waiting in the hall for Corliss to show up, or they might be waiting inside till Corliss knocks on the door. Meanwhile, we've never been here before. We don't know whether 5C is to the right or left when we get off the elevator."

"Gotcha," Flynn said. "So we get off on four first, check the layout, then we go up to five."

"Only if there aren't any access stairs between floors."

Flynn said, "What do you mean access stairs?"

"Where the stairwell doors aren't locked from the inside. In some buildings you can open the door to get *into* the stairwell, but you can't get *out* except on the *main* floor."

"We're wasting time here, Field."

"Knowing the terrain, and your partner, is never a waste of time. If they *do* have access floors, then you'll go up them while I take the elevator. I'll give you ten seconds to get into position, in case someone is actually waiting in the hall."

"Okay. Then what?"

"When you hear the elevator open, you come around the corner just as I come out. If there's someone in the hall, well, you know the routine. He'll know I'm not Corliss and I'll shout, 'Police officers, get on the ground!' You'll take custody of the guy in the hall while I go through the door."

"Good plan. Let's do it."

"No, not yet. If there's no access to the fifth floor via the stairwell, we have to have a backup plan. Plan B."

"Jesus, this is gonna take all—"

"It'll be worth it, trust me. It's like dog training. If you try to go too fast, you end up making mistakes."

"Enough with the dog training. What's Plan B?"

"Plan B is we both get off on the fifth floor, but you get off the elevator first."

"Why me first?"

" 'Cause I look more like a cop than you do. You look like someone's uncle coming over for a visit. So in Plan B, you get off, look around like you don't know where you're going. If someone's in the hall, you ask where 5A is. Or whatever we've found out on 4 is past 5C. When the guy points you to 5A, you go past him. Meanwhile, I'm holding the 'Doors Open' button. I count to five and come out holding the shotgun. After that, the routine is the same."

"Okay. Let's get up there before they get suspicious."

I pressed the Doors Closed button. As they closed I said, "Don't worry about it. In buildings like this you're always waiting for the elevator."

We went up. As the elevator slowly rumbled past three, Flynn said, "What if no one's waiting in the hall?"

"Then we just tippy-toe to 5C and bust the door down."

We got to the fourth floor. The doors opened. I said, "You case the joint while I hold the elevator."

He got off and came back a few seconds later. "4C is down that way," he said, pointing past me to my right, opposite the elevator. "And there's two sets of stairs, with no doors at all. I'm going to take the stairwell that comes out behind 5C."

"Good idea."

"Yeah," he groused, "like I don't *know* that? Give me an extra ten seconds before you go up."

"Gotcha. Oh, and Flynn?" He looked back at me. "Turn off your cell phone."

He unclipped it from his belt, opened it, pushed a couple of buttons, looked at me and said, "I put it on vibrate. She could still be out there somewhere trying to call us."

"I hope you're right."

27

I got to the fifth floor. The elevator doors opened. I came out and found the Rasta boy I'd seen earlier that day, waiting for me in the hall. Or I should say, he was waiting for Corliss. I was not Corliss, though. And I had a shotgun.

He reached into his jacket, but Flynn, all 250 pounds of him, crept up from behind on little cat feet and put the Colt automatic to the back of his head.

"Take it out slowly and drop it," he said.

"Fuck you, mon," he said, and kept going for his gun.

Flynn clocked him on the back of the head, just above the neck so as to make contact with flesh and bone, not dreadlocks. The kid moaned and fell like a lump.

Flynn shrugged at me. "It was either that or shoot him."

I whispered, "Good choice."

Flynn frisked him, got his weapon—a Glock nine mil, took out the clip and set it on the floor, then shuffleboarded it down the hall. He stood up, grasped the Glock's muzzle, pulled back the slide and ejected a single round from the chamber. Then he put the safety on and dropped the empty weapon into one of his big pockets. He pulled a pair of riot cuffs out of his other pocket and put them on the kid's wrists. He stood up and we both looked over at the apartment door. It was open just a crack. There were voices and music coming from inside. We hugged the walls and went toward it. Flynn frowned, cocked his head the other way, listened, stopped me with a hand gesture, and pointed toward the elevator.

I heard it groaning up the shaft.

He signaled for me to cover the far side of the elevator, then signaled that he would cover the near side. We did that and stood there waiting, hugging the wall again.

The elevator door opened. Eddie Cole, medium height and build, with longish sandy hair, wavy not straight, wearing jeans and a black leather jacket, got off the elevator. I knew it was him because he had Jamie with him. He had his left arm around her waist, holding her left arm tight to her body. With his right hand he held a gun to her rib cage.

"Hold it right there," Flynn said, and showed him his gun.

"Uncle Horace, oh my god, I'm—"

"Back off, Sheriff," Cole said. "I got a gun on her."

I stuck the shotgun in his back. "Mine's bigger."

"Oh, Jack—" She tried to turn around.

"Drop it and let her go," I told Cole.

He dropped it—another Glock—and let her go.

"Come around behind me, honey," I said.

She came around behind me and pressed herself into me. It was the nicest feeling I can remember. I think I started breathing again for the first time since the restaurant.

Flynn repeated the routine he'd done with the Rasta boy's Glock, kicked Cole's clip down the hall toward the first one, then said, "Assume the position, flat on the floor."

Cole got down on his knees. "You assholes are going to regret this."

"I don't think so," I said, kicking him down into place, hard. "Do *you* think we'll regret it, Sheriff?"

"I don't see how."

"Ow, goddamnit! I think I cracked a tooth."

"Jack, Uncle Horace, I'm so sorry. It was so stupid of me to disappear like that. And then my battery was dead and I couldn't call you, and I followed him here, but I guess . . ."

She chattered on, explaining what had happened while I handed Flynn the shotgun and got another pair of the plastic handcuffs out of my pocket, put one knee on the small of Cole's back, hard ("Ow! You fuckers!"), then got him up to his feet.

"Jamie," I interrupted her spiel, "you can tell us what happened later. Okay?" I took the shotgun back from Flynn.

"I'm sorry," she said. "I was babbling."

To Cole, I said, "Anybody else but you and Bob Marley over there got guns?"

"Fuck you!"

I jammed his face against the wall. "I'm sorry, I didn't hear you? Are there any more guns inside?"

"Shit! You broke my nose." It came out sounding like "doze," not nose. "This is police brutality."

Bang! More blood on the wall. "It *would* be if I was a cop, but I'm not. Now, do you want to answer the question?"

He sighed. "There's adother guy inside. Adother Somali. They're dot from Jamaica. They just act like they are."

"Jamie, you wait here and call 911." She nodded. "Flynn, give her your cell phone." He did. "Okay, let's go inside. I'll go left/high, you go right/low."

"Right/low. Gotcha."

We went to the front door of apartment 5C, which was still open, just a crack. I could have pushed it open with my toe, but instead I used Eddie Cole's broken "doze."

We went through. I had Cole in front of me, holding him by the collar with my left hand, holding the shotgun in my right. Flynn came through on the right side, crouching low.

Cole screamed, "Dod't shoot! Dod't shoot!"

"Police officers!" Flynn shouted. "Stay where you are!"

"Put your hands in the air!" I said.

There were half a dozen people in the front room, most of them smoking rock cocaine. The rest were waiting for their turn. The only light came from some lamps in various corners. There seemed to be a fog hanging in the air—free-base smoke. When we came in, someone dropped a glass bowl and pipe on a glass coffee table, and the bowl broke. Someone else, in the middle of a hit, dropped his butane torch onto the green shag carpet. The torch was still lit and the carpet started to go up in flames. I pushed Cole over in that direction, then put my right leg in front of his left ankle, tripped him and pushed him down onto the carpet, using his body to put out the fire.

"Ow! Goddabbit! It burds, it burds!"

"Everybody stay calm and put out your torches. Then lie flat on the floor with your hands behind your head."

There were four or five people in the dining room, which was off to the right. They had their hands in the air. One of them still had a lit torch in his hand. "Turn off your torch, sir. And put it down on the table!"

He did, then said, "What's gonna happen to us?"

"For now, you're all going to come in here and lie flat on the floor! You got that? Everybody."

They nodded, got up from their dining room chairs, shuffled into the living room and lay down.

I heard something creak, behind a door, off to the left, which probably led to a bedroom. "Sheriff, how much penetration does this baby have?" meaning the shotgun.

"It could blast through that door, I guess."

I shot at the door.

"Come on out with your hands up and your weapon visible!"

There was a pause. "Okay, mon. I'm coming! Don't shoot!"

He was another Somali kid, dressed like a Jamaican. He came out with his hands in the air, holding a brother of the two other Glocks in his right hand.

I said, "Put the safety on, take the clip out, and toss the puppy over here on the couch." I pointed to my left. He did as he was told. "Now, toss the clip over." He did that too.

We heard sirens approaching from not far away.

"Now lie down, flat on the floor, with your hands behind your neck." He did that too.

While I took possession of our third Glock of the night, Flynn, tired of the music, went over to the stereo and turned it off. Cole was moaning into the carpet. I think he was saying "Sudsabitches," over and over.

I suggested to Flynn that he meet the brothers in blue out in the hallway so they would know what's up.

"I'll keep an eye on the party," I said.

Then we heard someone moaning in the other room. "You stay here," I said. "I'll go check it out."

I made my way carefully into the soft darkness of one of the bedrooms and found Tulips lying in bed, moaning. I turned on a lamp. She turned away from the light, but before she did I could see that her face was badly bruised.

I called out to Flynn, "Sheriff, get Jamie in here. And call an ambulance." I heard him call Jamie as I sat on the bed next to Tulips. "What happened?" I said.

"I—I fell down," she said.

"No you didn't. Eddie Cole beat you up, didn't he?" She shook her head. "Don't worry about him, he's going to jail."

"But I need—I need some stuff."

"You're going through withdrawal?"

She nodded.

Jamie came in. "What is it? Oh, my god." She came right over to the bed and began examining her.

I went to the door to give them some privacy. After a bit, Jamie came over to me and said, "She's hurt pretty bad. She's got some broken ribs which may have caused internal bleeding. Plus, she's going through—"

"—withdrawal, I know."

"And I think she's been raped, repeatedly."

I put my arms around her and we held each other. "Don't let me go," I said. "Because if you let me go, honey, I'm going to go out there and kick the crap out of that piece of shit."

She held me tighter. "Don't do it, Jack."

"I won't."

"Though I almost wish you would."

"I know. At least he's going to jail now, for a long, long time, thanks to you."

It was about then that the cops arrived.

28

They got Tulips in the ambulance and rounded up everybody else, including Cole, for booking. As for me, it was the second time in twenty-four hours that I had to give a statement to the Lewiston PD. Halfway into my first interview, though, Flynn, bless him, being a county sheriff and a charitable soul, suggested to the detective questioning me that *he* give the statements for both of us. The detective agreed.

Jamie, meanwhile, had to give her own statement. But she was a kidnapping victim and therefore emotionally distraught, and so they didn't take up too much of her time. They said they could get her whole story later, down at the station house.

She gave it to *me*, though, on the ride home in her new car, with me at the wheel. At first she tried to cuddle up next to me, but the console got in the way. She tried a couple of different angles with her hips going first one direction, then another, until she finally gave up, reclined the seat back and settled for holding hands, when I wasn't using mine for steering. Her story went something like this:

As she was coming out of the ladies' room at the Waterworks, she saw Eddie Cole in the pub, talking to a "customer." The customer gave Cole a magazine, and Cole gave him a paper bag. Then Cole got up and headed for the back exit.

Jamie decided to follow him. At first she thought of coming back into the restaurant to tell me and Flynn about him, but she decided she could do that from her cell phone in the car—that if she didn't follow him right away she might lose him.

Cole got into his Mercedes, which was parked in the lot behind the pub. She crossed through the lot to the street, got in her car, and began to follow him. She'd tried to call me and Flynn after she got her car started, but found out the phone's battery was dead, so she decided to tough it out on her own.

Apparently, Cole had several deliveries to make, because he took a meandering route, occasionally stopping to talk to someone waiting at a street corner—again, exchanging such items as a magazine or newspaper for a small, brown paper bag—occasionally stopping at a bar or a hotel. (This explained why Flynn and I got to Cole's place before *they* did, even though we'd taken a detour to the old mill.)

Finally, Cole headed toward Lewiston, with Jamie not far behind. When he arrived on his block, he pulled up across the street from his building, but a few buildings down. Jamie pulled to a stop behind him, directly in front of Cole's building. Cole got out of his car, put a cigarette in his mouth, then acted like he didn't have a match. There was a convenience store where Jamie was parked. He walked toward it, as if he were going inside. She took her eyes off him for a moment, not wanting to make eye contact, and he suddenly appeared at her car window, pointing a gun at her head.

"Get out of the car," he'd said.

She'd done so.

"Who the fuck are you?" he'd said.

She'd told him.

He laughed, still holding the gun on her. "How *is* old Oren? I haven't seen him in quite a while. He go straight?"

"He's trying," she said.

He seemed to be thinking through his options. He looked

her over. She was freezing without her coat on. She was also gorgeous. Finally, he said, "What the fuck. Let's go upstairs and have a little fun. Huh, baby?" That's when he put his arm around her and jabbed the gun into her rib cage. "Don't try anything and you won't get hurt."

She did as she was told, trying to think of a way to get the upper hand. Wait until we get inside the building, she told herself. He won't shoot you there, not with all the other tenants around to hear the shots. When the elevator doors opened and she saw the stairwell, she thought, When he gets off the elevator, push him down and run like hell for the stairs.

Which is when the cavalry arrived.

"Well, you were a brave little puppy, honey."

"Brave and stupid," she frowned.

"That's what puppies are like. At least *some* puppies. I hope you learned your lesson, though."

"I sure did. I'm not cut out to be a detective."

"No. It's like being a doctor, you *learn* your craft before you practice it."

Her eyes searched mine. "What does that mean?"

"It means, if you had known the proper way to tail someone, you wouldn't have stayed so close behind him that he figured out he was being followed. And he wouldn't have trapped you."

"But I was afraid I might lose sight of him."

"I know. I used to be the same way. It's a beginner's mistake. The rule is, it's better to let someone you're tailing get away than it is to stay too close and let them spot you."

She sighed. "But that's just the thing. I don't know all the rules, so I shouldn't even *try*."

"Well, I'm inclined to agree after tonight, but only because you really put me and Flynn through the wringer. Still, it all turned out okay in the end. And at least Eddie Cole is going away for a long, long time."

"I hope so."

"And *you* said you weren't afraid of him."

"I wasn't. At least I didn't think I was. Not until tonight." We didn't say what we both were thinking—that what had happened to Tulips *could* have happened to her. Or worse.

We drove in silence for a while. The fallen snow made the trees and passing towns look all cozy and warm under its white, sugary blanket. Jamie yawned and closed her eyes.

"You know," I pointed out, "if we'd gone to Señor Froggie's, none of this would have happened."

She chuckled and said, "You really do love their enchiladas, don't you, Jack?"

"Remember, I grew up in Southern California."

"I know. Just outside of San Diego." Then she sighed and added, "The only thing is, if we'd gone to Señor Froggie's, Eddie Cole wouldn't be in custody right now and Tulips probably wouldn't have made it through the night."

I shook my head. "I love it when you're right." There was a pause. "She's that bad, huh?"

She nodded. "And it's still touch and go. By the way," she added, in that sleepy voice she gets late at night, "you know what Flynn said to me before we left?"

"What?"

"That he was proud to have been your partner tonight."

"No kidding. Well, ain't that something?" I thought it over and started to chuckle. "Oh, now I get it."

"Get what?"

"Why you did what you did."

"Why I did what?"

"Tailed Eddie Cole. It was to make me and Flynn go after you. You were pairing us up like two guys in a buddy movie."

She sat up straight. "I was not!"

"Sure you were. Maybe unconsciously, but you knew

when you disappeared that we would team up and try to find you."

She hit me. "No, I didn't. Besides, you're forgetting one important fact. I intended to call the two of you on my cell phone as soon as I could. I didn't know my battery was dead."

"Well, of course *you* didn't know that, honey. But your unconscious *mind* did."

"Oh, you and your Freudian analysis of everything. Anyway, I know one thing: I'm never going detecting ever again."

"Oh, yes you are."

"No I'm not."

"Sure you are. Tomorrow night, remember? We're breaking into the auto salvage yard outside of Belfast."

"Oh, no! I forgot!" She sighed, thought of something, then started to laugh. "But that's not the same thing. Tomorrow night I'll have *you* along." She kissed my hand.

"Right. And that's the way it's supposed to be. And that's the way it's going to stay."

"Yes, my handsome hero." She held my hand to her cheek.

29

It was eleven o'clock, Thursday night. "Ready?" I asked.

Jamie said, "Ready as I'll ever be." She seemed a trifle nervous, though still excited. We were in the mud room. I helped her on with her yellow parka.

We were on our way to break into the salvage yard where Judge Merton's and Dennis Seabow's cars were being held. Jamie had been unable to make a comparison between the spectra-whatever that was used to convict Seabow at trial and Seabow's hospital blood work because of red tape. Seabow had given permission for her to look at his medical records, but the hospital was swamped and probably wouldn't be able to get around to pulling the files till Monday, they said. I don't know if that's what was on her mind, or if she was still having bad memories of her experience with Eddie Cole.

"Come on," I said, "it'll be fun. It'll be just like the time we broke into Sam Kirby's house, looking for clues."

"Yes, and remember what happened that night? We had to crawl out on the roof, you fell off and nearly broke your neck, and actually *did* break my $500 pair of Manolo Blahniks."

"I didn't break the *pair*, just the one shoe."

She snorted. "Do you actually think there's a difference, you idiot?"

We got out to the car, but I noticed there was no light

coming from the little window to the right of the kennel door. Sloan was supposed to be inside, keeping an eye on the dogs and studying for a midterm exam at my desk.

"Hang on a sec. I want to go check on Sloan." Jamie followed me to the kennel building.

I opened the door, turned on the light, and found Sloan and Leon lying on a blanket in front of the reception desk. Sloan's top was off, though her brassiere was still fastened. The skin around her mouth was red, as though she'd just come in first place in a rhubarb pie-eating contest. She quickly grabbed her top and covered herself, though her slender arms and shoulders were still naked. She jumped up and ran to the back of the building and locked herself in the utility closet.

Leon looked up at me. "Nice timing, Jack. I was just about to reach second base."

"Leon, shut up. That's no way to talk. And I'll deal with you in a second. Sloan, come back out here!"

"Please don't fire me, Jack," I heard her cry.

"No one's going to fire you. I just want to talk to you."

There was an embarrassed silence.

"Sloan!"

"It's okay, Sloan," Jamie called out. "You didn't do anything wrong."

"Nothing," I muttered, "except that she's twenty-one and Leon's only sixteen."

"Hey, I'm big for my age."

"Shut up, Leon. Sloan, come back out here."

Jamie touched my arm. "Let me go talk to her."

She went to the back. Leon put his shirt on. While he was doing that, I came over, leaned my back against the reception desk and used it for leverage to slide down to Leon's level.

"So, what's going on, Leon?"

"Nothin'. We was just foolin' around, you know?"

"You want to tell me about it?"

"Not really, nah." I could hear Jamie talking to Sloan through the closet door.

"Oh . . . big *man*, about to reach second base, huh? And now you don't want to talk about your exploits?"

"Exploits?" He sighed, shook his head. "Okay, so me and Sloan was just talking and shit and then I told her I thought she was pretty and I kinda kissed her, you know? And she got all soft and sexy-like, and I said, 'Yo, let's go out to the carriage house and play some music,' and she says, nah, she's got to keep an eye on the dogs, so I goes out and gets us a blanket. Then a little while later, you and Jamie walked in."

"Well, we need to have a talk about this."

"I don't know what's the big deal. The dogs is all asleep now anyway. Nothin's gonna happen to them."

"Remember what happened to Thurston?"

"Yeah." He hung his head. Thurston was Tim Berry's basset hound, who'd been dognapped by Sam Kirby back in December.

Leon was right, though, in a way. The way most kennels operate is that after ten or eleven at night, the dogs are pretty much cozied up and sleeping in their individual kennels. There's no need for someone to constantly keep an eye on things overnight, not unless one or more of the dogs is sick, in which case they should probably be kenneled with a veterinarian, not me. But I like to be on the safe side. I have audio monitors in my bedroom, kitchen, and living room; all hooked up to a microphone in the kennel building. This hadn't stopped Sam Kirby from stealing Thurston, but without the monitors, we would have never known what had happened until the next morning. And even then we wouldn't have known it was Kirby who'd taken him.

Jamie came back, shaking her head.

"Look," I said to Leon, "there are some things you need to know. First of all, your body is going through some pretty strong changes right now, and you have to know how to handle things." He looked away. "So never go all the way unless you're prepared for the responsibilities of parenthood. You have to always keep that probability in the back of your mind. Things can happen and get out of hand and protection doesn't always work. Another thing, always let the girl set the pace of how fast or slow you go. If she moves your hand away from a certain part of her body, don't keep trying to move it back. She'll do that for you if she wants. And always treat her with respect, before, during, and after. And don't be playing her. If you're going to *act* like a man about sex, then you've got to *be* a man about it. That means you take responsibility."

Jamie was smiling at me, though I hadn't intended for her to overhear this.

"Okay," Leon said, a little exasperated, "I get it."

I stood up. "I don't think you do, Leon. Now, you're not responsible for what Sloan does or doesn't do. But you're at least partially responsible for putting her in the position that's got her so upset right now, don't you think?"

He thought it over. "So, I guess I should go talk to her?"

"That's right."

He stood up. "But, yo, what'll I say?"

"Well, there are two words that always make things better whenever a woman is upset—you just tell her you're sorry."

"Yeah, but what if I didn't do nothin' wrong?"

"It doesn't matter. You always say you're sorry. Trust me. It works every time."

"Jack, that is such bullshit," Jamie said.

"What do you mean?"

She shook her head. "It's so sexist and manipulative."

"It is? Oh, I'm sorry, honey. I didn't realize that."

"Well," she smiled at me, "that's okay."

I turned to Leon. "See? It works every time."

Jamie hit me.

30

Later, after Leon and Sloan had got things worked out (and I was very proud of how Leon handled it, by the way), Jamie and I left for Belfast.

Then, once we were on US 1, she said, "Did you really mean what you said to Leon back there, about the responsibilities of parenthood?"

"Of course. I almost always mean what I say to him."

"So, when we make love, do you think about that? The fact that I might get pregnant?"

I laughed. "I guess you got me on that one. No, I don't actually think about it while we're making love, but, yeah, it's always somewhere in the back of my mind. Or should be."

She looked out the window. "Do you want to have kids?"

There was a pause. (It was me, making the pause.)

"Jack?"

"I don't know," I said. "Do *you*?"

"I don't know." She shook her head. "Actually, yeah. I think I'd like to have children." She looked at me. "And I think that you, my friend, would make a wonderful father."

"Fine, then we'll have kids. How many do you want?"

She smiled. "I don't know. Two or three, I guess?"

"Good. So, we'll make us up two or three miniature Jacks and Jamies, and use them to populate the house."

She laughed. "You'll probably put leashes on them and make them sleep out in the kennel."

"That's right, honey, leashes and collars. You do realize, don't you, that it's going to be very hard for you to juggle being a mother and a chief medical examiner at the same time?"

"Jack, I'm only a part-time medical examiner."

"Yeah, *now*. Today. But after we prove that Dennis Seabow was framed, and that Dr. Reiner dropped the ball by not ordering an autopsy on Marti MacKenzie's body—"

"—I'll probably be fired."

"Or promoted. And, you know, I have some very influential friends in the Governor's Office . . ."

"I hope you're not referring to Grant Goodrich."

"Are you kidding? But I do have a plan, actually, to endear myself to his cousin, Judge Merton's widow. Is this where I turn?"

"No, it's the next light. And why would Judge Merton's widow be endeared to you, other than the fact that you're just terribly endearing in general?"

"Ah-hah. You shall see. Now, you were the one who cased this joint we're breaking into, so I hope *you* have a plan." I pulled the car up next to the front gate of LeClerc Automotive. It was set back about thirty yards from the road, probably because of some zoning restriction—in Maine they like to keep eyesores like LeClerc Automotive as far away from public view as possible, without being overly harsh in a way that might hurt business. The place was surrounded by a chain-link fence, which was itself surrounded on three sides by pine trees.

It was, frankly, a junkyard. A used car dealership? An auto parts store? No. Though it was a place where you might find a used radiator or alternator for a '72 Plymouth, or a set of tires—all recaps, mind you—for a '59 Caddie convertible. Maybe a hood ornament, maybe a taillight, or a gearshift knob for a '65 Mustang. They saved everything and threw away nothing. Not unless it was useless or broken.

Good. Dennis Seabow's Honda Accord and Judge Thayer (Terry) Merton's Cadillac Deville would be intact, with every ding, dent, crimp, blotch, or blemish available to look at and examine. Oh, sure, once the case (or cases) were solved, they'd sell off every fender panel, car seat, and floor mat to whoever wanted or needed them. But as for tonight? Me and Jamie were the only customers on the lot—or just out*side* the lot, that is.

"How do you propose to get in? Do you have a plan?"

"You think you're the only undercover genius on the planet? Yeah, I've got a plan, and it's a good one."

"Okay, so what is it? From what I see, we've got a chain-link fence with barbed wire on top, and a gate with two or three heavy chains, connected to several huge, motherfucking locks."

"Technically, Jack, those are several Medeco brand locks, not 'motherfucking' locks."

"Fine. And how do we get inside the fence? TNT?"

"You doubt my abilities because of last night? You think I don't know what I'm doing here?" She opened her car door.

"I apologize as always. Lead the way, Wonder Woman."

She hit me. Sometimes I think it's her only, or at least her preferred, expression of affection.

"Can you pop the trunk, please?" she said.

"No, it's a Suburban. But I can open the back door for you."

We got out and went around the back. Inside was a large black nylon bag, which Jamie unzipped, with something of a flourish. In the bag was a bolt cutter—about four feet long—a wire cutter, a box of liver treats, a Polaroid camera complete with film cartridge, a book of matches, two Power Bars, a bottle of Gatorade, a measuring tape, some tampons, and a couple of flashlights, with extra batteries.

"Nice packing, James."

"Thanks, Sherlock."

"Three questions. Wire cutters?"

She pointed to the barbed wire atop the fence. "Just in case the bolt cutters don't work. Plan B is we climb over."

"Good thinking. And the tampons?"

She sighed. "I'm having my period, or didn't you know?"

"Sorry, I should have known that, yes. I apologize."

"That's okay. Wait a second, you just did it again, didn't you?" She sighed. "That apology thing you told Leon about?"

"Yeah, but I'm truly sorry, honey. Really I am."

She sighed again. "What am I going to do with you?"

"And the liver treats?"

"Oh, didn't I tell you about the guard dog?"

"A guard dog? You expect me to control an unknown animal? who's probably a vicious killer? with nothing but liver—"

"A vicious killer? I thought you said dogs can't be—"

"I know, I was making a joke, honey. Though I do value several of my tendons and would not like to have them severed and eaten tonight. What kind of dog is it?"

"Do I know? I think it's a 500-pound Rottweiler."

"That would be a first." I opened the can of liver treats and jammed as many as possible into the left pocket of my Levi's jacket. Then I reached into the right pocket and pulled out a tennis ball. "If you had ever listened to anything I've ever told you about dog training, you would have brought a few tennis balls like this along, instead of the liver treats."

She put a hand on my arm. "Jack, why would I need to do that when every coat, jacket, or parka you own has at least one dirty tennis ball hidden away somewhere in one of its pockets?"

Impressed, I said, "Wow, you *did* think this through."

She put her arms in the air. "I have great, magical planning abilities that you, my friend, know nothing about."

"I apologize completely. I am truly sorry."

"Oh, shut up." She zipped up the nylon bag, took it out of the trunk, and threw the strap over her shoulder—very James (or, should I say, Jamie) Bondlike of her.

"So, what's the plan?" I asked.

"Well, I'm going to use the bolt cutters to make a hole in the chain-link fence, then worm my way through it, examine the two cars, measure and take pictures of everything I can, while you keep an eye out for, and hopefully control, the guard dog—who, I'm led to believe, is a terribly vicious killer."

I shook my head. "This is going to end in disaster. Did I mention, earlier, my undying affection for my testicles?"

She shook *her* head. "I'm already quite familiar with that aspect of your nature, Jack, believe me. Let's rock and roll."

"Wait. Did you just say—"

"Yes, I did. And I'll thank you not to rain on my parade. I'm already feeling a little nauseous about this." She headed around the corner, toward the back of the junkyard. "I mean, nauseated."

"If that's the case, then you should have packed some Midol." Again, with the hitting. "Is he on a *chain*, at least?"

"Who, the dog? God, I hope so. But don't worry too much. You can handle him. You can handle *any* dog, remember?"

We began to feel our way around to the back, pressed between the chain-link fence and the pine branches. I said, "You know that talk we had earlier? about us having kids? How is it going to help if I lose my equipment?"

"So, we'll adopt. And stop worrying about your precious testicles already." She stopped and unstrapped the bag. "This should do," she pointed, "there's the tarp, right over there."

She got out the bolt cutters.

"Do you need me to do that?"

"Why would I need *you* to do it? You do *know*, don't you, that I have a gym membership at the Samoset health club?"

"Yes," I said, raising my arms. "And I am also aware that you use it mainly for the exercycle, not weight training. Also, you use it to have little sex parties with me in the whirlpool." This time I successfully dodged the back of her hand.

She shook her head and got the bolt cutter open, then clamped it around one of the links of the fence, toward the bottom. She tried to close the handles but couldn't do it.

I waited a respectable amount of time before taking over. In half a second I had the first link cut wide open.

"Show-off."

"It doesn't mean you're not stronger than I am. It's just the way masculine muscle mass is concentrated in the back and shoulders, and the way a woman's arms flare out at the elbows to allow her to hold and nurse a baby. It's gender genetics."

"Oh, shut up. Let me try the next one." She took it from me and tried again, squeezing as hard as she could. No luck.

"Honey, now your *cleavage* is in the way."

"What? I don't have any cleavage." She put her hands up to demonstrate. "I'm wearing a sweater and a parka."

"I don't care how many layers of clothing you wear, my dearest, in my mind you always have the most wonderful cleavage. Ow!" I dodged her hand again, but got stuck in the back by a pine bough. Meanwhile, someone else was creeping up on us from inside the fence. He was very quiet and discreet about it too. All except for the low growl coming from his enormous throat. I looked at the dog then back at Jamie. "That's your 500-pound Rottweiler?"

She took a deep breath. "Looks like it."

"Honey, don't you know? That's a Dogue de Bordeaux."

She stared at me. "How in the world would I know *that*?"

"Because, my darling, how many times have I tried to get you to watch *Turner and Hooch* with me?"

"You really love that movie, don't you?"

"Not really. But I love the scenes with the dog. Anyway, that's a 'Hooch' dog. A Dogue de Bordeaux." I crouched down and looked at the dog. "Hey, baby. How are you?" He wagged his tail. "Are you a good boy?" he was still growling but he began to shift his shoulders back and forth and look at me kind of sideways. I got down on all fours, did a play bow, and some other things. The result was that Hooch soon stopped growling and actually began licking my hand through the fence. (And I didn't have to use the liver treats.)

"Okay." I stood up and handed Jamie the treats. "You feed him these while I get the rest of the fence cut."

"You *are* going to go through first, though, right?" She had that scared little girl look on her face again.

"Yes, I'm going to go through first. And kind of crouch down like I did, or just sit there in the dirt while you feed him. If he growls at you, just praise him and talk silly."

She did as she was told, and a few minutes later we were both inside the junkyard, me running around and playing fetch and tag with Hooch, and Jamie examining the two automobiles.

When she was done and we were getting ready to leave (the same way we came in, of course), Hooch wanted to come along.

"Did you get what you needed?" I said, holding the gash in the fence open for her.

"I sure did." She got through, turned around and said, "Ah, honey, look—he wants to come with us."

I turned and saw it was true. Hooch was standing there, his sad, droopy eyes practically begging us to take him along. "I wish I could take you boy, but I can't." He wagged his tail. I looked at Jamie. "I really can't take him, can I?"

She shook her head and laughed at me. "We've already ruined these people's fence, Jack. Let's not steal their dog too."

"I know, it's just that I feel bad for him, having to stay out here alone all night."

"I'm sure he has a dog house and a warm blanket."

"I hope so." I looked back at Hooch. "Sorry, boy. You be a good boy and stay here. You stay." I edged my way sideways through the hole in the fence, and when I was through he came over, trying to follow me. I looked at Jamie. "Can I at least give him my tennis ball?"

Arms up, she said, "What do *I* care what you do with it?"

I handed the tennis ball through the fence to Hooch, and he took it very gently in his mouth. "Okay, good boy. You take that back to your bed and chew on it, okay? You rip the cover off that thing. Maybe I'll see you tomorrow. Chew it good."

"Jack, what the hell are you doing? Aren't you the one who says that dogs don't have the so-called cognitive architecture necessary to understand and use language?"

"Yeah, so?"

"So why are you wasting all this time *talking* to Hooch like he can actually understand what you're saying, when we should be getting the hell out of here?"

"It's not my *words* he understands, honey. It's the tone of my voice and the mental images those words create."

"What? You think you're sending him mental images?"

"Of course. I do that with *all* the dogs I train. I don't know how I do it, exactly, but watch . . ." I turned back to Hooch. "Go on, take that ball back to your bed, Hooch. Go on! Take it to your bed and chew the skin off."

Hooch tilted his head, chewed on the tennis ball, then turned around and trotted off, out of sight.

I looked at Jamie. She shook her head. "That has to be a total coincidence. Or maybe he already learned what 'go to your bed' means." (We found out later this wasn't true, that the LeClerc brothers, who were from Montreal, had trained him in French, *and* with a piece of one-by-three, the bastards.)

We made our way back to the car.

"So explain this to me, just so I don't think you're totally crazy, okay? You were using *telepathy* on Hooch?"

"Partly. That and emotional . . . I don't quite know what to call it, emotional consonance, I guess, since that's the opposite of dissonance. Dogs are very telepathic and very emotional. Watch out for that branch, honey."

"So they don't have the cognitive architecture necessary for language, but they do have it for telepathy?"

"Sure. Telepathy is a lower function of consciousness than language, which requires symbolic and conceptual thought, both of which dogs are incapable of. Telepathy just means 'distant feeling' in Latin. It's a natural biological function, to be able to feel something someone else is feeling. Most animals have it, even humans, though we're less reliant on it because we've developed the use of language, which is a more exact form of communication. Anyway, that's *my* theory." We got to the Suburban. I opened the back. "Here, let me get that bag for you. Haven't you ever picked up the phone and said, 'That's funny, I was just *thinking* about you'? It's the same phenomenon."

"No, that's just a coincidence when that happens."

"Maybe. And you're right. It's a damn hard thing to prove. I think it has something to do with the limbic system." I took out my key chain and beeped the car doors open. "And I wish I knew *how* I do it, because I can't do it all the time."

The car was parked parallel to the highway. Jamie went around the back side, closest to the fence. I came around in front and heard a mosquito or bumblebee whiz past my ear. Only it wasn't an insect, it was a bullet, because a split second later the driver's side window broke into a million pieces, followed immediately by the passenger side window breaking too.

"Get down!" I shouted to Jamie, then hit the dirt myself and rolled under the truck.

"Are you okay?" I heard her say a second later.

"I think so. Just a skinned knee."

We heard a car door slam from across the road, but couldn't see anything. The sound seemed to be coming from behind some pine trees. Then a car engine started and a dark car—probably black, I couldn't tell for sure, nor could I tell the make or model—fishtailed onto the pavement and drove off at high speed.

I came around the vehicle over to Jamie's side. We got up and dusted ourselves off and held hands and got our emotions settled and under control as best we could.

Still a little jangled, but ever the smartmouth, Jamie said, "I thought you told me you were telepathic."

I laughed, hard. It wasn't that funny, but the laughter helped lighten the moment. "Telepathic, not *psychic*, honey. And I doubt if whoever was just shooting at us was trying to send me telepathic messages about what he was doing. Now, listen, how did you find out those two cars were being kept here?"

"What do you mean?"

"Somebody just tried to kill us. Whoever did it, didn't want us to find the evidence in those cars. So, how did you know they were here? Was it in the police report, or the—"

"No, Barry Porter told me." It suddenly hit her. "Oh, no! Oh, *no*! I don't believe it. He *couldn't* have! *Barry*?"

"Well, don't jump to any conclusions. It might not have been him. He may have told Seabow, who *is* his client, after all. And Seabow could have mentioned it to one of his cellmates." I looked around. "Who the hell knows how someone knew we were here, but—my god, would you look at that?"

Jamie followed my gaze. She put a hand to her chest. "It's Hooch! He came to save us! Good boy, Hooch!"

He was standing at the right front corner of the fence. I crouched down and he came trotting over to me. He seemed to have something in his mouth. He dropped it at my feet.

Jamie and I looked down at what it was. I smiled up at her. She looked back down at me, amazed.

It was a tennis ball, with all the skin chewed off.

"Good boy, Hooch," I said, and he wagged his tail.

31

We got Hooch back inside the junkyard, rolled a tire out through the hole in the fence, then used the string from a couple of Jamie's tampons to kind of tie some of the severed links in the chain link shut as best we could, then leaned the tire against the hole so Hooch wouldn't be able to get out again. We hoped.

We said our good-byes to our new best friend in life, then got out on the open road.

"What now?" Jamie asked. "And Jesus, turn the heater up."

"It's up all the way already. I'm sorry, but I just had my car windows shot out by a bullet that very nearly took my ear off. And why are you being so mean to me tonight?"

She glared at me. "What are you talking about?"

"You were saying some very mean things, calling me an idiot, and taking every opportunity to hit me. What's up with that?"

She sighed. "I'm sorry. It's probably because I get nervous on these expeditions." She looked sad and small, which had not been my intention. I started to feel bad to have brought it up. I would much rather have had to deal with a few slight blows to the spleen and a few negative comments than with seeing that sad look on her face. "I was the same way when I broke into Sam Kirby's house with you, remember? Only then, I hadn't been invited."

I nodded. “I see. Then there was the time you caught me going through Wade Pierce’s office.” Wade Pierce had been her divorce attorney, and at the time was a key suspect in the murder of Allison DeMarco. “You were kind of the same way then.”

“I know. I’m sorry.”

“No, no, it’s okay. I just didn’t understand before. Now I do. In fact, it’s kind of cute, in a way. Do you feel like going out to the murder scene before we go home?”

“Which one? And why is it cute?”

“Where Marti MacKenzie was killed. It’s the only murder scene we know of for sure, since we have no idea where Judge Merton was actually killed, we only know where the body was found. And *I* thought you were being mean because you didn’t love me.”

“I *do* love you.” She still looked sad and hurt. “I just—I don’t know. Tonight was supposed to be *my* expedition, you know? I wanted you to see how good I could be at these kinds of things.”

Hearing this just sank my heart. “Honey, you were *great*.”

She looked at me. “You didn’t make me *feel* like I was.”

My heart sank even more. “I didn’t?”

“No, you made fun of me. ‘Why did you bring your tampons?’ ” she imitated my voice. “ ‘Your cleavage is in the way.’ ”

I resisted an impulse to say, Well it *was*. Instead, I said, “You’re right. I should have showed you how to use the bolt cutters instead of taking them away from you. Your only problem was that you were trying to use your arms and elbows instead of your back and legs, and you can’t get enough leverage that way.”

“So I could have done it myself, if you had taught me how?”

“Probably.”

She shook her head. “And the other thing is, I want you to

appreciate me. And furthermore, on deals like this, I don't *want* to be the Bond girl, you know, Jack, I want to be James *Bond*."

I laughed, though not too hard. "But you *were*. I guess I should have said something earlier, because I distinctly remember thinking how Bondlike you were tonight."

"Really?"

"Yes. Not only Bondlike, but Q-like, and M-like, and—"

"Okay, Jack, don't go overboard."

"Well, anyway, I was very impressed with you."

"Really? You really were?"

"Yes, I was. Though you have to remember that James Bond, for all his panache and skill, never had to crack open a safe or break into a villain's lair while carrying around a beautifully formed and quite ample, I must say, pair of woman's breasts."

She hit me.

"And did I mention the words sexy? delicious? perfectly round? exquisite? irresistible? haunting my dreams at night?"

"Yeah, you can stop now before you get to melonlike."

"Ah. You *do* understand me. You *do* love me."

"Well," she started to smile again, which made my heart relax, "I was *really* impressed with how you handled that dog."

"Hooch? Well, I don't think that was me, honey. No, I think he's just one helluva damn wonderful dog. Here we are."

We pulled up to a kind of Y intersection near a railroad bridge, surrounded by bare trees and tall, brushlike branches.

"What do you want to do?" she said.

"I don't know. Get a feel for the place? Try to picture how it happened?"

"Are you going to use your magic telepathic abilities?"

"Maybe." I looked at the crossroads. There was a triangular patch of, what would have been, in the summertime, grass, though it was now just a patch of, well, fallow grass. Beyond that was the tree Marti MacKenzie had been pinned up against when the police found her trapped between it and Seabow's car. I remembered all this from the police photos. We had passed the diner Farrell Woods told us about on our way over, and were now parked a few yards short of where Marti MacKenzie's car was found that night.

I said, "So, what was she doing here that night?"

"The police report said her car had broken down. The hood was up when Sergeant Loudermilk arrived. The carburetor was faulty."

"Mm-hmm. And her car was parked about right here, where *we* are, so she'd probably been coming from the same direction. But she lives in Lewiston, which is the other way."

"So she wasn't coming from home."

"Right. Now we know, or suspect, that she was going to confront Merton or Cole about the blackmail scheme. Or maybe she wanted *in* on it—you know, to get her hands on some of that Goodrich money."

"Okay," Jamie said. "So how do we find out?"

"I don't know. I guess we have to find the 'bull nose' and examine her diaries."

"What's the 'bull nose'?"

"I don't know. A bar? A restaurant?"

"Okay, well let's just say, for the time being, that she was here meeting Judge Merton or Eddie Cole that night."

I shook my head. "Late October, after ten at night, leaves falling, ghosts and goblins of Halloween around the corner? She's going to meet a creep like Eddie Cole here? In the dark? Unless she was buying drugs. But then she'd have met him closer to home—in a bar or a coffee shop."

She nodded. "So, it was probably the judge."

"It was probably the judge. But even though she *knew* him—she was his law clerk, after all—she probably wouldn't meet him here at this isolated crossroads either. Not on a scary night like that. Do we know what the weather was like?"

She looked through her notes. "Well, there was a slight drizzle that night, it says, with patchy fog."

"Oh, yeah. Great place for a meeting. What was she wearing when the body was found? A raincoat? A slicker?"

"A simple brown suit," she read to me, "with an ecru blouse and a green tie. A raincoat and scarf were found in the back seat of her car."

We sat and thought about it for a while. What was she doing at this crossroads? Why was her raincoat in the back seat?

"The diner is just down the road," Jamie said.

"I was thinking the same thing. We just came from that direction, just as she did—probably. And it's a much safer place to confront someone over a blackmail scheme."

"So, maybe she was at the diner. And so were Farrell Woods and Dennis Seabow. We could ask them if they saw her."

"Yeah, but they might not remember her."

My cell phone rang. She gave me a look. "Probably Kelso," I said. I answered the phone. "Gee, that's funny," I said to Kelso, with a look toward Jamie, "I was just thinking about you."

He ignored my comment, then told me what he'd found out about agent Bermeosolo. "What do you want me to do with it?"

"Two things. First, leak it to the press. Second—and I don't know if you can do this or not, but I'm assuming you can, or you know someone who *could*—I need you to plant an e-mail on his computer, dated six months ago, showing that he knew the locations of some of these hard-core hydro houses in Portland and went after some mom-and-pop type local pot growers instead."

Kelso told me he wasn't a computer genius, made the usual invectives, diatribes, and caveats, then said, "Well, I do know someone who *could* do it. In fact, he could rig a whole system of internal memos from Bermeosolo right up to the President if you wanted. But it costs me a thousand dollars every time I simply make a phone call to this guy. And why do you want to burn these pot growers? Are you trying to emulate Eliot Ness, perchance?"

"You know, Lou, you really should have been a songwriter."

"Yeah, I'm Cole Porter, reincarnated." He hung up.

"What was that all about?"

"I don't know," I said, and I really didn't. "I'm trying to get Farrell Woods and his people out of the jam they're in."

"Why?"

I shrugged. "I don't know. How can you not love a guy who names one of his dogs Townes Van Zandt?"

"Sometimes I just do not understand you."

"Look, I'm trying to keep Farrell Woods from going to prison. If not for *his* sake, then for the sake of those ten damn beagles."

"If you say so. Now what about the murder?"

I shook my head. "What can you tell me again about the wounds on Marti MacKenzie's body?"

"You mean without an autopsy?"

I shrugged. "Well, gee, have you done an autopsy since I spoke to you last?"

She huffed at me. "Now who's being mean?"

"Sorry."

She looked up at the ceiling of the car, trying to remember. "Well, there was a fracture of the skull."

"Right or left side?"

"Very good, Jack. It was the right orbit. I told you that, remember? Then there was the pelvis fracture."

"This was a major, bone-crushing event, as in a major car accident, or just a slight fracture, like a fall from a ladder?"

"Very good, again. It was a minor fracture, at best."

"Mm-hmm. And the last wound, I think there were three?"

"Uh, yeah, you're right. It was a bruise to her abdomen, on the right side again. Just over the liver, by the way."

"And you said the blood work—"

"—showed that there was major liver damage, yes."

I thought it through. "So, we've got a left-handed guy, who went Neanderthal on her ass with a tree branch, a crowbar, or a baseball bat, or something, and that's the cause of—"

"A baseball bat? Yes, Jack, but my brother played baseball! And even though he's right-handed, he always batted lefty."

"Very good, Jamie. So the killer isn't necessarily left-handed. You are a brilliant woman. I mean, person."

"So, my brilliant detective—slash—future husband and father-of-my-children-to-be, who do you think killed her that night?"

"Well," I said, laughing somewhat, "we have several suspects at hand. Randy Corliss, who hated her guts, and who, if he'd wanted to kill her—which he apparently did—would have beat the crap out of her. But with him I don't think there would have been only three wounds on the body—she would have been turned into a meat pie. Not only that, but I doubt if he would've come up with this elaborate, cockamamie scheme to frame Dennis Seabow. Not unless there's some bad blood between them that we don't know about. He would've just dumped the body and been done with it."

"Okay, so what about Eddie Cole?"

"Again, same thing. I don't believe the way she died indicates Cole's involvement. Not in her murder, anyway. A guy like Cole, who's running his own little criminal enterprise?

If he were to stage a murder, he'd do it in such a way that anyone in his organization thinks twice about screwing him over. There would not be, in any conceivable scenario that I can think of, a frame of someone else. He would want everyone to know that he'd killed her and that he was above the law."

"I think you're absolutely right. I hadn't thought about it in quite those terms, Jack, but—"

"Hey," I shrugged my shoulders, "this is what they used to pay me for, back in the Big Apple."

"So, it *had* to have been Judge Merton."

I nodded. "That makes the most sense. She tells him she's on to his blackmail scheme with Eddie Cole. He says, 'Let's meet at the diner around closing time.' She says, 'Okay,' then waits for him, but he doesn't want to be seen so he calls her on her cell phone—we need to find out if she had a cell phone, and then we need to check the records of her incoming calls for that night."

"Right. Or for the pay phone at the diner."

"Good point. So," I went on, "the judge says, 'My car broke down. I'm at the intersection. Can you pick me up?' "

Jamie nodded. "She says, 'Okay. I'll see you in a few minutes.' She gets her raincoat and scarf off the coat rack at the diner, or off the back of her chair, she runs out to the car, throws them in the back seat, then drives to the three-way—"

"—he meets her. They get in his car and start to talk things over. She gets upset. He becomes enraged. She gets out of the car. He follows her, grabbing a tree branch from the ground, or a crowbar from the trunk—"

"Not very likely. It would take too much time."

"No, you're right. Or a baseball bat from the back seat, and starts whacking away at her, furious that she won't keep quiet."

"She falls to the ground dead, or dying, and he freaks out."

"He doesn't know what to do. He drags the body out of sight and makes a phone call to someone who can help."

"But who?"

"That, my dear, is the hundred thousand dollar question."

She shook her head. "I watch the Game Show Channel, Jack. It's called *The Sixty-Four Thousand Dollar Question*."

"You watch The Game Show Channel?"

She shrugged. "Sometimes things get boring at the lab."

"Okay, so anyway, he calls someone to help him get rid of the body. Maybe Eddie Cole, maybe Randy Corliss, maybe someone else. Now let's think this through."

She smiled at me. "You know, I love doing this with you."

"Thanks, honey. Now, if it's Corliss, I don't see it. Not unless he needed the judge for something."

"Really? Why not?"

"Well, I met the guy. Unless there's something in it for him, he's just not interested. So, let's say the judge calls him and says, 'I just killed Marti MacKenzie. You've got to help me hide the body'—or whatever. Corliss is simply going to say, 'She's dead? Good. Kick her once for me,' and hang up."

"You're sure about that?"

"Yeah, I think he would probably say something exactly like that. He's an asshole's asshole and proud of it."

"Okay, so what about Eddie Cole?"

"You're right. That's a good possibility. Cole doesn't want his get-out-of-jail-free card going down the tubes, but does he arrange the accident with Dennis Seabow? I don't know. That's the thing I just can't figure out, you know? I mean, how does *he* get set up for the drunk driving rap—this Seabow? Who knew he was at the diner, passed out behind the wheel of his car?"

"No one but Farrell Woods. Do you think he could've—"

"Anything's possible, but I doubt it. Besides, we don't know for sure that no one else knew Seabow was there. You know, Woods had people after him, the DEA, maybe Eddie

Cole. Seabow was ratting for the DEA. There could have been surveillance of his meeting with Woods, wire-taps, hidden video cameras. But then again, someone could have just come along, and showed up in the parking lot after Woods had already slipped him the Rhohypnol. They would have found him unconscious inside his car."

I thought a moment. "Is there any chance that Seabow wasn't totally unconscious? That maybe Woods hadn't given him a big enough dose to keep him under for more than a few minutes?"

"Not the way he described the event. If someone is given or takes a small dose of Rhohypnol, they don't pass out. They just get all loose and rubbery and slobber a lot. If the dose is strong enough to make the person pass out, they're out. They won't wake up for hours, and *then* they start to slobber. That's why, after I'd read the police report, I had a suspicion it was Rhohypnol not alcohol that caused Seabow's condition, remember? When Woods first told us about slipping him a rufie, and I said I'd already suspected as much? When a drunk comes-to his mouth is dry. He *can't* slobber."

I told her that I *did* remember and that I was proud of her for thinking of it.

"Thanks. But who would've found Seabow in his car? Everyone from the diner had gone home."

"Oh, I don't know," I smiled, suddenly realizing something, "a passing motorist who gets curious when he sees the car and comes over to the parking lot to investigate?"

"That doesn't seem likely. A passing motorist might notice the car, but would just pass by. There'd be no reason to stop."

"Unless it wasn't just a passing motorist." I smiled again.

She shook her head. "I'm not following you."

"What kind of person, driving on a lonely road, late at night, stops their car, gets out, and investigates a solitary vehicle in the parking lot of a closed diner late at night? I'll give you a hint. They would be carrying a flashlight and be wearing a gun, a badge, and a uniform."

"Of course! A state trooper." She thought it over. "Heidi Loudermilk? You think she covered up for the judge?"

"She's on the list. At least for now."

"But, Jack, come on. She's a State Police officer."

"And the judge was a dirty judge. Anyway, we don't know anything yet for sure. Not till we find out what's in Marti MacKenzie's diary."

"And if Judge Merton knew Sergeant Loudermilk."

I shook my head. "It might not have been like that. She might have investigated Seabow's car, decided he'd just had too much to drink, gotten back in her cruiser and gone up the road, letting him sleep it off. Then she comes across the judge just after he's killed the girl, maybe while he's doing it, but before he's had a chance to call anyone like Eddie Cole or Randy Corliss, or 911, for that matter. She pulls over. He's out of his skull, crying, 'I didn't mean to kill her, I can't go to jail, my wife's family will kill me.' Then *she* says, thinking of the drunk just down the road, 'I can make it look like a drunk driving accident,' and the rest is her just staging things, including getting the judge to make a phony 911 call about a drunk driver, maybe on a prepaid cell phone."

"But why would she do it?"

"If she has the least bit of larceny or deviousness in her nature, she would be thinking, 'The judge is rich, or has a rich wife, if I help him get away with murder, then . . ."

"Blackmail."

I nodded. "A hundred thousand dollars worth. But this is all just speculation, my honey lamb. There might be a jealous ex-boyfriend that's been stalking her. Maybe the boyfriend was jealous of her affair with Dennis Seabow."

"She was having an affair with Dennis Seabow?"

"She might've been. We don't know. Maybe the boyfriend was Farrell Woods. We won't know which direction to go until—"

"—we read her diary."

"Exactly. Anyway, I'm starting to get a headache just thinking about all this—wait a second," I said, looking into the rearview mirror. "Do you believe this?"

Jamie turned around and looked over her shoulder.

Hooch was trotting toward us, his face tired and stressed with the miles he'd traversed to find us—still, he was a beautiful sight and a beautiful boy.

Jamie looked at me. "Face it, Jack. That dog loves you."

"And, at this point, me him."

We got out of the car and Hooch started running toward us. I crouched down and said, "Good boy, Hooch! Good doggie!"

To Jamie I said, "How the hell did he find us?"

"Simple, you idiot—sorry, I'm not supposed to call you that anymore—but don't you see? It's a matter of telepathy."

"It is? You think?"

"Sure. You've been sending him mental images of him coming home with you, and like some of us, he just can't resist you."

"So," I smiled, as Hooch came even nearer to the car, "what do we do? We can't keep taking him back to the junkyard. He'll just keep escaping and trying to follow us home."

"You're probably right. I guess the only thing to do now is to take him back to your place. Do you have an empty kennel available?"

"I sure do."

"Then, in the morning, you can start making some phone calls, telling the police and local vets how we—or, better yet, you, leave me out of it—found this dog wandering around, and that now you're trying to find his owner."

"And I can play with him till his owners come?"

"Yes, Jack," she laughed. "You can play with him to your heart's content. Until his owners come."

Hooch came smiling up to us, and I said, "Hey, you want to come home with us, Hooch?"

Jamie must have seen something in my eyes, because she said, "Oh, no, Jack, you're not going to let him sleep on the bed with us! Not on the bed! Jack!"

"But he's a nice doggie."

"He's a nice doggie who weighs 300 pounds!"

"More like 250. And it's a big bed."

She sighed. "Either way I just know I'm going to wake up in the morning with a double tib/fib from him sleeping on top of me. If I *do* wake up, that is."

"Are you kidding? You're not gonna wake up at all tomorrow morning, honey, because you're not going to get any sleep tonight. Do you know how loud these dogs snore?"

"Jack, no!"

32

Judge Merton's funeral service was held at noon on Friday in the Camden First Congregational Church. Jamie and her mother, Laura—both of whom had been invited by members of the widow's family—allowed me to tag along.

"Just please, Jack, don't try to bring any dogs with you."

"Oh, come on, honey—who would bring a dog to a funeral? Although, come to think of it, Roark *is* family."

"Jack," she sighed, "don't even think about it."

On the ride down the mountain I *did* think about it, though. What would be the harm? Wouldn't having a few doggies running around the chapel, sniffing each other's bums and trying to get the pastor to give an ear scratch kind of demournfulize the proceedings? Well, of course it would. But since that's the whole point of a funeral—to mourn the passing of a loved one—maybe the presence of dogs would be more suited to an Irish wake—where they drink, and sing, and dance—than to a funeral. In fact, I wouldn't be surprised to learn that dogs are often welcome at, or even required to attend, the wakes in Ireland.

Jamie had spent the morning looking over the evidence she'd gathered at the salvage yard. The measurements of Seabow's bumper and the girl's injuries didn't match. At breakfast she said, "Plus, I found these in each of the cars!"

She held up two plastic evidence bags.

I peered through the plastic. "Well, they look like seeds of some kind. In fact, they look kind of like hops."

"Very good, Jack. They are in fact seeds from what's called a hop tree, because the seeds look just like hops. This one," she held up one bag, "was found in the windshield wiper well of Judge Merton's Cadillac. While this one," she held up the other bag, "was found inside Dennis Seabow's front door."

I took the Baggies from her. "So?"

"So? *So?* Hop trees do not ordinarily grow north of Massachussets, Jack. Not very often. And also—*so*—Marti MacKenzie's body was found pinned against a hop tree, one of the few, if not the only hop tree in the entire State of Maine!"

"How do you know all this?"

"The Internet. You know, it wouldn't hurt you to—"

"Yeah yeah."

"Well, it wouldn't. If you were online, you wouldn't need to keep bothering your friend, Lou Kelso, to do things for you."

"I like bothering him. And as for these seeds," I handed back the Baggies, "they seem pretty circumstantial to me."

"Maybe now, yes. But once I do the DNA on the tree at the scene and on these two seeds . . ."

I was impressed. "That's very clever. Still, it doesn't prove definitively that the judge was there that night. It would only prove that he, or his car, had been there at some point in time."

"Yes, okay, but how did this seed," she held up one of the Baggies, "get inside Seabow's car door, if he was passed out behind the wheel?"

"Good point. But couldn't it have gotten inside when the police arrived and opened the door? A defense attorney would certainly argue that point to the jury."

Suddenly depressed, she put the Baggies down.

"Don't feel bad. It was a brilliant idea. It was just the wrong case."

"What do you mean?"

"Doing a DNA analysis of two seeds? found in two different cars? That's exceptionally brilliant. *I* would've never thought of that. It just doesn't help us with this case very much."

She sighed, then smiled and said, "It *was* a good idea, though, wasn't it?"

I agreed that it was, and said, "What *I'd* like to know is if you can pinpoint the type of blunt object the killer used."

She nodded. "Well, here, look at these photos." She spread them out on the kitchen table. "She was struck once in the head, here, and once across the abdomen—you see the bruising?—that was a very hard blow, which probably damaged the liver."

"And the blood work showed liver damage."

"Exactly. Then this last injury, to the pelvis, may have been done postmortem. Notice that there are no bruises."

"So? What was the murder weapon?"

She leaned back and smiled at me. "Due to the size and nature of the bruising, I think it was probably a Little League baseball bat. I can't say for sure, but that's my best guess."

I thought it over, then smiled. "Joey Stevens is about the right age to play Little League. And he's Merton's grandson." I gave her a pointed look. "We need to find Joey Stevens's bat."

Then, as we continued on our way to the funeral, my mind went to how the LeClerc brothers, owners of the salvage yard Jamie and I had broken into last night, had called me earlier that morning. Or at least how Serge LeClerc had called on behalf of himself and his brother Marcel.

"Hey, yeah," he said, "the police in Belfast say you got a dog at your place, you. A big orange dog, him?"

"A Dogue de Bordeaux?"

"Dat's da one," he said. "Not much of a dog, him, but we'd like him back, no?"

"What do you mean he's not much of a dog? He's a great—"

"Him don't chase away da peoples who break in last night."

"Someone broke into your house?"

"No, no. Me and my brudder, we own a salvage yard? Jean Claude is supposed to be da guard dog, but he's no good, him. Too friendly all da time to customers. I guess we'll have to beat him some more, no? Maybe dat'll do da trick."

"Or maybe you should get another dog. I'm a trainer, you know. I could train one for you. Maybe a Rottweiler?"

He thought it over. "No, I beat him first, den we see."

"Well, he's at my kennel." I sighed. "You can pick him up any time." I hated sending Hooch (or Jean Claude, apparently his real name) back to that kind of life.

"Jack," Jamie interrupted my reverie, "your tie is on perfectly straight. Stop tugging at it."

"Sorry. I'm not used to wearing them."

"And what's that bulge in your pocket?" I drew a tennis ball out of my sport coat and showed it to her. She laughed. "You're impossible."

When we got to the church, the organ was playing Bach and the chapel was a sea of black. A few people—probably strangers to Judge Merton's true character—had their hankies out.

It was a closed coffin and quite beautiful: made of rosewood and mahogany with gleaming brass details. In a way, it reminded me of a small yacht, only this boat was designed to take the man to his final peace. Supposedly.

We found some room on a pew across the aisle from Ron and Beth Stevens, who were there with two of their three kids, Joey—nine, with dark brown hair and eyes—and the seven-year-old girl—I think her name is Emily or Elizabeth, with blond hair and blue eyes and a pale, almost parchment-like complexion. (The five-year-old was too young to come.)

Beth, with shoulder-length, medium brown hair, wearing a black skirt and suit jacket with a white cotton blouse, had tears streaming down her cheeks. She was one of the few people in the room with a legitimate reason to cry: she was the judge's daughter, after all. Her husband, Ron, balding, with short-cropped nondescript-color hair and watery eyes, was also wearing a black suit. He tried to comfort her, just as I'd seen him do the night the body was found. And just like that night, she shrugged her shoulder away from his comforting hand.

I looked around and saw a few other familiar faces dotting the room. Flynn was there—it was just part of his job. So was Sergeant Loudermilk. I also recognized the prosecutor and the judge from the Dennis Seabow case. Kind of ironic, I thought. Then I looked behind us and saw Eve Arden. They scowled simultaneously when they saw me. They were dressed in matching black outfits and both had their hankies out, though their eyes were dry. Evelyn was the taller of the two, I think. Or maybe that was Ardyth. I could never tell the two of them apart.

Something else caught my attention. The Stevens kids were battling for space, surreptitiously—or so they thought—jabbing each other with their elbows and kicking at each other's ankles under the pew. Beth's seat was on the aisle. Next to her was Ron, then Joey, and then Emily (or Elizabeth). After more fighting from the kids, Ron finally leaned over and told them to knock it off (I assume that's what he was doing—I couldn't hear from where I sat). He got some sass back from the girl, so he gave her a swat. She squealed then kicked her brother again, even harder than before.

"Hey! Quit it!" Joey said, a little too loudly.

Beth leaned over to Ron, and he got up, grabbed the kids, and took them outside.

I leaned into Jamie. "I think I'll go have a cigarette."

She chuckled and shook her head. "How many times do I have to tell you, Jack, you don't smoke."

"Ssshh," Laura said.

"Listen to Mommy, sweetheart. Besides, I got me some detecting to do." I got up, sashayed past mom and daughter's knees, then walked up the aisle toward the back of the church. I stopped at Eve Arden's pew for a moment. Leaned over to them and said, "You ladies are looking especially lovely today." Then I looked back up front and said, "So sad, isn't it?"

They nodded, somewhat carefully.

I got outside where there was a sidewalk leading to the street and another leading around the side of the church. I heard voices coming from that direction. I followed them around the corner and found the coach giving the two kids a stern talking-to on the finer points of funeral behavior.

The bright morning sun etched a lattice of tree shadows into the dead lawn which embraced the north side of the chapel. The effect was neither eerie nor pretty. It was just a February morning in Maine.

"And the least you could do," the coach was saying "is have consideration for her feelings. She's very sad right now."

The girl said, "You mean because Grandpa died?"

"That's right, Emily. And the last thing she needs is to have you guys knocking each other around at his funeral."

I approached them, took the tennis ball out of my sport coat pocket. "Hey, Joey," I said, "you like baseball?"

He squinted his brown eyes at me like I was nuts. I showed him the ball, threw it to him, and he caught it.

"How's Roark?" the coach asked. I don't think he really cared how the dog was. It was just something to say.

"Fine. I think Beth wanted me to bring him by later."

Joey's scowl brightened to a smile. "Hey, I remember you," he said. "You own the kennel where Roark stays when we go on vacation." He threw the ball back. Hard.

"Hey!" I caught it. "Good arm." To Ron, I said, "He's got a slight fracture over his left eye. Nothing serious." I took a slow, easy windup and threw the ball back to Joey.

Ron said, "From what, the accident?"

"Probably," I said, knowing it was more likely that he'd been hit hard by someone right-handed (probably the judge's killer), as discussed previously with Jamie. But I didn't want Ron, or anyone else, for that matter, knowing that *I* knew the dog had been hit in the face. Not until I knew the killer's identity for sure. And I certainly didn't want the kids to know that their doggie pal had been mistreated.

Joey threw the ball back, and I said, "So, Joey," I threw it back, "you never answered my question."

"What question?" He tossed it back.

Emily said something to her father and he shook his head. "I said no."

"Do you like baseball?" I threw the ball.

He caught it. "Yeah." He made it sound like a question.

Ron said, "Joey's team made it to the playoffs last year."

"That's pretty good."

"We didn't *win*."

We tossed the ball back and forth and I learned that Joey played third base for the Lions and had the second best batting average on the team.

"That's great, Joey. Your grandpa ever watch you play?"

He shook his head and threw the ball back. "Just the playoff game. That we *lost*."

"What kind of bat do you use, aluminum or wooden?"

"Aluminum," he said, like it should've been obvious.

"Yeah? Do you use a team bat, or your own?"

"My own," he said sourly. "Till it got lost."

Ron said, "We'll get you a new bat for spring training."

Emily said, "Dad, I want to go home."

"We *can't* go home, honey. Not until the funeral is over."

She pouted some more. And while they discussed why not, and how long before it was over, and why does a stupid funeral have to take so long, and while Joey and I kept tossing the ball back and forth, me making it a bit more interesting by adding variations to each toss—a high pop fly, a slow ground ball, etc.—I found out that Joey last saw his bat the day of the playoff game (which I later found out was held the afternoon of October 18—the same day Marti MacKenzie was killed), that he'd hit a home run with it in the fifth inning, that after the game the family had gone home in their grandpa's car, and that the bat went missing the next day.

"Maybe you left it in your grandpa's car."

"Nah. My mom called him and he said it wasn't there."

Score one for Jamie. A big one.

Ron and Emily stopped arguing long enough for Ron to say, "What's all this about your bat, Joey? I told you we'd get you a new one."

"No," I smiled, "that's my fault. I'm an ex-detective. When I heard his bat went missing, I kept asking him questions, trying to solve the mystery." I came over to them and gave Emily the tennis ball, then took Ron by the elbow and said, "Mind if I have a few words with you, in private?"

"What's this for?" Emily said.

"What about?" Ron said.

"That's why it's private." To Emily, I said, "It's a ball. You and your brother can play catch while your dad and I talk."

"With a stupid girl?" Joey said. "No way."

Emily threw the ball at his head, but missed. He stepped forward to hit her and Ron stepped in between them. "Okay, now, knock it off. Emily, you go get Mr. Field his ball."

"But Dad!"

"Just do it."

She huffed, turned with a flip of yellow hair, then ran off across the dead grass to get the ball, which had ended up at the trunk of a very old oak tree. She leaned down, picked it up, and brought it back to me.

"No, Emily, sweetie," I said, "that's for you and Joey to play catch with while I talk to your dad."

There was more argument, mostly from Joey, until I told him that all great ballplayers took time to teach younger players how to play the game. Babe Ruth even taught his sister.

"That's right," Ron said, agreeing with my fabrication.

The kids started tossing the ball back and forth, with Joey giving his sister some pointers. Ron and I walked away.

"So, what's this all about, Jack?"

I said, "You've been having an affair with one of your students." He had no idea I'd seen him with her in the high school parking lot.

His face turned red. He looked over at the kids, then tried to look back at me, but couldn't meet my eyes. "I don't know what the hell you're talking about."

"Un-huh. And I'm guessing your wife knows about it and is threatening to divorce you, right?"

"That's—that's not—that's . . . how did you find out about this? Is she paying you to—"

"No one's paying me. I just keep my eyes open. Now, normally this kind of thing wouldn't concern me. I mean, it bothers me, you taking advantage of a teenage girl, but it's none of my business, so—"

"If you only knew," he huffed. "She's the one who's been pursuing *me*. I'm telling you, this girl knows what she wants and she gets it . . . besides, she's almost eighteen."

"Almost is still a felony. Plus, she's a student. I mean, come on, Ron, the whole thing is sleazy, or hadn't you noticed?"

He hung his head. "I know, I know, but I just can't help myself. She's so incredible." He looked sadly back at his kids again.

I wanted to slap him. Slap him silly, if you must know. But I didn't. I just said, "Maybe you should think about Emily, about her when she gets to be that age and has some pervert of a teacher diddling *her*. How would that make you feel? And by the way, did you extort a hundred thousand dollars from your father-in-law, the Friday before he died?"

"What? What? A hundred thousand dollars? Are you kidding? That old bastard—God rest his soul—wouldn't give me a dime. In fact, he *couldn't* give me a dime. Not without my mother-in-law's approval."

This was what I was really interested in. "Are you sure about that?"

"Yeah, he hated me. Why would he give me any—"

"No, I mean about needing his wife's approval. Are you sure that Mrs. Merton—"

"—controlled the purse strings? Absolutely. They had a special checking account where she could sign any check on her own, but he couldn't. He had to have her countersignature."

I feigned disinterest. "Mmm-hmm. So where were you last Friday between three and six?"

"What? You think I need an alibi?"

"Just answer the question."

He thought hard, then smiled suddenly. "We had a match in Bangor that afternoon. We left right after school and got back around seven o'clock."

I gave him a hard look just for the hell of it, then said, "Okay, I'll have the police check it out. But if you're lying—"

"I'm not lying, I swear."

The organ music started up again inside the church. We looked over at the kids and saw them having fun together, playing catch.

"Are you going to tell anyone about this?"

I paused. "No, though I probably should. And if she were any younger, I *would*. But it cuts both ways. This conversation never happened." I checked my watch. "I'd better get back inside."

He looked over at the kids. "Let me get your ball back."

"That's okay. I've got plenty more."

Jamie said she had things to do after the service. Since Laura and I both wanted to go to the cemetery for the burial, I suggested that we try to hitch a ride with someone at the church. Jamie said fine, she'd call me later to see how it went, and we kissed our good-byes and she left.

"Sheriff Flynn could give us a ride," Laura said as we came outside the church.

"Yeah, or Sergeant Loudermilk, for that matter."

Laura gave me a funny look, then said, "Oh, I get it. Your interest in attending the burial has nothing to do with paying your last respects to Judge Merton."

"What respects? And you?"

"Me? Oh, at my age you get a bit morbid about these things, I suppose." She took my arm. "But I must admit, I'm also itching to watch the great detective at work."

"You think I'm going detecting, do you?"

"Aren't you?"

"Well, I had an idea or two in mind." I shrugged. "But if you want to see some real action, you should come watch me train a dog sometime."

33

We caught up with Sergeant Loudermilk at the parking lot next to O'Neal's, a cozy Italian joint on Bayview Street. She had one of her big mitts on the door handle.

"Hi," I blushed, or tried to, "we sort of got stranded."

Her car was a black Chevy Malibu. A guy's car. Or a girl's car, I suppose, if she was a girl who was into cars.

She looked at me like I was from Mars. "I'm sorry?"

"Our ride took off. We were hoping to go to the cemetery. Are you headed that way?"

She looked me over, shook her head and sighed. "Do you folks need a ride?" She opened her car door.

"Hey, thanks," I said, and Laura and I got in the car—me in front, Laura in back.

Loudermilk got in and settled behind the wheel.

"We really appreciate this," I said. Laura murmured in agreement. Loudermilk started 'er up and I said, "While we're on our way to the cemetery, maybe I could ask you a few questions, if you don't mind."

"What kind of questions?" She checked the rearview mirror and started to back out into the street.

"About the Dennis Seabow case. His attorney asked me to look into things, and I noticed that—"

She put on the brakes, half in the parking lot, half in the street. "The Seabow case? That's over, done, history."

"Well, his attorney is filing an appeal, and I was noticing

that you were the first officer at the scene. Are we going to sit here all day?"

She huffed, shook her head, and backed into the street. She put on the brakes, jammed it into drive, then peeled out. "Appeal? What appeal? It was an open and shut case. The bastard got what he deserved."

"You're probably right," I said as she turned left onto US 1 and got in line behind the procession of cars, all driving slowly with their headlights on high beam, "but there were some discrepancies in your testimony—I had a chance to read the trial transcript. My fiancée asked me to look into it and—"

"Your fiancée?" Laura said. "Oh, Jack, that's wonderful news."

"What discrepancies?" Loudermilk said.

"Well, it isn't official yet, but we've talked about it."

Laura said, "Jack, I think that's just terrific."

"Can we get back to the Seabow case?"

"Nah, I don't want to bother you with this. You're probably all overwrought by the death of your friend and all."

"Who, Judge Merton? I wouldn't call him a friend exactly."

"Is that right? That's interesting. Hey, this is a really nice car. How long have you had it?"

She sighed. "I bought it last year."

"Yeah." I ran my hand across the dashboard. "A sweet ride. It's a Malibu, isn't it?"

"Yes. And why do you think it's interesting that—"

"Isn't the Malibu mostly a guy's car, though? I mean, no offense, but most women don't really go for the fast, muscle-type car, do they?"

I went on for a while in this indirect fashion. It was an interrogation technique I'd learned years ago, when I'd first started out with the NYPD. On my first tour, on graveyard, I was paired up with an old Irish drunk named Sully Smith, who had the annoying habit of asking a perp a question and then changing the subject in the middle of his answer, like so:

"So, Octavio, you understand your wife's in the hospital from a knife wound? The doctors say she may not live through the night. And *she's* saying *you* stabbed her."

"That lying bitch, I did no such thing! She's got it in for me because she thinks I've been banging her cousin—"

"Listen, do you want some coffee or something?"

"No, man. I'm okay."

"All right. All right. You're okay. Sorry, I can't get this pen to . . . oh, there it goes. I thought it was out of ink." And he would start writing. "So, you've been banging your wife's cousin. What's her name?"

"No, no, man. I just been telling you that that's what my wife thinks, but it ain't the truth, man—"

"Oh, right. Sorry. So the reason you stabbed your wife is because she's been telling lies about you and her cousin."

"I didn't stab her, man! That's what I'm trying to—"

"Jeez, you know, that's a nice crucifix. Mind if I have a look at it? I was brought up Catholic myself. Can I see it?"

He just wore the suspect down with his unfocused, drunk act until the suspect finally confessed out of pure frustration. (By the way, Octavio's wife died, he got fifteen years, and his wife's cousin was waiting for him when he got out of jail. Ain't life wonderful?)

Loudermilk finally said, "I want to know what discrepancies you think there are in my testimony."

"Oh, I wouldn't worry about that. You know, this Seabow thing, it's an open and shut case, like you said. I doubt if his attorney can make a case out of something as simple as a tiny detail that you probably just misremembered."

"Misremembered? What detail?"

"Like I said, it's nothing. Just the squealing tires."

"Squealing tires?"

"Mmm-hmm. At the trial you said you heard Seabow's

tires squealing on the asphalt, just before he hit Marti MacKenzie."

"That's right. What of it?"

"Well, it's just that in the crime scene photos, there don't appear to be any skid marks on the pavement at the scene. Say, what kind of gas mileage does this baby get?"

She sighed. "I never said I heard the tires squeal immediately before the accident. It could have been several hundred yards up the road. He was going pretty fast."

"That's not the impression you gave in your testimony at trial. I mean, about exactly when you heard the tires."

She thought it over. "Maybe, you know, with all that happened, I put the two together. I seriously doubt if anyone took photos further up the road than a hundred feet or so."

"I guess that's it. It's funny, isn't it, how the mind plays tricks on you?" I paused as she followed the fleet of cars and turned into the cemetery north of Rockport, which overlooked the crashing waves and the rocky coast of Maine.

"Still," I said, "it's kind of puzzling, though."

"What is?"

"Well, in the transcript of your radio call to the dispatch office, you mention the tires five seconds before you discover the accident. Now, I don't know how fast you were driving that night—I'm assuming pretty fast—but I have to tell you, I seriously doubt . . . well, isn't this a nice place to be buried?"

Laura said, "Yes. It's lovely."

The procession stopped. Laura and I prepared to get out. Loudermilk was staying put for the moment. "Look, Mr. Field, I don't know what you and Seabow's attorney are trying to pull here, but I can assure you I heard those tires squeal, trust me. I've been doing this job for the last three years in Maine, and I worked five years before that with the Boise Police Department." She pronounced it "Boyzee," like most people.

"You're from Boise?" I said pronouncing it "Boycee," the way they do in Idaho. "Isn't that something. I knew you weren't from around here. I thought I detected some sort of accent when you talk."

"Well, that's why. I grew up surrounded by potato farms."

"Is that right?"

"I'm a Boyzee girl, born and bred. And whatever kind of sleazy trick Seabow's attorney is trying to pull, I can assure you it won't work. The evidence is solid against him."

"Well, you know how defense attorneys are. He's got it in his head, this thing with the squealing tires, and I had to ask you about it. Sorry, if I bothered you with it."

"It doesn't *bother* me in the least." She opened her door, ready to get out. I stopped her.

"There's just one other thing. I listened to the tape, you know, of your conversation with Dispatch? And, it's a funny thing, I could hear your siren going, and when you stopped and got out, I could clearly hear your footsteps in the fallen leaves."

"So?"

"So, nowhere on that tape did I hear any squealing tires."

"I'm sorry?" She was stalling.

"There's all this detail on the tape except for one thing: there are no squealing tires."

She moved her tongue around in her mouth. "The sound of the tires was probably covered by the siren, that's all."

"Covered by the siren?"

"Yeah. Drowned out by the siren. Did you think of that?"

"No, I didn't." I pretended to think it over, nodded. "You're probably right. I hadn't thought of that. Of course, of course." I looked at Laura. "I couldn't hear the tires because of the siren. That makes perfect sense." I paused. "Wait," I said. "But if *you* heard the tires squealing over the sound of the siren, why didn't it show up on the tape?"

"Uh . . ." She sighed. "I don't know. It's—they're very

low-quality tapes. They don't pick up everything. Now, if there's anything else you need to know," Loudermilk said, "I'll be glad to clear it up for you. I was *there*, Mr. Field, so I know what happened that night."

Yeah, I thought, getting out of the car, and so do I. I also know that you, sister, are *not* from Idaho.

34

There's a feeling of finality you get when you see the coffin go into the ground and watch that first, token shovelful of dirt being poured into the grave. I had a feeling of finality too, about the Seabow case, and about who helped Judge Merton get away with murder. Was there really any point in proving he'd killed Marti MacKenzie, I thought, now that he was buried in the cold, cold ground? Who really benefited from that knowledge? The state? His family? Seabow did, certainly. But Jamie and I almost had enough evidence together at this point to get Seabow a new trial, and all without revealing who actually killed the girl that night.

And what did it matter who killed Judge Merton? He was not the pillar of the community that many thought him to be. In fact, if anything, just the opposite. It could be argued, given that he was a murderer, that he deserved what he got. So why care who done him in? Well, because. It's just the way the system works. Let's say a good citizen kills a rotten one; does that mean the good one doesn't pay for his crime? Sorry, it doesn't work that way. Not unless you're filthy rich. And sometimes, even then, you can't get away with it. Of course, in a perfect world there would be no lawyers or cops or judges. But, honey, this ain't a perfect world.

I caught up with the widow Merton as she was about to get into the back of her limousine. Beth Stevens was with her.

"Mrs. Merton," I said, stopping her, "I'm Jack Field. I'm sorry for your loss."

"Thank you," she said, but it was just her mouth moving.

"I wonder if—" I stopped, then went on. "I know this isn't the best time, but I wonder if I might ask you a few questions about the circumstances surrounding your husband's death?"

She stared hot coals at me from behind her black veil. "You can't be serious."

"I am, though. Couldn't we just sit in the back and talk for just a minute? Time is of the essence."

"What does that mean?"

"I'll tell you once we get inside."

Beth said, "It's all right, Mama. I trust him."

She looked at Beth, then at me. "Very well, one minute."

We got in the back of the limo—I got in first and slid across the seat, which is the proper, mannerly thing to do, though most people aren't aware of it. Once she got settled in and Beth closed the door for her, I laid it on the line: "Your husband killed a girl named Marti MacKenzie back in October of last year. Were you aware of that?"

"That's a horrible and impertinent question."

"He was involved in an illegal activity and she knew about it. She went out to meet him that night, and for whatever reason, she ended up dead. And he was the one who killed her. In fact, he used your grandson's Little League bat to do it."

"Why are you torturing me with these gruesome fantasies?"

"You knew about it. I know you knew because you helped him get rid of another blackmailer by allowing him to withdraw a hundred thousand dollars from your joint account."

"Stop it, please! Beth!" she called outside, but the smoked-glass window was rolled up tight and her voice was weak with fear.

"I'm not saying any of this to hurt you, or to get you into any trouble with the law. In fact, I want to help you if I can." I went on to tell her that I wanted to keep her husband's name out of the papers in regards to Marti MacKenzie's death, if at all possible. With her family's connections it seemed like a good bet that I could. "But she had a family too. And an innocent man is in jail for something your husband did."

"What," she gasped, "what do you want me to do?"

"First, tell me about the money—the hundred grand."

She sank back into her seat. "What do you want to know?"

Beth knocked on the window. Mrs. Merton rolled it down and said, "Not just yet, dear. We're having a conversation."

"But, Mother, everybody's waiting."

"Well, let them wait. I'm busy with this gentleman." She rolled the window back up. "I'm all yours," she said.

She told me that on the night of the murder her husband came home late, woke her up and confessed the crime to her. He said he hadn't meant to kill the girl, but had lost control and hit her with his grandson's bat—he didn't remember how many times. Then he told her that someone had come along and helped him hide the crime by making it look like a drunk driving accident. This good Samaritan buried the bat somewhere near the scene under a pile of leaves, and wanted to be paid a lot of money for helping out—$250,000.

"Wow. A quarter of a million dollars? There was no mention of that in any of the police reports."

I could see a faint smile taking shape behind her veil. "I am fortunate to have a very discreet relationship with my bank. No one else knows about that money but you and the bank manager."

"And the good Samaritan, whoever he is. Or she. Did your husband tell you who it was?"

She shook her head.

"Did he tell you he was being blackmailed?"

"I don't understand. The first payment wasn't blackmail. It was simply a payment for services rendered."

Maybe she didn't know anything about Tulips and Eddie Cole. That was okay by me. I wasn't going to tell her. "What about the hundred grand?"

"That," she said, "was blackmail. I shouldn't have helped him the second time. In fact, I asked the bank to put invisible dye on the money so it couldn't be spent." (There are three kinds of dye used by banks: the kind that explodes when you open the briefcase, the kind that instantly shows up on the skin as soon as you touch it, and the kind that can only be seen with ultraviolet light, which was the kind on Merton's money.)

"Did the judge know about the dye?"

She shook her head. "But I think the blackmailer must have found out somehow. I'm afraid that's what got my husband killed." She clutched my hand. "I'm responsible for his death, Mr. Field. Just as certainly as if I'd killed him myself."

I looked at her for a moment. It was hard to get a really good look at her eyes, hidden as they were behind the veil. I wondered if she *had* killed her husband, the way Mrs. Murtaugh had suggested. Or had had him killed. I looked down at her gloved hands, one of which was now holding one of mine. Her hands were too small to account for the bruising around the man's neck. Still, she could have hired someone to do it. Somehow I didn't think so, but it *was* possible.

I said, "So you killed him, did you?"

"Oh, I didn't do the actual deed, Mr. Field." She tilted her head to look at me. "Or hire someone to do it, if that's what you're thinking. But I killed him just as sure as we're sitting here talking." She let go of my hand and leaned her head against the window as if drained of all ability to sit upright.

"You can't dwell on that. You didn't know what would happen. Did he tell you who the second blackmailer was?"

Her head shot up. "The second blackmailer?"

"Yeah," I said. "There had to be two different people."

"Why do you think that?"

I shrugged. "The first payment was for services rendered, like you said. Whoever framed Dennis Seabow . . . he's the—"

"I know who he is."

"Well, whoever framed him was just as guilty of murder as your husband."

"I don't understand."

"It's called felony murder. You don't have to actually commit the murder to be guilty. You just have to be involved. And since she was just as guilty as he was, there would be no reason for her to keep asking your husband for money since she couldn't very well expose *his* crime without exposing her *own*."

"You think it was a woman?"

"I know it was."

"That's strange." She looked off into the distance.

"Why is it strange?"

"No reason." She put out her hand. "I think you've taken up enough of my time."

"You're right, but I just need to know one more thing, about the second blackmailer?"

"There was no second blackmailer, Mr. Field. It was the same person. My husband said so. If it hadn't been, I wouldn't have had the bank put dye on the money. In fact, I probably wouldn't have paid the money in the first place."

"Maybe your husband knew that, and only told you it was the same person to get you to go along."

"Trust me, Mr. Field. It was the same person. There was no second blackmailer." She put out her hand again.

I shook it, got out of the limo and stood there for a few moments scratching my beard. What she'd said didn't make sense to me, but I couldn't come up with a reason for her to lie about it either. Maybe the judge had lied to her about it or maybe my instincts were just wrong. Maybe there really was no second blackmailer. It came down to two witnesses who were telling two different stories: Mrs. Merton and Roark.

I should've trusted Roark—dogs don't know how to lie.

35

I was in the kitchen, listening to an old Michael Franks LP, frying up a couple of salmon fillets for a late lunch (or early dinner), using a nonstick pan—no butter or oil—when I heard Jamie come in the front door.

"Come kiss me, Jack. I've just done something wonderful. Hello, Frankie! Hello, Roark! Good dogs! Jack?"

"Sorry, I'm busy in the kitchen, honey. Come on back."

"It smells delicious. And when are you taking this dog home?" She'd hung her loden coat on a hook in the mud room, and now came toward the kitchen, followed by the two dogs who circled and sniffed her, wagging their tails. She untwirled her gold woolen scarf from around her neck and draped it over the back of the easy chair. "He does *have* a home, doesn't he?"

"I'm going to take him home tonight. Right after he helps me and Maggie find the murder weapon. Did you bring the blood?"

"And that's not all I brought." She held up a smallish brown paper shopping bag, the kind with its own handles.

"You do know, don't you," as I turned the salmon over, "that there are plenty of hooks for your scarf in the mud room?" I peeled back the skin from the two fillets and pulled them off to the side of the pan.

She came in the kitchen door. "Oh, Jack, I am not going to

let your anal retentiveness about my housekeeping habits ruin my good mood. Not with what I've got in this bag." She pulled out four or five small pink diaries, the kind they sell at variety stores. "Voilà! Marti MacKenzie's diaries!"

"Wow, way to go! Where did you find them?"

"I'll tell you, but first, that smells soooo good. What's in it?" She put the diaries down on the kitchen table.

I told her it was made with my own marinade of soy sauce, cranberry juice, honey mustard, and a touch of shredded ginger. "Though, it's not really a marinade since I just brush it on and cook the fish right away."

"Mmmmm, smells and sounds delicious. Oh, and look, you made two. Too bad I'm not hungry."

"One's for Leon," I said. "You can always have a taste of mine if you like. So where did you find them?"

"Did you know," she sat down and began unlacing her boots, "that a bull nose is a carpenter's term? It refers to the curvy part at the bottom of a set of stairs. You know, the part that kind of butts out past the banister?"

"You mean that little extra curlicue on the bottom step?" I turned off the flame and put the salmon steaks onto two plates to rest, each with a sprig of dill, and each next to a pile of red Maine baby potatoes and baby carrots smothered in butter.

"That's it. And it's a perfect place to hide, oh, I don't know, some diaries? Say, five of *these* little babies?"

While she said this I opened the cabinet, found a bottle of applesauce, twisted the cap off and, as I dolloped some onto Leon's plate, said, "Have you read any of them yet?" then closed the lid and took the bottle over to the fridge.

"Oh, yeah . . . it's all here, baby. Listen to this—"

While she tried to locate the passage she wanted to read, I put some sour cream on top of Leon's applesauce, then put my plate on the table, with an extra fork for Jamie, left

Leon's plate and a glass of milk next to the stove, went back to the fridge and said to her, "I'm having a beer. You want one?"

"Yes, thanks," she said, flipping through the diary.

I opened two bottles of Pilsner Urquell and handed her one. She took a sip. I went to the phone and used the intercom to call Leon. "Dinner's ready," I said, then came over and sat next to Jamie and started to eat.

"Okay, listen to this, 'Well, I'm at the diner and, as usual, JM is late.' Oh, I forgot to tell you, this is from October eighteenth, the same night she died. So we were right! She *was* at the diner that night! She says, 'How many times was he late to court when I worked for him?' JM, that's Judge Merton!"

"Mmm-hmm," I mumbled, chewing my food. I had a dilemma on my hands here. How was I going to tell Jamie that we didn't need the girl's diaries anymore? She was so happy, so pleased with herself, but if I didn't tell her, it would be the pool game all over again. And I didn't want that.

"Honey, save the rest for later. I want to know how the hell you found the diaries in the first place."

"Oh," she closed the diary, "okay, well first I spoke to her father. I had to discuss some things with Ian Maxwell, you know, because of that thing with my dad. So we were on the phone."

"You and Maxwell."

"Right. So, he's half talking to me and half talking to someone in the background about getting a better price for board feet of some kind of wood, so I figured he must be talking to Moon MacKenzie, and he is, and I ask if I can talk to him."

"Wait, you're having an important business discussion with your father's billionaire partner and you ask to speak to his carpenter and he hands him the phone?"

"Uh, no, even better. He asks me where I am and has his own private, and very handsome, helicopter pilot fly to my mom's house! and pick me up and take me out in the middle of Penobscot bay! actually much further than that!"

"I don't believe this."

"I know! So, Maxwell and I have our discussion, which he wanted to have done personally in the first place, because there are some documents he wanted me to give to my Dad, then I ask if I can meet privately with Moon MacKenzie and we talk while he's installing a custom balustrade into this unfinished stairway. This beautiful stairway. Oh, Jack, you've got to see this house. It's like . . ." She stopped. "Well, anyway, I told him about his daughter's diaries and the bull nose, and he walks over to the bottom step and lifts the top off with the cap of his boot. 'That, my dear; he says, 'is a bull nose.' "

"What do you know."

Leon came in followed by the two Pomeranians, Scully and Mulder. He picked up his plate, looked at it, and said, "*Salmon?* Ah, man . . ." to no one in particular. Then he went to the door, held it open for the two dogs with one foot, and left. He never even looked at me.

"You're welcome," I said over my shoulder.

"What's that all about?"

I shrugged. "Near as I can figure, Sloan isn't speaking to him so he's not speaking to me." I chuckled.

"You think it's funny?"

"Sure it's funny. He's a kid." I laughed some more.

"Have you tried to talk to him?"

"Of course. But I can't very well talk to him if he won't talk to *me*. Don't worry, sweetheart. He'll get over it. So what did he say about Seabow possibly being framed?"

"Who, Moon MacKenzie?" she asked.

I nodded.

"Well, he was actually quite pissed at first. Your vegetables are getting cold."

"Sorry." I began eating again.

She took another sip of beer, then went on. "But I told him about some of the evidence, and that if we can find her diaries we'll know for sure."

"Well, it's too bad we don't really need the diaries after all. Though I suppose he'll be happy to have them."

"What do you mean we don't need the diaries?"

"I tried to call you before but your cell phone wasn't working."

"I know. I've been having trouble with it. It wasn't the battery after all. So why don't we need the diaries?"

"Because Judge Merton confessed."

"How can he confess? He's dead."

I explained about my talk with the man's widow and she got a small look on her face. "You did this on purpose."

"No, I didn't. And I just realized: we know who killed Marti MacKenzie but we still aren't a hundred percent sure who killed Judge Merton. Or who helped frame Dennis Seabow." This wasn't a lie, exactly. I was pretty sure of who it was, but not a hundred *percent* sure. "Maybe there's something in those diaries that'll tell us that. But I want to hear more of your wonderful adventures while I do the dishes."

We went to the sink and she told me that after she'd taken the return flight home by private helicopter, she looked at the police report again and found that Marti MacKenzie was living in a kind of sorority house, off campus, at the time that she died. (Though it wasn't actually a sorority—since she was an unwed mother—but that part wasn't very clear to me.) So anyway, Jamie went there and, what do you know, there was a beautiful stairway with gorgeous steps and not one, but two bull noses. One on either side of the bottom step. She asked permission to open them up, and the diaries were right there.

"Now, honey," I said when she was done, "don't be so disappointed about my talk with Merton's widow. Just think what would have happened if the judge *hadn't* confessed to her, or if she'd refused to talk to *me*. You did wonderful detective work today and you should be proud of yourself. You can't always predict where a certain piece of evidence is going to lead.

"Now you start looking through those diaries for more clues while I feed the dogs."

"That reminds me, where's Maggie?"

"Upstairs having a time out, though not the way you think." I opened the bin where I keep Frankie's food, and he and Roark, who'd been asleep in the living room, got up, stretched briefly, shook themselves, and came loping hopefully toward their provender. "I've been working with her tracking skills, which is why I asked you to get me some of Marti MacKenzie's blood. It's just that sometimes a dog's hunting instincts can be sharpened by spending a few hours alone before taking her out to work."

"You're locking her up to make her hunt better?"

I shrugged. "Fasting her too. It'll build her drive to a much higher level. It's done all the time with hunting dogs."

"If you say so."

I got the kibble into two bowls and the dogs went to town.

Jamie, looking through a diary, said, "Here's something."

I came over. "What?"

"She mentions an SL who also may have known about Cole's blackmail scheme. See? Look, right here."

"I don't recall anyone with those initials."

"Think, Jack. JM for Judge Merton, SL for Sergeant Loudermilk? She says she's afraid of her too. Where are you going?"

"I forgot to tell you: Sergeant Loudermilk is a liar and I need to have Kelso do a background check on her."

"How do you know she's a liar?"

"Because she claims to be from Boy-zee, Idaho."

"So?"

"So, no one from Boise calls it Boy-zee. It's pronounced Boy-cee. Plus she said she grew up surrounded by potato farms, and there are no potato farms within three hundred miles of Boise, Idaho. It's in the western part of the state, and all the potato farms are in the eastern part." I speed-dialed Kelso.

"How do you know all this?"

"Because my grandmother has a sugar beet and alfalfa farm in Kuna, Idaho, which is just west of Boise. We used to go up there every summer. My dad would take me trout fishing up in the Cascade Mountains. Yo, Kelso, it's Jack."

I filled him in on the situation with Loudermilk. When I was done, I hung up and said, "I'm going to go upstairs and floss. You want to come up?"

She gave me a look and said, "No. Why would I?"

"I don't know, I thought we could fool around when I'm done."

"That's very romantic," she sniggled.

"If you don't want to, that's fine." I went to the door.

"Jack, I'm sorry. I'm just not in the mood." I stopped in the doorway. She looked up at me. "Do you really want to?"

"Yeah, I do. Really bad."

"Why?"

"I don't know. Your helicopter story turned me on."

She laughed. "Okay, then." She stood up.

"You mean you will?"

"Why not?" She smiled. "It's like . . . what's it like?" She thought a moment. "It's like when someone says 'I need to get a new car battery. You want to come along?' and you do. You just go along for the ride." She took my hand.

I chuckled. We went to the staircase, followed by Frankie and Roark, who had just finished eating.

As we climbed the stairs I said, "So this is just another trip to Sears for you, huh?"

"I don't mind. I mean, hey, if you need a new battery—besides, you deserve a freebie once in a while."

We stopped in the middle of the stairs. I put my arms around her, pulled her long hair up and kissed her on her neck and throat. She likes it when I do that. She melted into me for a moment, then stepped back, leaned against the banister, pulled her sweater up over her head and let it fall behind her, down to the first floor. Then she turned her back to me and held her hair out of the way so I could work the hooks on her brassiere. It was at this point, I think, that the dogs went past us and into the bedroom. (My mind was on other things.)

Oh, and I never did get around to flossing.

36

A thick fog had rolled in from the bay. We were sitting, holding hands in my Suburban at the MacKenzie crime scene, with the emergency lights flashing, enjoying the warmth of the heater and the tunes coming from the listener-sponsored station in Blue Hill. They were playing an evening of acoustic music by British singer and guitarist John Martyn.

"This is very pretty," Jamie said, letting go of my hand to turn up the volume. "But what the hell is he singing about?"

"I know. I can't understand a word either."

She sighed and took my hand again. "That was nice, earlier on the stairs."

"I know." I kissed the palm of her hand and then the small of her wrist. She pulled my hand up to her face, kissed it, and held it there. A moment passed. A very pleasant moment.

"Is this going to work?" she said finally.

"The way everything else on this case has worked? Probably not. But we've got to try." I let go of her hand and cracked open the door. "You stay here with Frankie and Maggie. Roark and I are going to take a look around first."

"Jack, why? I thought this was Maggie's show."

"I don't know. Maybe Roark can find it on his own. It was Joey Stevens's bat, after all."

I left the engine running, got out, opened the back door

and called Roark. Frankie wanted to get out too, so I said, "No, Frankie, you can't come." He whined and looked cute. "I don't care how cute you look, honey boy, you cannot come."

"Will you stop talking to the dog like he understands you?"

I laughed. "It really bothers you when I do that."

"Yes. Especially since, according to you, dog's have no Broca's area."

"You're absolutely right. I should just give them commands and not talk to them as if they understand." To the dogs, I said, "Frankie, stay. Roark, come."

Roark, the boxer boy, jumped out of the car. He was wearing a navy blue and dark green wool plaid doggie coat. He also had on a collar with an attached light that blinked off and on when you flipped the switch. I flipped it, and Roark's collar began to blink, just like my emergency lights.

I closed the car door and said, "Hey, Roark!" He wagged his stub. "Where's Joey's bat?"

He looked around in the fog for Joey.

"You want to help me find it? Huh, good boy?"

He did a play bow and barked.

"Good boy! Let's go find it!"

I led him straight to the hop tree, the one the girl had been "pinned against." (She hadn't really been pinned against it, but had probably been tied to it, since, according to Jamie's interpretation of the photos taken of the body, there appeared to be ligature marks around her wrists.)

I scanned the area and tried to imagine where someone might have thrown the bat. There were so many possible places. This is futile, I thought. How do I know Loudermilk didn't come back for it and then dispose of it somewhere else? Because, I replied to myself, she had gone to a lot of trouble to make the murder look like a drunk driving accident, so in her mind there would be no reason for anyone to search the area for a small aluminum bat with blood on it.

So Roark and I searched the bushes, and clomped (me) and bounced (him) around in the snow for about twenty minutes before I decided it was time to bring in a specialist—the Maggie girl.

She was in a crate in the back of the car. I put Roark in the back seat next to Frankie.

"No luck, huh?" Jamie said over her thermos of coffee.

"Not yet."

"But, Jack, what if you don't find it?"

I shrugged. "That's the way it goes sometimes. You never know which piece of evidence will clinch a case for you. You never know if you'll even find that one piece. The idea is to keep plodding on as best as you can."

"You're in a positive mood."

"There's that too. Sometimes you can't shake the blues, or the feeling that you'll never get anywhere."

She smiled. "I guess that's why I'm here, huh? You want me to get out and help you guys look?"

"Not for now. For now it's just me and Maggie and . . ." I patted the pocket of my down vest. ". . . Marti MacKenzie's blood. You stay here and keep warm." Then I nodded my head at the radio. "And let me know if you figure out any of the words to anything he's singing."

"Not much chance of that," she said. "I don't know, maybe he's not singing in English. Maybe it's a foreign language."

"No. I have a couple of his earlier records, on vinyl. My theory is he just gets so far into the music that the words seem irrelevant to him."

She laughed. "I get it. So the music, which is a function of the right brain, short-circuits his Broca's center, which is located in the left brain?"

I chuckled. She was on to something. "I think you're

close. I don't think the music short-circuits the Broca's, though. I think the corpus collosum just gets in the way."

"Corpus collosum?" she said. "You really do know a thing or two about how the brain works."

"Honey," I said, "the reason I went to Harvard medical school was to become a psychiatrist, remember?"

"I do remember." She touched the back of my hand.

"Wish us luck," I said.

She did, and I took Maggie, on lead, to the center of the triangle, then reached in my pocket for the vial of Marti MacKenzie's blood. She stared at me intently, wondering what was in my pocket. I showed her the vial, took the cap (or the cork, or whatever you call it) off and waved it under her nose, which began to twitch as I did so.

I put the cap back on and said, "Okay, Maggie, find!"

She stared at me intently, her little beagle tail sticking straight up in the air and quavering. She barked (or I should say, she howled) at me. "Woo-woo-woo-*woo*! Woo-woo-woo-*woo*!"

"That's right, Maggie, find!"

She just stood there, howling, so I uncorked the bottle again and gave her another sniff. She drank in the aroma with her nose. I recapped the bottle and put it in my pocket.

It seemed to me, for some reason, that the leash was holding her back, so I took it off, threw it over a nearby tree branch, where it hung in the air like a noose. She stared up at me until I said, "Where is it? Where's that smell?"

Then she lifted her nose to the air and moved her head around in semicircles, then looked up at me and howled again.

Uh-oh, I thought, I haven't trained her well enough. She's never going to be able to do what I want her to do. This whole thing is a waste of time. All these thoughts jumbled through my head at the same time.

Now, if this were an actual police investigation, the place would be knee-deep in personnel, searching and scouring over every square inch of the area, following a predetermined grid pattern. There would be metal detectors and trained bloodhounds. The place would be, as they say, crawling with cops. But I didn't have that luxury. First of all, doing an official search would've tipped off Loudermilk, and I didn't want this to be on her radar, fearing that she'd take whatever was left of the $350,000 she'd gotten from the judge and leave town. She'd done something similar a couple of times before, according to Kelso, although her name hadn't been Heidi Loudermilk from Boise, Idaho, then; it was Jana Baumgarner and she was from Tulsa, Oklahoma.

Baumgarner had killed her husband when she was nineteen, then left town, only to be arrested two years later in Idaho. She had been taken into custody by a Boise cop by the name of—you guessed it—Heidi Loudermilk. But the *real* Heidi Loudermilk was five-foot-five, had brown hair and brown eyes, and, in all probability, knew the correct pronunciation of her hometown. Not that it did her much good. She went missing the day she took Jana Baumgarner into custody. Baumgarner had probably killed her, and had definitely stolen her identity.

Of course, I could've just reported this information to the Maine State Police and had her sent back to Tulsa, or to Boise, for that matter, to stand trial for her crimes in those localities. But those were old cases, cold cases. There was no guarantee she'd be convicted. If I had a smoking gun in the Merton case, or the Seabow case, I could put her behind bars and almost guarantee that she would stay there. I needed to find that bat. But it didn't look like Maggie had the foggiest idea what I wanted her to do. Face it, Jack, I told myself, you're a fraud. For all your theories, for all your successes with dogs like Satchmo and Henry, you don't have what it takes. You're just not good enough. In the words of Farrell Woods, I was screwed, glued, and tattooed.

I stood there feeling miserable and helpless, staring down at Maggie, who was staring up at me and periodically howling while her leash still dangled from the tree branch.

Then the wind changed and she got this look in her eye. Her tail stopped oscillating. Her head and shoulders were up, her nose was twitching with the wind currents. She was going into phase transition. (Since phase transition is a property of an emergent system, it may seem out of context to relate it to an individual organism—i.e., Maggie. But the fact is, the nervous system is also self-emergent, so Maggie didn't go into phase transition, but her nervous system *did*.)

She howled again, not at me this time, but at the wind, and then ran straight across the road to what my grandmother in Idaho used to call a barrow pit—basically just a ditch by the side of the road. Phase transition meant that she was the pack leader now. Or her nose was. So, like a good doggie, I grabbed her leash from the tree and followed her.

She began digging furiously in the snow. I turned and called out to Jamie. "I think we've got something!"

She got out of the car. "What? I can't hear you!"

"Come on over here! Switch off the engine first!"

"Okay!" She got back in the car.

Maggie had now started a very determined attack with her front paws. The snow was flying between her back legs.

Jamie arrived and I hooked Maggie to the leash and gave her a tennis ball as a reward. She took it in her jaws and shook her head around, "killing" it.

I handed Jamie the leash then dug at the snow with my gloved hands, found some tree branches under the white stuff, moved them out of the way, and found a pile of decaying leaves underneath *them*. Beneath the leaves was a small, aluminum baseball bat, with what looked like a bloodstain

right in the sweet spot, which is where good hitters meet th
ball when they hit a home run. Maggie had just hit a hom
of her own. She was the Babe Ruth of doggies.

"That's amazing," Jamie said. "How did she smell it fro
clear over there?"

I shook my head. "I'll be damned if *I* know. Just the mag
of a beagle's nose, I guess."

She handed me Maggie's leash. "Let me have it," she sai
of the bat. "I'll take it to the crime lab and start running tes
on it tonight."

"Not a chance," I said, handing back the leash. I put th
bat back where I found it and began covering it over with th
leaves, then the branches, then the snow.

"Jack! What are you doing?"

"Setting a trap. Call Flynn and have him meet us at Baum
garner's—I mean Loudermilk's place in an hour."

"But if her fingerprints are on the bat, then—"

"—the defense will argue that she handled the bat at som
previous time, having nothing to do with the murder. N
Trust me. If I'm right, we'll have an airtight case again
her."

"What if you're wrong?"

"Then we're screwed, glued, and—"

"—tattooed. By the way," she said as the three of u
headed back to the car, "I figured out some of the words t
one of those songs."

"Really?"

"Un-huh. It was called 'Sweet Certain Surprise.' "

I laughed. "That's fitting, because that's exactly wh
we've got in store for Ms. Jana Baumgarner, a.k.a. Hei
Loudermilk."

37

The timing couldn't have been more perfect as far as I was concerned. We caught Sergeant Loudermilk in her driveway just as she was leaving for her evening patrol—4:00 P.M. to 12:00 A.M. The overt crew included me, Flynn, and Jamie. We spoke to her directly. The covert crew included sheriff's deputies Quentin Peck and Trudy Compton, and Camden police detective, second grade, Carl Staub. They were lurking in the shadows, each in an unmarked car, keeping in constant contact through a secure radio frequency. It was their job to keep tabs on Loudermilk in case she decided to pull a Judge Crater (i.e., disappear).

"Hey, I'm glad we caught you," I said, smiling at her.

"What is it now?" she huffed.

"You sound like you're not happy to see me."

"Should I be?"

"Probably not, since we've got some new information that might discredit your account of what happened the night that Marti MacKenzie was killed."

"Not this again. I already explained to you about the squealing tires."

"Yeah, I know. It's not the tires. It's something in the photos of her body. I think Jamie should explain."

Jamie stepped forward. "I'm convinced, given the girl's height and the height of the bumper on Seabow's car, that the car didn't cause her injuries."

"Honey, I was there. I saw her pinned against that tree by his car, and found him passed out behind the wheel."

"Yes," I said, "which was all part of a clever plan by the killer, or killers. She was actually killed with a baseball bat. Or so Jamie thinks."

"That's right," Jamie said. "The kind they use in Little League. The funny thing is . . . well, I think Sheriff Flynn should tell you this part."

He shrugged and played the dumb county sheriff act to the hilt. "Well, I don't know how much stock I'd put in my ex-niece-in-law's version of things, but if it wasn't the damndest thing. Soon as she tells me about this damn theory of hers, we get a call at the Sheriff's Office, from someone who says they saw somebody burying something the night Marti MacKenzie was killed."

"Right near where it happened," I said.

Loudermilk gave us a tired look. "Why are you telling me this? A witness comes out of nowhere, five months after the girl was killed, and you believe them?"

"Well," I said, "that was the same attitude we got when we took this to the State Police. They weren't interested."

Flynn said, "That's why I've organized a search team, through my office, to comb the area around the accident site, looking for that baseball bat. I feel kinda bad, since you were the first one on the scene that night, and the whole thing is your baby, so to speak. So I thought I ought to at least invite you to the party. We're gonna start around sunup tomorrow."

She thought it over. "Well," she said, "I think it's a waste of time, but I'll be there, if for no other reason than to laugh in your faces when you don't find anything."

"Well," Flynn plied her with his Yankee charm, "I'm not saying we will or we won't, but we'll be happy to have you with us, if you decide to come along."

She remained uncharmed. She said she had to get to work and would we mind vamoosing her driveway? We did so.

She got in her cruiser and drove off, followed, quite unobtrusively, by Carl Staub, Trudy Compton, and Quentin Peck.

"Think she bought it?" I asked Flynn.

"Hook, line, and sinker," he smiled.

Jamie asked, "Do you think she'll go straight there?"

He shook his head. "She'll probably stick to her regular route, up the coast to Searsport, then north to Hampden, west to Waterville, and back over here to Belfast. I'd say we've got a good hour and a half before she shows up at the accident site. It'll be dark by then too."

"Well," I said, "let's get over there now just in case."

"I've already got somebody sitting on the place."

"Who?" I said.

"A couple of detectives from the Belfast PD. Greg Remillard and Tom Shelford. Both smart as hell and both rarin' at the bit to bring this bitch down. Sorry, Jamie."

"Don't apologize to me. I don't mind the B word, as long as it's used in the proper context. And Ms. Baumgarner is the proper context, as far as I'm concerned."

Flynn was right. Loudermilk didn't show up until well after six-thirty. We were out of sight, with our floodlights hidden in the bushes and clipped onto the lower branches of some of the bare trees.

She parked her cruiser, got out, looked around, then went straight for the spot where the bat was buried. As soon as she dug it out of its hiding place—BAM!—all the lights came on and she was caught like the proverbial deer in the headlights.

Flynn and I were the first to approach her.

"What have you get there, Sergeant?"

"Well, I got to thinking, maybe you were right."

"Really?"

"So I came here to have a look around. And I found this." She showed us the bat.

"Except you didn't look around, Jana. You went straight for the spot where it was buried." By this time everyone else had gathered around—Greg Remillard, Tom Shelford, Quentin Peck, Trudy Compton, Carl Staub, and Dr. Jamie Cutter. "Did you all see how she went straight to the spot where the bat was buried?" Everyone agreed that that's what they had seen. "Now, how could you have known where the bat was, if you didn't bury it there?"

She hesitated. "Because, like I said, I just came out to search the area, and as luck would have it—"

"Did anybody here see her search the area?"

Everyone shook their heads.

"No, see, you went straight for that spot. I mean straight *for* it. And if all these witnesses weren't enough, we've also got it on videotape."

She seemed on the verge of trying another lie, then threw the bat at me, missed, drew her revolver and aimed for my head. Quentin Peck, of all people, got off a shot before she did. He hit her in the shoulder, causing her to drop her weapon. In less than a fraction of a second Shelford and Remillard had her facedown in the snow and began cuffing her. She screamed in pain, and it turned out later that there must have been a sharp rock under the snow, because she'd fractured her cheekbone.

"Just one more thing," I said to the two detectives, then turned to Jamie. "Do you have the Woods lamp ready?"

"I sure do."

Shelford and Remillard got Loudermilk to her feet.

"What's this all about?" she wanted to know.

"This will prove that you also blackmailed and then killed Judge Merton. Jamie?"

Loudermilk laughed a sour laugh. "The hell I did."

Jamie turned on the ultraviolet light.

I explained to the two detectives. "The money Judge Merton paid her was sprayed with a kind of dye that only shows up under black light. As soon as Dr. Cutter shines that lamp on her hands, you'll see them glow a bright blue."

"Hah!" said Loudermilk.

Jamie ran the Woods lamp over Loudermilk's hands and there was no blue glow from the dye. I was stunned for a moment, then realized: "Of course. It was her cousin. Her goddamn cousin."

"What are you talking about?" Jamie said. "I thought—"

"I know. So did I."

Flynn said, "What the hell?"

"Hey," I shrugged, "even the greatest detectives make mistakes sometimes. Fortunately, this one can be rectified."

He asked me how.

"Give me twenty-four hours and I'll show you."

He thought it over. "Okay, you got it."

Remillard and Shelford put Jana Baumgarner into their cruiser.

"And listen, Sheriff," I said, "can you give Jamie a ride home? I need to take Roark back to the Stevens house."

Jamie said, "I don't mind the drive."

"Well, there's more to it than that, honey. I think I should tell Beth about Tulips—she *is* Beth's half sister, after all. And I don't know if she'd appreciate the two of us telling her. It just feels like something I should do alone."

"I think I should go. What do you think, Uncle Horace?"

He twitched his mustache a couple of times. "My feeling is, you can't go wrong having Jamie along, whatever the deal is."

"Okay. I guess I'm outnumbered."

We drove to Camden without much conversation. At one point Jamie asked me who I thought had killed Judge Merton, since it appeared that Heidi Loudermilk hadn't done it. I told her, and she said, "Well, that would be convenient, wouldn't it? You could get back at him for—"

"It isn't about that. He just fits, that's all. He has very large hands, he wears a ring on his right hand, which would account for Roark's hairline fracture—since my feeling is the killer hit Roark during the murder—and then there's the fact that Roark is scared out of his wits by this guy."

"But how are you going to prove it?"

I laughed. "Don't worry. I have a few ideas in mind."

"If you say so, Sherlock." She smiled and hugged my arm.

We got to Beth and Ron Stevens's house around eight. The kids were still up and happy as hell to see Roark again. They were hugging him and kissing him and petting his head.

"Be careful of his head, you guys," I said. "He has a bad ouchie over his left eye."

"An ouchie?" Beth smiled.

"Isn't that what you call it?"

"I suppose it will do. Thanks for taking care of him."

"You're welcome. There's just one other thing. I need to speak to you about it in private."

She followed me and Jamie down the walk toward the street. I could see Ron, standing in the front window, watching us.

"What's this about?" Beth asked.

"Well, I don't know if now is the right time to tell you this or not, but I think you should know about it sooner or later, and the sooner the better, in my opinion."

"Okay. What is it? Is it about Ron?" she asked, looking over her shoulder toward the house.

"No. I suspect you already know about that. It's about your father. He had a mistress when he was serving in Vietnam. And she had a baby. And that baby was adopted by a family in Seattle, or somewhere in Washington State, I don't know for sure where. And she's living in Maine now. She came out here a few years ago, looking for her dad."

She thought this over. "You're saying I have a sister?"

"A half sister, yes. Her name is Amy Beckwith. That's the name her adoptive parents gave her. Everyone calls her Tulips. She's a smart girl, and very talented. She sings with a local blues band. The thing is, she got in with a bad crowd and is addicted to drugs. Then this guy she was hooked up with—Eddie Cole—he beat the crap out of her the other night, and she's in the hospital right now, recovering from her injuries. Not to mention going through severe heroin withdrawal."

Beth took a moment to absorb all this. "What hospital?" she said, and I wanted to cry. What a beautiful thing to ask.

"It's in Lewiston," I said.

She nodded. "If I decide I want to meet her, would you come with me? The two of you?"

"Of course," Jamie said, touching her arm. "We'd be happy to introduce you to her."

She nodded again, thinking things over. "Did my father know about her?"

I sighed. "He knew, but I don't think he ever met her. He was too afraid of what your mother's family might do."

"We're all afraid of that." She stood there a moment, thinking. "So, I have a sister. Funny thing," she smiled, "I always wanted a sister."

38

A good part of the next day—Saturday morning and afternoon—was spent "auditioning" dogs for a little demonstration I had in mind for that night. Flynn said it sounded intriguing, but that this was also one of his weekends to fly to Buffalo, so he begged off.

As for the auditioning, it basically amounted to testing the dogs for aggressive tendencies toward other dogs, and toward a human being, namely me. Dale Summerhays, the crazy old bird who runs the Mid-Coast Animal Rescue League, was an enormous help. As soon as I told her what I wanted to do, she got excited and called everyone she knew who owned a pit bull, Rottweiler, Doberman pinscher, or German shepherd. The cars and vans were in and out of the driveway for most of the day. Everyone who brought a dog to the "audition" was very keen on the idea.

"When will people realize," said Dale, between phone calls, "that it isn't the dog that's to blame, it's the owner."

"Not only is it not the dog," I said, "it most certainly is not the *breed* of dog."

"Exactly," she exulted.

She was also instrumental in getting promises of a good turnout from the local media. We were timing the event early enough in the evening to make it on the eleven o'clock news, and Dale, through her connections, was able to ensure that this would happen.

Not every dog who auditioned made it to the final cut, but by the end of the day we had about twenty dogs, which I thought was enough to prove my point. And to catch a killer.

Darryl Deloit dropped by, in the midst of all this madness, to drop Henry off for a two-week stay. There were two pairs of skis in a ski rack on top of his white BMW.

"Hey, Jack," he rolled down the window, "Annie checked herself into a clinic in Vermont." He got out of the car. "I'm taking a couple of weeks off to go be with her."

"Really? That's great."

"Well, it's mostly thanks to you, I think. Oh, and she asked me to tell you that Henry is a totally different dog now. He and Annie have become best friends. No more biting."

I laughed. "That's good to hear."

We walked up to the kennel building and got Henry situated in one of the kennels, the one with the pine tree motif.

"Of course, they don't actually let you see the patients at the clinic," Darryl said as we went back outside, "but I thought it might be nice for her to know I'm nearby."

"That *is* nice." We got to his car. I looked at his skis. "Plus they have some great skiing in Vermont, huh?"

He shrugged. "Actually? I prefer the snow in Utah."

I had to give him that one.

"But yeah," he smiled a chagrined smile, "what am I supposed to do all day while she's in recovery? So, I thought, you know, I'd bring the skis along." He got back in the car. "Take good care of Henry," he said, and drove off.

At some point Jill Krempetz called. She'd been talking to some people at the DHS—that's the Division of Human Services—and they thought it might be a good idea for me to take Leon back to New York sometime between now and our first court date. They wanted me to let him see his grandmother, which I had no problem with, and to check out the possibility of him moving back to New York permanently, which I did have a problem with.

Leon, meanwhile, still wasn't talking to me. I got the feeling that he really liked Sloan a lot and was feeling a little heartbroken. Taking a trip together might give us a chance to talk and work things out.

Farrell Woods showed up late in the afternoon. Since Loudermilk and Eddie Cole were in custody, and since Gary Bermeosolo—the DEA asshole who'd been pestering his growers—was catching flack from the press and from his bosses, Woods felt safe enough to finally come pick up his beagles. I told him what I had planned for the evening, and he said, "Count me in."

I had an idea. "Can you get them to howl on cue?"

He laughed. "Like that's hard to do with beagles? Watch this." The dogs were circling around his truck, sniffing and scratching and doing beagle-type things.

"Ten-hut!" he said. They all stopped what they were doing and came running over to him. "Beagles, ready?" They wagged their tails. "Get set, and howl!" He did a little howling himself to start them off, and they went to town. It wasn't "The Camptown Races" or "Oh, Danny Boy," but it was a joyful noise. In fact, Frankie heard them and came running out to join in.

At some point Audrey—who'd seen the cars coming and going and wanted to know what the deal was—came over from Mrs. Murtaugh's place to find out. I told her, and she immediately volunteered Ginger for a place on the evening's roster.

"Perfect," I said.

At the end of the day we had five Rottweilers, six pit bulls, two German shepherds, three Dobies, one Newfoundland, one great Dane (Achille), and one Airedale (Ginger). Not to mention ten beagles.

Oh, it promised to be an unforgettable evening.

* * *

Finally, it was Saturday night. The Olde Timey Boyz were on stage, singing their first number—"Ida, Sweet as Apple Cider." We could hear them as we came in through the backstage door—me, Jamie, Shelford and Remillard (the two Belfast detectives), along with Frankie, Farrell Woods and his ten beagles. A stage manager tried to stop us but Shelford and Remillard showed him their badges and he let us through.

Woods got the beagles situated behind the curtain and had them all sit, just as we'd rehearsed. Jamie and I took our positions on stage right, while Shelford and Remillard took theirs on stage left.

I gave a nod to Woods, and he instructed his beauties to start howling—all ten of them. They made quite a racket.

I went out on stage, followed by Jamie. The Olde Timey Boyz, in their striped shirts with sleeve garters and straw hats, were angry and confused, as was the audience. They'd all come to hear some old-fashioned American music, not ten howling hounds. I raised my arms and said, "Ladies and gentlemen, we're sorry for the disturbance." Backstage, Woods quieted the beagles. Shelford and Remillard appeared stage left. "Sorry for the interruption but we need to do a demonstration here tonight. These two gentlemen are from the Belfast police, and we're hoping to arrest the man who killed Judge Merton. He's right up here on stage right now." I spoke to the man in the technical booth at the back of the theater. "Could we have the lights dimmed, please? This should only take a second." After a moment, the stage lights were dimmed. Jamie turned on the Woods lamp and shone it on Grant Goodrich. His hands turned a bright blue. There were also blue finger-sized streaks on his trousers, mustache, striped shirt, and even on his straw hat.

He looked down at his hands, looked over at Shelford and Remillard, then out at the audience. He leaped off the stage.

"House lights up!" I shouted. "Pit bulls ready!" As Goodrich ran toward the back exit, twenty people came through those same doors, each with a pit bull, Rottweiler, or Doberman pinscher, etc., on lead.

"Release the hounds!" I shouted.

The owners of the dogs all unleashed their animals. This stopped Goodrich in his tracks. He turned and ran back toward the stage, but didn't quite make it. All twenty dogs came after him, like something from one of his worst nightmares. They trapped him at the foot of the stage, jumped up on him and knocked him down. He was screaming, "Make them stop! Please! I did it! I killed him! I confess! Please make them stop!"

All the dogs actually *did*, though, was lick his face, or rather, his mustache. (Just like Frankie, they seemed to enjoy the flavor of his mustache wax.) The local camera crews came running up, with their hand-held lights and cameras and got some very interesting close-ups of Goodrich being "licked to death." Otis Barnes was there too, with a still photographer. He stood slightly apart from fracas, then looked over at me and smiled.

Shelford and Remillard climbed down off the stage, handcuffed Goodrich and got him to his feet. The dogs were still crazily trying to lick his mustache. I almost felt sorry for the poor bastard. Almost, but not quite.

Then I had Woods release the beagles, and they howled and circled around the auditorium, full speed, like greyhounds at the dog track, chased by the rest of the dogs. The audience went nuts. They *loved* it. In fact, there wasn't a dry seat in the house.

Jamie, laughing, took my hand. "You are something else, Jack Field. Is this how you solved your cases in New York?"

I shook my head. "We're in Maine, darling. The people up here are a whole different animal."

"You got that right."

* * *

Goodrich confessed again, back at the station house, but claimed he'd only killed Judge Merton because his cousin had paid him a hundred thousand dollars to do it. His story could not be corroborated, though, since Penelope Goodrich Merton disappeared, along with five million Goodrich dollars that were eventually traced to an offshore account in the Cayman Islands.

The Camden PD finally searched the area behind Gilbert's Publick House and found the two bullets that had been shot at Woods. They were a match, ballistically, with a throw-down automatic Loudermilk kept hidden in her garage, so it turned out that Heidi Loudermilk, a.k.a. Jana Baumgarner, was the person who'd shot at Farrell Woods, and at me and Jamie. She claimed she hadn't been trying to kill us, just to scare us off. It didn't matter. It still added time to her sentence.

On the down side, later that night we got a report that Eddie Cole had escaped from custody on his way to the state prison in Warren. He was said to be headed toward the Canadian border, but this was an unsubstantiated rumor. He could have just as easily been headed for Mexico (which is a small town in central Maine).

Beth Stevens called and told me she wanted to meet Tulips, her half sister, so on Sunday, Jamie and I met her at the hospital in Lewiston and made the introductions.

We left her in Tulips's room, where they started getting to know each other, and we were walking down the hall when I heard a familiar voice: "Hey, where's a fucking nurse when you need one! This is bullshit! Nurse! You fuckers!"

Jamie and I went into room and found Randall Corliss in bed, with both arms in a cast, held up in the air over his head.

Corliss smiled at me. "Hey, Field. I heard you solved a couple of cases without me. Nice going."

"Jamie, this is Randy Corliss, the dickhead cop I told you about. Corliss, this is Dr. Cutter."

"Nice to meet ya."

"What seems to be the trouble here?" Jamie said.

"I need a fucking nurse, that's what."

"Okay. I'll see what I can do."

She left, and Corliss watched, or rather scoped out her ass as she left the room. "Man," he said, "what I wouldn't give to have those legs wrapped around me sometime. Or to have those gorgeous lips of hers—"

Before he could finish, I picked up a squirt bottle of disinfectant soap and squirted a big glob into his open mouth.

He screamed, of course. So I gave him a drink of water, which only made his mouth foam. The foam ran down his chin and onto his cast. He started choking and his face turned red.

"Corliss, I told you not to talk about her like that or I would wash your mouth out with soap. Remember?"

"Fthwuck you," he said, his mouth still foaming.

"You're welcome." I held up the water glass. "Want some more water?"

Epilogue

It took a week for Seabow to be released. Corliss was not only fired, but arrested for his illegal involvement with Eddie Cole. And Jamie's divorce finally came through. We celebrated with dancing and champagne at the Seaside Inn, followed by more fun in the hot tub at the Samoset. This time I let Jamie have her way with me. There was no one else around.

After a bit she said, "What about your heads-up, remember? You're supposed to propose to me now."

"Oh," I laughed, "you expect me to get down on one knee right here in the hot tub and pop the question just like that?"

She pouted, or pretended to. "That's the general idea."

"Un-uh, honey. When I propose to you there'll be fireworks and an orchestra with enough music to wake the mountains. And I'll have bought you a beautiful ring from Tiffany's, which I will have hidden in some wonderfully unexpected and surprising place for you find."

A smile warmed her face. "You've got it all planned out."

"Not all of it. Just the general idea."

I took the next weekend off. Mrs. Murtaugh had recuperated from her surgery and said she was fine to take care of things. Audrey and Ginger had gone back to Boston, much to Frankie's disappointment, and mine.

At any rate I took Duke, I mean Leon—I always call him Duke when we're in New York—down to the city to spend

some time with his grandmother. I didn't want him to mov
back—I wanted him to stay with me, I'd grown kind of a
tached to the kid—but I knew it was in his best interest
make the decision on his own, with all the elements intact.

While he was up in Harlem, I was taking care of som
business matters downtown and doing a little shopping. La
that night Kelso dragged me to a damn cabaret show.

"I don't want to sit in a bar watching you get drunk, wi
some boy singer onstage camping it up at the piano."

It wasn't like that at all. His name was Billy Stritch and h
sang Cole Porter and Johnny Mercer and Rodgers and Ha
and George and Ira and his voice was reminiscent of M
Torme. His piano playing was pretty good too.

Duke and I—I mean Leon and I—got back late Sunda
night. He was in a conflicted state, so I didn't push him to
hard or even try to talk to him. He knew the score. He woul
let me know what he wanted, whether it was just to tal
things out or to let me know of his final decision. Either wa
I wanted to be okay with whatever he decided.

Jamie called around ten-thirty and asked if she coul
come over and spend the night. I guess she missed me. I tol
her, fine, I'd love to see you, then started building a fire i
the fireplace as soon as I hung up the phone.

Later, after the embers had died down and we were u
stairs in bed, the silence drove me crazy. That and Jamie
snoring. (Not to mention the fact that this was now or neve
Finally I threw the covers off and went downstairs, dress
in just my pajama bottoms, followed close at heel b
Frankie. I jumped on top of Jamie's bumper—that of h
new Jagwire—and in no time at all the car alarm went o
Frankie and I ran back upstairs and I found her sitting up i
bed, the covers wrapped around her naked body, her fa
swollen with sleep.

"What the hell?" she said. She seemed to mean it.

"I don't know what came over me. I guess, you know, b

ing in New York this weekend, and coming back here to all this silence—I guess I just kind of missed the noise of the city."

She stared at me. "Are you crazy?"

"I think so. By the way—and don't worry, I'll go down and turn it off, can you throw me your keys?—I bought you a little something this weekend."

"Fabulous." She threw me her keys. "Now, could you just let me get some sleep? Is that too much—"

"The thing is, I got you a little trinket at Tiffany's when I was in New York. So, if you could kind of rummage through your underwear drawer there while I'm downstairs shutting off your alarm, you might find a little baby-blue box hiding amidst the silk and satin. Remember I said there would be fireworks when I finally proposed to you? Well, I couldn't arrange for any fireworks, and I couldn't wait till the Fourth of July, so I did the next best thing: I set off your car alarm. I hope you don't mind. Anyway, while you're looking through your undies I'll just go downstairs—"

"You did what?" She was still half asleep.

"And don't worry, you don't have to answer yes or no right away. Just try on the ring."

"What? Jack!" she said, but I was gone.

I danced down the stairs, ran out into the cold, and used Jamie's key chain to shut off the alarm. I never did make it back upstairs, though: Jamie—wearing nothing except one of my T-shirts—tackled me in the living room.

I guess she liked the ring.

"So," I said a few minutes later, "does this mean yes?"

"Yes," she said, grabbing my face and kissing me all over. "Yes, yes, yes, yes, yes."

Suddenly, we heard something or someone scratching at the front door. I got up on one elbow to listen. Jamie did too. Frankie lifted his head up and wagged his tail.

"Don't answer it," I said, "it's Kristin Downey."

She laughed. "You idiot. She's not coming till next week, according to you. And besides, I don't think she'd be scratching at the door at two in the morning."

"You don't know her like I do."

She hit me. "Oh, shut up and go see who it is."

I got up, went to the door, opened it and found Hooch standing there, panting and shivering.

"Who is it?" Jamie called out from the living room.

"It's just Hooch, honey," I said over my shoulder, "better put another log on the fire."

Author's Note

The dog training techniques Jack uses are based, in part, on Kevin Behan's *Natural Dog Training*. And there's a funny story about my editor, Erin Richnow's family dog, Lace (a springer spaniel), who lives back home in Texas:

Erin and I were talking one day on the phone and she happened to mention that Lace was kind of out of control, crazy, and exhibiting pica, which means she was eating nonfood items. Erin asked me what advice I could give to her mother about the dog. I laughed because there's a chapter in *A Nose for Murder* where Jack deals with just such a problem. Erin, who'd read the book as an editor, not looking for training advice, had apparently missed Jack's technique in this chapter, so I told her to have her mother play fetch and tug-of-war with Lace every day, to always let her win at tug and to praise her very enthusiastically for winning.

Her mother took my advice, and Lace is no longer crazy and is no longer eating things she shouldn't.

Stimulating and then properly satisfying a dog's prey drive, in a controlled manner, can cure almost any type of behavioral problem, from fear to aggression. It's a shame that more people don't understand this.

Also, the technique used by Jack regarding the pug Henry is based almost exactly on two actual training experiences of mine, the first involving a cocker spaniel named Dodger, the second involving another cocker named Isabella. In each case playing fetch and tug-of-war stopped the dog from biting its owner.

I should also mention that part of the technique Jack uses with Henry is based on "The Jolly Routine," invented by William Campbell. Campbell, in some ways, has been very influential on my training method even though I find that very few of his techniques are totally effective, and that none of them is as effective as Kevin Behan's *Natural Dog Training* techniques.

I also wanted to mention my college classmate and friend, Orson Scott Card. In the introduction to the definitive version of his novel, *Ender's Game*, he tells of how he wrote the short story that eventually became this marvelous book, longhand on a notepad, and that he still writes the same way today.

When I first read that introduction, several months ago, my computer wasn't working very well and I realized—yeah, you know, that's how *I* used to write. So I forgot about getting a new computer, or getting my old one fixed, and began writing *Murder Unleashed* longhand, with a LePen on a yellow college-ruled legal pad, just as I used to do back in college when I wrote my first short story for a creative writing class, and when I wrote my first screenplay for Tad Danielewski's film workshop.

So I began to write furiously on subway trains and buses, on trips between my apartment (at the time) in Marble Hill and my meetings with dog-training clients all over town. Then I would come home and try to "download" my subway-rattled heiroglyphs onto my peevish computer and add a little polish and a rewrite or two (or twenty, or thirty).

Later, after I finished reading *Ender's Game*, I e-mailed Scott and said that the kind of books he writes may well be transformational, while mine are purely transportational (meaning they're the kind of light reading you take with you on the bus or the train or on a plane trip).

It's kind of ironic too, since you may be sitting on the number 9 train right now, or on the M57 bus, reading this, not knowing that I'm in the car ahead of you, or sitting in the back of the bus, working on my next novel. The same may be true even if you *don't* live in New York. I could be in your town for a book tour, using local transportation, writing away on my legal pad on my way to a radio show or a newspaper interview, while you're reading this book to pass the time on your way to work. Or I could be *flying* to your town, sitting in first class (I wish), doing the same thing, while you're back in coach, letting Jack and Jamie take your mind off things (like turbulence, a faulty engine, or that suspicious-looking guy in front of you).

At any rate, I have Scott Card to thank for reminding me of how I used to write back when we were classmates, back when I was first learning how to tell a story in prose form.

It's the only way to travel.

—Lee Charles Kelley
February 21, 2003

(You can contact me via e-mail at thekelleymethod @yahoo.com or you can visit my website: LeeCharles Kelley.com. (Be sure to remember that Kelley is spelled with two "E"s. Also, Kevin Behan's website is dogman@natural dogtraining.com.)